THE BREAKER

THE BREAKER

ROMAN REPUBLIC SERIES BOOK THREE

PENELOPE SKY

This is a work of fiction. Names, characters, organizations, places, events, and incidents are either products of the author's imagination or are used fictitiously. Otherwise, any resemblance to actual persons, living or dead, is purely coincidental.

Published by Montlake, Seattle

www.apub.com

EU product safety contact:
Amazon Media EU S. à r.l.
38, avenue John F. Kennedy, L-1855 Luxembourg
amazonpublishing-gpsr@amazon.com

ISBN-13: 9781662539275 (paperback)
ISBN-13: 9781662539268 (digital)

Cover design by Caroline Teagle Johnson
Cover image: © Michelle Lancaster PTY LTD

Printed in the United States of America

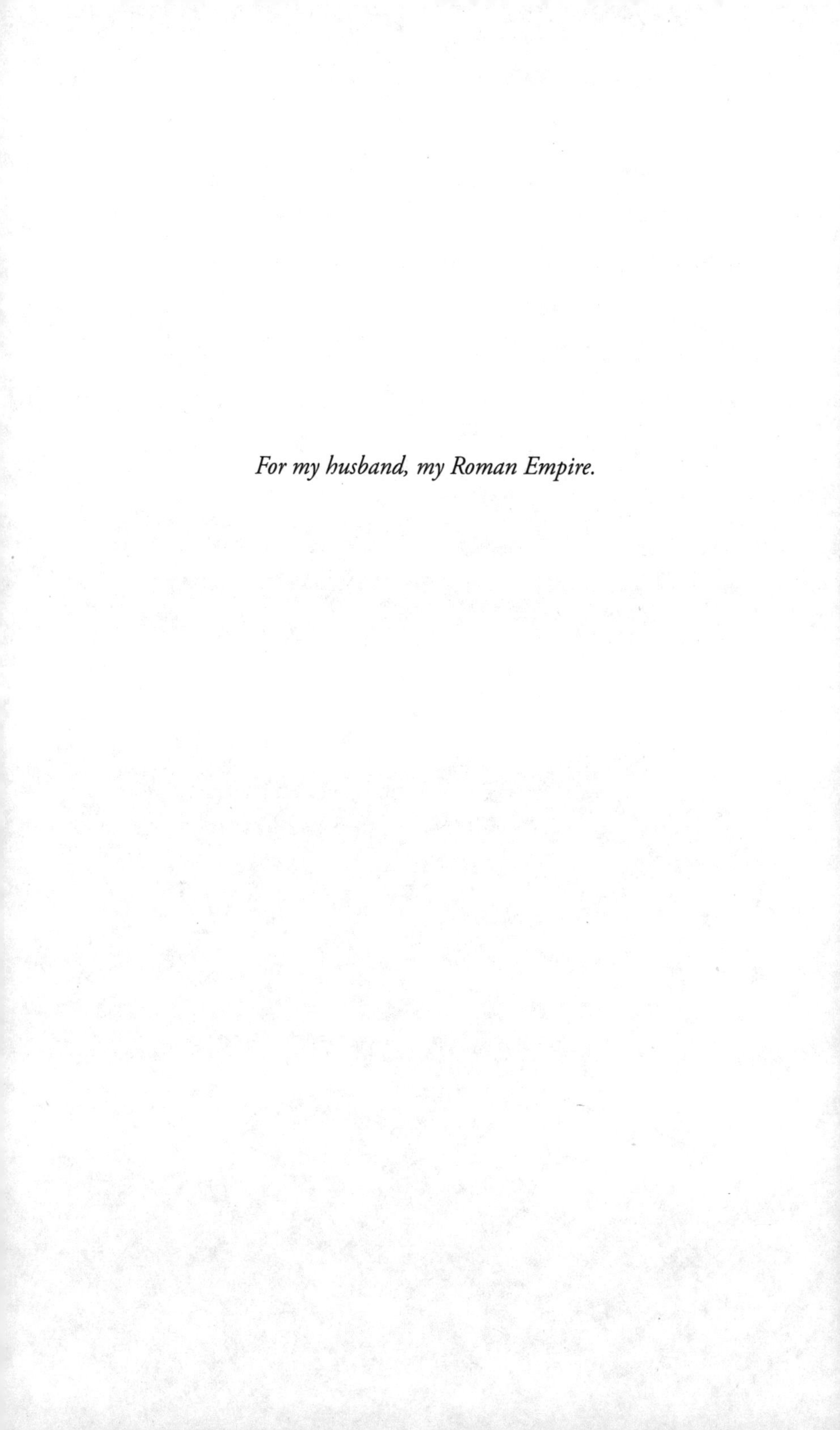

For my husband, my Roman Empire.

Chapter 1

Constantine

"Thanks for this, Santino." I admired the contraption he'd made with Medusa's measurements, a walker that would allow her three legs to move freely but her fourth to be supported with a wheel. We'd gone to school together, and he'd become a contractor and could pretty much build anything.

"So you're in town for a while?" He crossed his arms over his chest before he leaned against the counter of his front office. His receptionist was in the back on her break.

"More than a while," I said. "More like permanently."

"Yeah?" he said with a raised eyebrow. "Your mother must be ecstatic."

"Haven't told her yet, but yeah, she will be." Her scream would probably split my eardrums.

He pushed off the counter with his hips. "Let me know if it needs adjustments. Happy to swing by."

"Thanks, man."

I put the seats down in the back of my Range Rover, placed the walker inside, and then headed back toward Taormina, up the mountain over the village, where my villa was nestled on the cliff face. It was still an extraordinary property with nine thousand square feet divided among the three floors, but the palace had felt like a city in comparison. Sometimes it bothered me to know Darius was shitting in my toilet and fucking his whores in my bed . . . but I had what really mattered.

When I returned home, I carried the walker through the entryway and the main common room with twenty-foot-tall floor-to-ceiling windows that showed the sea in the distance. The main floor had two different living rooms, an office, and a formal dining room, and then upstairs was where the bedrooms were located.

Aurelia sat on the rug on the floor with her back to one of the couches, next to the dog bed, and she gave Medusa soft, loving strokes across her cheek to help her relax. A cup of coffee sat on the table, and it still wafted with steam like she'd just made it. She looked at the walker when I put it down in front of them. "Wow, that's it?"

Medusa opened one of her eyes and stared at me, but she didn't get up to greet me like she normally would. She was still in pain, even with the meds, so she wasn't quite herself.

It killed me to see her like that, but I knew I just had to be patient and I'd see her running around again. "Yeah, now she'll be able to get around on her own. I know she misses being a dog."

She looked down at Medusa and stroked her cheek. "Yeah."

Most women liked dogs, but they liked the little ones you could carry in one arm or stuff in your purse. Medusa was a full-grown seventy-pound German shepherd. More like a wolf than a dog. But I knew Aurelia loved Medusa as much as I did. I could see it in the way she cared for her as if she'd had her since she was a puppy. It was so real it couldn't be faked. "Baby girl, let's give this a try." I patted my thigh so Medusa would get up.

She lay there and released a breath through her nostrils.

"Maybe later," Aurelia said. "She's having a hard time today."

When I'd brought Medusa home, I'd just wanted a dog around the house. I never expected to love her like this, to feel like she was a piece of my heart outside of my body. I'd take another bullet to fix her broken leg if I could.

I moved to the other side of Medusa, my arm resting over the cushions of the couch so I could touch the back of Aurelia's neck, and together, we sat with our dog.

Aurelia continued to pet her fur as she looked at me, wearing nothing but one of my T-shirts, without makeup, doing nothing else except caring for Medusa since she woke up. With the light coming through the windows before us, her eyes were lit up in a glorious way, and she was fucking stunning. "How's your arm?"

"What do you mean?"

Her hand paused momentarily in Medusa's fur. "You were shot, remember?"

"Oh, that," I said with a smirk. "Yeah, I already forgot about it."

Her eyes did that thing where they shifted back and forth frantically as if I'd just said something crazy. "Isn't getting shot painful?"

"Not at all. Now getting *a shot* . . . that's the worst."

"Are you serious right now?"

"Any time I've been shot, it's been in the middle of chaos. Adrenaline is high and I'm focused on killing someone, so it's impossible to feel anything. You just feel your body jerk back from the speed of the bullet, but that's it. But when you need a shot at the doctor's office, you just have to sit there and wait for them to stick a big-ass needle in your skin. It's the worst."

"The worst?" she repeated like I was a nutcase. "A shot can't kill you."

"Well, I've been shot a lot, and it's never killed me."

"Yet."

"Well, those days are behind me, so that was probably the last one." Something I wouldn't miss. Sometimes when I flew commercial, the bullets I hadn't been able to get out set off the metal detectors. That was always a gun story to tell airport security.

"At least you're feeling good."

"I don't even notice it." I looked down at Medusa, a dog I loved even though we'd never said a word to each other. I had her back, and she had mine. If I hadn't taken that bullet, she would have died. In the moment, I didn't think twice—and I'd do it again.

"How many times have you been shot?"

"This year or . . . ?"

She released a sigh and shook her head. "Jesus . . ."

I grinned. "I'm just messing with you, sweetheart. I've probably been shot . . . four times? Maybe five?"

"Maybe? You aren't even sure?"

"Well, I've been stabbed a lot too, so after a while, you get things mixed up."

"Oh my god."

"Yeah," I said with a chuckle. "Good times."

"Does your mother know all this?"

"God no," I said quickly. "Give my mom a heart attack."

"Maybe it's for the best that we're here, then."

A painful bomb of guilt dropped on my heart, and I looked at Medusa again, doing my best to hide the pain from her . . . and from myself. "Yeah. Maybe it is."

~

Medusa was much more animated the next day, so I helped her into the walker and locked it into place. It took her a second to figure out how it worked, but she was a smart dog, so a couple minutes later, she figured it out. She was able to move around the house without putting weight on her injured leg, and instantly, her tail started to wag again.

I smiled like a proud dad who'd just taught his kid how to ride a bike. "Attagirl." I opened one of the enormous back doors, and she walked right out onto the patio to explore, the sound of her wheel audible everywhere she went.

"Aww, she loves it." Aurelia moved past me and stepped onto the patio, wearing a sundress with a long slit up her thigh that exposed one of her toned legs. Her hair was in loose curls down her back, and she'd already taken to Taormina so well, like it was her home. She took a seat on the couch and watched Medusa head to the gardens.

I sat down beside her, my arm moving around her shoulders, and together, we sat in the shade and watched our dog be happy again.

Her hand automatically moved to my thigh in my sweatpants.

We hadn't made love since we'd arrived here. The longest dry spell we'd ever had. I hadn't initiated anything because I'd been too emotionally exhausted to be in the mood. She didn't try anything either—maybe because she was too preoccupied with Medusa's well-being to think about it either. But despite the lack of intimacy, I'd never felt closer to her, never felt my soul come so in tune with someone else's.

I headed into the village the next morning.

The first thing my mom did every day was visit my brother at the cemetery. Well, visit his headstone, actually. Because the grave was empty, and the coffin had probably disintegrated years ago.

And the man who'd killed him was living in my house.

A sharp pain moved through my chest at the realization, and it was like swallowing a rock as a pill.

Her next stop was Rosticceria Da Cristina, where she worked in the office because she didn't trust anyone else to handle the books or the supply orders or the staff schedule. When I got to the front door, I went to push it open but realized it was locked.

Because she always locked it after she came in, unlike me.

I still had a key, so I unlocked it and let myself inside. "Ma, it's me!" I yelled so she wouldn't freak out at the sound of the door.

"Con!" My mother's frantic voice came from down the hallway.

"Yeah, I'm home."

I heard her quick footsteps, and then a moment later, she appeared nearly at a run. "Oh, I'm so happy." She clapped her hands quickly, then gave an excited scream when her eyes landed on mine. In dark jeans and a blouse, with a gold cross that hung around her neck, she came to me with her arms outstretched and hit me with her momentum.

I caught her with a chuckle, my arms hooking around her and giving her a tight squeeze. "I'm happy to see you too."

She squeezed me back, then cupped my face and gave each of my cheeks a kiss, probably leaving lipstick marks there. "My boy." She patted my cheeks. "Is Aurelia with you?" she asked hopefully.

"Yeah, she's at the house. Medusa is hurt right now, so someone needs to be with her at all times."

She looked happy at the mention of Aurelia, but the news about my dog changed her mood. "Why is she hurt?"

"She broke her leg."

"Oh, that poor baby. But why did you bring her here?"

I took a step back from her. I was so close, I could smell her perfume. "That brings me to the reason for my visit today . . . we've decided to move back to Taormina."

Her face was like a fireworks display, explosions and sparklers going off in her eyes. Her hands cupped her mouth, and she took a step back as she tried to process the greatest news she'd ever received. Even her eyes started to smart because having me close was her dream, a dream she'd never forced on me. She stood there and started to breathe harder and harder, like she really might burst into soul-racking sobs. "Oh, Con, I can't remember the last time I was this happy."

Now I felt guilty for two different reasons. One, I wasn't back in Taormina because I wanted to be there. And two, I still felt like shit for leaving Rome and letting the Skull King turn it into his playground. Whatever horrible things happened to that city and her people . . . would all fall on me because I wasn't there to defend it.

"You mean it?" She dropped her hands and blinked to stop the tears. "You're here to stay?"

It pained me to do it, but I nodded.

Then the tears she fought so hard to defeat returned with a vengeance. "Oh, Con." She moved back into me and hugged me hard, hugged me like I'd just returned from service in war. Her face planted in my chest, and she cried for another moment before she composed herself. "All of my children . . . together."

Except it wasn't *all* of us.

Edric was probably in my old home at that very moment, because Darius was enough of a prick to move him there, to turn him into a nightstand like he promised, in the room where I used to sleep every night.

I'd made my decision and wouldn't turn back, but fuck, it was a hard decision to live with.

My mother pulled away. "What about work? Did something happen?"

She and I had a mutual understanding never explicitly stated that we wouldn't discuss my job. That I would let her bury her head in the sand because it was the only way she could cope. After the loss of one son, she wouldn't be able to breathe if she lost the other. So I didn't share the details, let her know as little as possible. "It's just time to move on."

Chapter 2

Aurelia

Once Constantine's staff were back to their positions, we had someone take care of Medusa while we were out of the house so she wouldn't be alone. She was doing much better now, and with her walker to assist her, she was in much higher spirits. It seemed that the immobility, not the pain, had been the source of her depression.

We got out of the cab and stepped into the village, and even though it'd only been a few months since I was last here, it felt different. Felt magical, special—and like home. I was a different person from the last time I was here, so I also felt like I was experiencing it for the first time.

Constantine took my hand and held it as we headed down Corso Umberto, the main road, and we passed the Duomo and the fountain with the horse statues on the right. It was where we'd met on our first official date, before he'd taken me into the village and introduced me to Bam Bar and La Focaccia.

I'd thought we were just a fling at the time, and now I hoped he would be my husband someday. The street was busier than it'd been in May because the high season hadn't started yet, but now it was late June, so there were a lot more people around window-shopping, ordering gelato, looking at the dishes and pottery from the boutique shops.

"Where are we going?" I wore a light-blue sundress and platform sandals. I'd taken only the essentials when we'd left, so I didn't have my full wardrobe, just my summer stuff. The rest of it had been left behind, and I imagined Darius had someone toss it all. But I'd brought the stuff that mattered, like keepsakes, pictures, and items that belonged to my mother.

"Daiquiri. The boys are meeting us."

"Oh."

"That a problem?" he asked as he looked down at me.

"Well, I can just head back if you want to hang out with your friends. I don't want to intrude—"

"Intrude?" He came to a stop and looked at me like I'd just lost my mind. "You're my woman, so you *are* one of the boys." He continued forward again, bringing me with him. "Come on, they'll love to see you."

"You think so?"

"Yeah. They've liked you since the day they met you at the beach. And if they didn't like you, I'd punch them in the face until they changed their minds." He gave me that handsome smirk, like maybe that was a joke . . . or maybe not.

We turned left and headed down the stairs, the white sign with the black writing visible, with the name **Daiquiri** printed. We'd been there before, and they had a cute stone courtyard with bright blue and yellow chairs with decorative pillows, music over the speakers, people enjoying their vacations with big mixed drinks with colored straws and umbrellas hanging over the rim.

He found the guys seated in the corner, and when they all spotted Constantine, they gave a shout in unison. They all stood to greet him, and a round of hugs and hand claps was exchanged. I recognized his cousin Antonio and his friends from the beach, like Aldo, Francesco, and Gianni. They all greeted me just as warmly, hugs all around.

We took our seats, and without taking his eyes off his friends, Constantine moved his enormous hand to the area just below my knee, his forearm the length of my thigh, being his normal possessive self. "It's good to be back in town. What have you boys been up to?"

They talked about work. They all seemed to be in the service industry, working in family-owned restaurants, with the exception of Aldo, who was an assistant manager at one of the nicer hotels. They shared some gossip about people in town, a couple who'd recently broken up, famous people who'd come into their restaurants recently, stuff like that.

"So, I hear you're in town for good?" Antonio asked.

"Yeah, I heard the same," Francesco said.

"Damn, word travels fast," Constantine said with a slight laugh.

"Well, your ma told mine," Antonio said. "And she blew up my phone with texts right away."

"So, is it true?" Aldo asked.

There was a flicker in Constantine's eyes, a momentary lapse in his happiness, a sting in his gaze. But it passed as quickly as it came. "It is."

"Man, that's awesome," Francesco said. "Now we can hang out all the time. Beach club every Saturday."

"You haven't been to a Sunday-night dinner in a while," Antonio said. "They've gotten bigger, if you can believe it."

"I can absolutely believe it," Constantine said with a chuckle.

"So, what changed?" Antonio asked. "If you don't mind my asking."

Me. He had to give up everything he loved . . . for me. And that made me feel horrible every day. I wanted to live a quiet life in Taormina close to his family and see a beautiful sunset every night, but I knew Constantine was destined for something greater. The blood of emperors ran in his veins, and he should be in Rome serving his country and his people—not letting it be destroyed by the psychopath who'd killed his brother.

Constantine paused for a heavy moment, like he actually considered telling them the truth. But instead, he issued a vague answer that was true but also empty. "It was time to move on." He glanced at his hand on my thigh before he gave me a gentle pat. "There are more important things in life than work."

~

"I can't believe this is happening." We walked down the street and turned slightly to the right, moving uphill as we ventured deeper into town. "I've thought about this granita every single day since we were here. I can't believe they don't have it in Rome."

He smirked. "If I'd known you wanted it that bad, I would have asked my chef to make it."

"Yeah, but it wouldn't be the same."

"He's from Sicily, so I'm sure it would be."

"You tell me this now . . ."

His hand moved to my ass, and he gave me a playful smack. "Well, now we can come here every morning to make up for your losses."

"Works for me. Can't wait until we can bring Medusa with us."

"She'll love it here."

We walked up to the restaurant and stood in line underneath the sign, and just like the last time we'd come here, the waiter knew who Constantine was and got us a table outside. They made small talk about family, and Constantine told him he was back in town for the foreseeable future. The waiter left the menus for us to decide what we wanted.

"God, I have anxiety." I looked at the flavors on the menu, then saw what they had written on the sign next to the kitchen.

"Over granita?" Constantine asked with a smirk.

"I've wanted this so long, I don't know what to do."

He turned to see what the flavors were for the day. "Their special is mulberry. I would get two scoops of that. It's pretty good, and they don't make it often. Probably because it's in season."

"Yeah?"

He continued to smirk. "You act like you're about to make a deal with some suits."

"That's exactly how I feel."

When the waiter came back over, Constantine ordered for the both of us. He got the same thing I did and handed over the menus.

I took in the scene, the beautifully painted tables made of volcanic rock, the bright sun in the center of their logo, the people who passed in front of the restaurant with their bags of souvenirs or sandwiches tucked in waxed paper.

Constantine watched me. "You love it here."

I turned to meet his stare. "I do. It's where I fell in love with you."

A little smile moved onto his lips. "That quick?"

"Oh, one hundred percent," I said with a chuckle, relieved that I could get all these big feelings off my chest. Relieved I didn't have to pretend he wasn't the man I wanted the rest of my life.

"Because you sure played hard to get a lot," he teased.

"I didn't want to jump from one relationship to the next. I wanted to do it right, because I knew you were the real deal. And I guess I never thought it would go anywhere at the time because, you know, you're hotter than the fucking sun, and I'm nothing special."

"Nothing special . . ." His smirk continued. "Sweetheart, if only you were in my head the first time I saw you. I couldn't believe my luck when I saw you again at the bar of the hotel. Felt like I won the lottery."

Psh, I was the one who won the fucking lottery. "You're sweet."

The waiter arrived with our glass bowls of granita and the basket that contained two brioche rolls. He placed a bottle of water for us to share and two cups before he walked off to help the other tables.

"Here we go." Constantine handed me a spoon so I could take the first bite.

I spooned the granita out, then smeared it on a piece of the brioche before I popped it into my mouth. "Oh god." I added more granita to the bread and proceeded to eat it piece by piece, and it got better with every bite. "It's sooooo good."

Constantine continued to watch me. "Not gonna lie, this is turning me on a bit."

"I'll happily eat granita off your dick."

This was one of those moments where he would usually smirk, but he continued his hard stare, made it slightly sharper. "You've got yourself a deal, sweetheart."

~

With the exception of Medusa still being hurt and needing her medications, that week felt like a vacation. Constantine took me out all the time, showed me spots we hadn't seen the first time we were there. That night, we got ready for dinner and returned to the hotel where we'd met for dinner at their Michelin-star restaurant, Principe Cerami. We were given a table outside on the terrace with unobstructed views of the sea. By the time we were seated, the sun had already set so we couldn't see the water for more than ten minutes before it was gone. Then the city lights along the coastline became our view.

Constantine ordered the six-course meal so he could try everything, but I stuck to the à la carte menu and ordered the artisanal spaghetti with tomatoes and salty ricotta cheese. Constantine chose the wine without needing to look at the menu.

I noticed that he'd ordered the tasting menu without even looking at what the selections were. "Did you review the menu before we came?"

"No. But I eat anything." He took a drink from his wineglass.

"We should put that to the test by having me cook for you."

He released a little laugh, and it sounded so charming. I didn't make him laugh often, so when it happened, it was special. "I'd eat anything you'd make, sweetheart. But you never have to cook for me. It's my job to have someone cook for you."

"No, it's not," I said honestly. "I'd be just as happy in a one-bedroom apartment with a microwave and a little stove."

"Well, I wouldn't be. I did that in my early twenties, and I'm not going back."

"I'm just saying you don't need to spoil me all the time."

"Yes, I do." He took another drink of his wine and looked out at the dark sea.

We fell into silence, and he continued to stare, looking at nothing in particular as far as I could tell. His mind seemed to be elsewhere.

And I suspected I knew exactly where it'd gone.

There were times when he was happy, when he smiled brighter than the sun, teased me and slapped me on the ass, and we were perfect together. But these moments continued to come back, and I suspected they always would.

I followed his gaze to the sea and saw a collection of small boats and their multicolored lights on the surface of the water. Blue, red, green, and yellow. I had no idea what they were for. "Do you know what they're doing out there?"

His eyes flicked away from the random spot he was looking at and focused on the boats. "Fishing for octopus. They're nocturnal and attracted to the lights."

"Oh, interesting. Have you ever fished for octopus?"

He shook his head. "I don't eat octopus."

"You just said you eat anything."

He smirked. "Well, it's the one exception."

"May I ask why?"

"Because I respect them. One of the most intelligent creatures on the planet, too smart to be food. I've seen them when I've gone diving before. They're different from fish and other seafood."

"That's actually really sweet." And really compassionate for someone who policed gangs and killed people for breaking his laws.

"You're welcome to eat it in front of me. Don't change your diet because of me. It doesn't bother me. My mom makes it every Sunday, so it's not an issue. Just my personal decision."

I didn't say it out loud so as not to make him uncomfortable, but if he didn't eat octopus, then I wouldn't either. I would stand by him in whatever he believed in. I knew if the situation were reversed, he would do the same.

He stared at the ocean again, still in his introspective mood. I noticed that ever since we'd left Rome, his phone didn't go off all hours of the night and he wasn't constantly sending texts. He was hardly on his phone at all now. There would've been no way for us to sit through a six-course dinner like this without his phone lighting up on the table every couple seconds.

The quiet was nice, but the calm was riddled with guilt. I knew it wasn't my fault that Darius had cornered me in the house, but I still felt responsible for Constantine losing his passion. He loved me enough to sacrifice it all without hesitation.

"I've been thinking about what to do with my time now, since all my clients are in Rome." I'd canceled all my shoots and told them I was no longer in business. I'd refunded everyone's money and had received some nasty emails, but I never told Constantine about any of that because I knew he'd lost far more than I did.

"I can get you accounts at the hotels. They always have weddings and events."

Oh, I hadn't considered his endless line of connections. "Actually, I was thinking of taking a break from photography."

The waiter came over and brought Constantine's first course, a soup.

Constantine turned to me directly. "Yeah?"

"Yeah. I started to get burned out toward the end. I like taking the photos, but sitting at a computer for hours and editing them is what wears me down. And working all hours of the day and nights and weekends gets old too."

He listened to me with his full attention, wearing a black button-up collared shirt that was stressed around his arms and shoulders from the muscles bulging there. He had a private gym in the house, and despite the turmoil he suffered, he continued to work out in the morning and later in the afternoon, keeping his muscle mass like he was still prepared for a fight. "Then don't work. Even after everything that happened, money is no issue, so don't worry about that."

I had no idea what his financial situation was, but I would never ask. He said the palace had been given to him, he hadn't bought it, so all his assets must be in other places. He already owned his place here in Taormina, and it was a twenty-million-euro home—at least. "It's not about the money. It's about purpose."

He continued that hard stare without needing to blink, a stare I noticed he never gave to anyone else. When he talked with his friends, he was animated and reactive, not quiet and intense like he was with me. He wasn't like that with Rocco either. Not his family. No one. "I can understand that. Have any ideas?"

"Actually, I wanted to know if I could help at the restaurant."

He blinked before his eyebrows furrowed. "At Rosticceria Da Cristina?"

"Yeah, I thought it could be fun. I could help in the kitchen. I could be a waitress in the main restaurant. I could spend more time with your mom. Just a thought. If you think it's a stupid idea, you won't hurt my feelings—"

"I don't think it's a stupid idea. Just surprised, is all."

"She doesn't have to pay me either. Free labor for her."

"If anyone should be getting free labor, it should be me." His eyes were serious, and then a playful smile moved over his handsome face.

"I can hold two jobs."

"Ambitious." His grin widened. "I like it. I'll ask her what she thinks."

"If she's not into it, I understand."

"I'm sure she'll be into it."

"I have literally no restaurant experience."

"Yeah, but she's all about running a family-owned business. That's why my cousins and sister work there."

"Well, I'm not family."

His eyebrows furrowed. "You're going to be my wife, so yeah, you are."

We'd never discussed this topic before. We'd just recently started saying we loved each other. But my heart raced as if he'd given me a beautiful diamond ring and proposed on the spot. There was nothing I wanted more than to spend my life with him, whether he was Emperor Constantine of Rome . . . or this Constantine.

He continued his intense stare. "I knew the moment I saw you."

Chapter 3

Aurelia

I got ready for the day and prepared to head to Osteria Rita with Constantine to visit his mother.

He threw on a T-shirt and jeans before he put on his shoes. Despite the heat, he didn't wear shorts. I'd never seen him in shorts since I'd met him. When we walked into the main living room, Medusa hurried over to him in her walker, wagging her tail like her typical happy self.

Constantine kneeled down and gave her a rubdown and kissed her on the head. "Sheila will be here in a couple minutes, baby girl." He stood upright again and looked at me. "Ready, sweetheart?"

"Yeah." I liked how we each had our own nicknames. And instead of being jealous of how much attention he gave a dog, it actually made me fall for him even more. "Actually, no. Um . . ."

He turned to give me his full focus. "What's up?"

"I don't want to make this weird . . . and I feel bad for even bringing it up—"

"Don't do that."

"Do what?"

"Drag your feet, prep me for bad news, draw things out. Just deliver the information to me. I promise I can handle whatever you're about to say." He said it all calmly, despite the fact that he'd just cut me off to rush me.

"I'm afraid I'm going to make you mad."

"The only thing that would make me angry is if you fucked some other guy, and I know that didn't happen, so just tell me."

"Um, okay," I said. "Does Isabella know you're living here? I hate to bring her up, but I'm worried working at the restaurant might upset her or something. I just have a feeling we're going to run into her sometimes, and . . . maybe you should give her a heads-up."

As he'd said, he didn't get angry at the mention of her. "I'm in a relationship with you, not her, so her feelings are not my concern. Honestly, I haven't thought about her once since we got here. Been too occupied with you and Medusa and all the shit that just happened. But word travels fast in this small village, and I'm sure she's heard the news by now. Her mom and my mom are still best friends."

I remembered that argument they'd had on the terrace. I should have been angry that she wanted the man I loved, but I felt no resentment toward her at all. And if she still went after him while we were here, I didn't think I could even be angry about it. Maybe it was because Constantine made me feel so secure. He'd made me feel that way since the day we met, something Enzo had never done. Or maybe it was because I really did feel bad for her. "Well, do you think this is a good idea—"

"We're not revolving our lives around her feelings. *Period.*" He turned away from me. "Come on, let's go. My mom is always fifteen minutes early, so even if we get there on time, we'll be late."

~

When we arrived at Osteria Rita, there was a line out the door, but Constantine walked past everyone and up the stairs like he knew his mother was already seated inside. Then he stepped aside and waited for me to come to his side before he took my hand and walked me around the corner to the other side of the restaurant. When a waiter passed, he smiled at Constantine and gave him a playful bump in the arm.

His mother was already seated with someone, a man dressed in a T-shirt with the restaurant logo on it, along with dark jeans. He didn't look like a waiter or one of the cooks in the kitchen, so he might have been the manager or the owner. And they were chatting away like they were well acquainted.

His mother's eyes shifted to us and lit up like Christmas morning. "Con is here."

"Dario." Constantine smiled as he embraced the guy with one of those hand grabs that guys did. "It's been a while. Looks like business is good."

"It's too good," he said with a laugh. "Seems like I'll never have a day off as long as I live."

"Dario." Constantine introduced me. "This is my woman, Aurelia."

I noticed he didn't use *girlfriend.* I couldn't picture him saying something teenagers said. "Nice to meet you, Dario." I shook his hand.

Constantine pulled a chair out for me and got me seated before he took the last unoccupied chair at the four-seater table.

Dario and Constantine's mother finished up their talk, and then he headed back to the kitchen.

His mother gave her full focus to me. "Oh honey, it's so nice to see you." She was the one who got out of her chair and came all the way over to give me a hug when I should have been the one to go to her. She hugged me and smothered me like a child, then pulled back to look at me. "You're so beautiful. Every time I see you, you get more and more beautiful."

"Aww, thank you." She was so damn nice to me.

She went back to her seat, beamed at her son, and then held his hand on the table. "This is so nice. Having you both here. I swear the sun shines brighter on Taormina these days. At least, it does to me."

Constantine smiled, but it was restrained, the kind that didn't reach his eyes.

I noticed it, and I wondered if she knew her son well enough to notice too.

"How's Medusa?" she asked.

"She's a lot better," Constantine said. "Got her a walker so she's able to zoom around the house again. That really picked up her mood."

"Yeah," I said. "She was pretty sad for a while there."

"There's nothing worse than losing your independence," she said. "Especially for someone like Medusa, whose entire purpose is serving others. How long is the recovery?"

"At least four weeks," Constantine said. "So we have a little over two weeks to go before she can put weight on it."

Sofia patted her son's hand. "She's lucky to have you, Con."

His eyes shifted away like he didn't deserve the praise, even though he'd taken a bullet for her.

No other man would have done the same.

"Okay, let's eat." She pulled her hand away and clapped them together. "It's a treat not to be the one in the kitchen."

The waiter came over, and Sofia ordered a bottle of wine for the table without asking what we wanted, something that Constantine did himself. She ordered an appetizer too, bruschetta with ripe tomatoes and torn basil leaves.

Sofia turned her attention back to us. "So, how have you liked being back in Taormina?"

"It's been great," Constantine said. "Been seeing the boys a lot. Love eating at my favorite spots. Aurelia has been at Bam Bar nearly every morning." He shifted his gaze to me and gave me a playful smile.

"Guilty," I said with a shrug.

"I love that place too," Sofia said. "I'd go there more often if I weren't working all the time."

"Speaking of work . . ." Constantine said. "Aurelia lost all her clients when we left Rome. I told her I would help her pick up accounts with the hotels nearby, but she said she wanted to take a break."

"Good," Sofia said. "Don't work too much like me." She smiled at me across the table, looking so different from Constantine that I had to assume he mostly took after his father. But he definitely had her hair, thick, luscious, and dark. She had an inherent sparkle to her eyes, beautiful full Italian lips. I could tell she would have been a total bombshell when she was my age. No wonder she gave birth to such beautiful children. "You don't need to work when my son can take care of you."

Any other mother would probably worry I was taking advantage of his wealth and being lazy when I wasn't even his wife, but not her. She was so accepting of everyone. The kindest soul I'd ever met.

"Actually, Aurelia wanted to know if you needed another hand at one of the restaurants," Constantine said.

"Really?" she blurted. "Why?" She looked to me for an answer.

"I just thought it would be nice to spend time with you and the rest of Constantine's family—and to have a purpose. I burned myself out on the photography gig toward the end. Hours and hours I've spent sitting at a desk, editing photos, and I just want a break. Something that keeps me on my feet." Since I was mostly on my ass . . . or my back. "You don't have to pay me or anything."

She still seemed surprised by the request. "Never heard someone ask to work for free." She released a quiet chuckle. "But of course you're welcome to help out. Do you have any restaurant experience?"

"No, not really."

"Oh, that's okay," she said as she gave a wave of her hand. "Waitressing is straightforward, and I'm sure you'll pick up quickly in the kitchen."

"Ma, if this doesn't work for you, please don't feel obligated to accommodate us," Constantine said. "The last thing we want is to inconvenience you."

"It's no inconvenience," she said quickly. "If Aurelia wants to learn the ropes, I'll be happy to show her. Besides, a pretty waitress always brings in more business, so . . ."

The next day, I headed to Rosticceria Da Cristina alone, and I was greeted by Constantine's cousin Antonio. "Hey, Aurelia." He was warm like his cousin, giving me a big smile and making me feel welcome whenever we were in the same room together. Probably out of loyalty to Constantine, he accepted me without question.

"Hey, Antonio. Are you the one showing me the ropes?"

"Yeah, if you're up for it. Pizza and arancini can be a stressful gig." He smiled to tell me he was joking, then nodded for me to join him in the kitchen. "Just shadow me for the day, and tomorrow, you'll get your hands dirty."

"Sounds good."

"Aunt Sofia said you can help prep in the morning and then work the lunch shift next door."

"Works for me." I followed him around for the day, watched him prep the pizza dough as the first task to give it time to rise in the dark pantry. Then he prepared the tomatoes and the ingredients for the sauce for the arancini. There were other kitchens in the back, so other people were working as well, probably on different things. "How long have you worked here?"

"My whole life," he said as he worked the rice balls with his gloved hands. "My mom brought me here when she worked during the day, and then I would help out after school with Con. Food is life and life is food."

"Good words to live by." I loved that Constantine had pursued his own interests in life, but he'd never forgotten his roots. He had a lot of love for his family and for the restaurant. I could tell by the way he spoke about it. He was a wealthy man but remained down to earth, and that just made him more perfect.

"Why do you want to work here?" he asked as he continued to work.

"I needed a break from photography. Just wanted to do something different."

"They said you are working for free."

"Yeah, I'm not taking money from Constantine's mother," I said. "And it's not about the money. I thought it would be a great way to spend more time with all of you. And I think Constantine needs some time to himself." We'd lived together for a brief amount of time, but he'd been working for the Republic and I was focused on my photography, so we weren't together every moment of the day. I worried that he needed his space and having me around too much would strain what we had. And I suspected he needed time to process what had transpired in Rome, and it was impossible to digest the heaviness while constantly in the presence of someone else.

"Really?" he asked with a chuckle. "Because it sounds like he can't get enough of you."

A warmth spread through my chest, and then a tingle followed down my arms. I was the luckiest woman in the world, and I never forgot that. Constantine looked me straight in the eye and said I would be his wife someday—like it was a prophecy that would be fulfilled. "Yeah, he's sweet."

~

My shift ended shortly after two, so I headed to Bam Bar afterward. I sat alone at one of the beautiful round tables with the sun in the center and ordered a granita by myself, double mulberry with a scoop of cream. I needed to be mindful of my figure because I was with a freakin' gladiator of a man, but it was hard to turn down the perfect treat after a long day at Rosticceria Da Cristina. I enjoyed the atmosphere and thought I'd catch on quickly, but it was eight hours of constantly standing, which was a change of pace for me.

As I waited for my granita, I watched the people walk by, and I had to pinch myself to remind myself that this was real—that I was back in paradise. I had been born and raised in Rome, but this place felt like home to me. Every time I felt that joy, it was riddled with guilt because I knew Constantine didn't feel the same way.

My eyes narrowed on someone in the crowd, a six-and-a-half-foot gorgeous man with dark hair who looked identical to Constantine. I had to blink several times, assuming he was like an oasis in the desert that wasn't actually there, but he was.

Then he smiled.

Oh, it was Constantine.

"Hey, sweetheart." He came to the table and leaned down to kiss me.

"Hey. What are you doing here?"

He took the seat beside me and propped his arm over the back of my chair. "Saw you were here after your shift, so I thought I'd stop by."

Maybe he wasn't tired of me. Maybe he didn't need his space.

"When I saw you head farther into the town, I knew where you were headed." He grinned widely, handsome as hell.

"Saw me?" I asked blankly.

"Your location," he explained.

I forgot we'd shared our locations with each other a long time ago. "Oh yeah."

"Is that okay?"

"Yeah," I said quickly. "I just forgot."

The waiter came with my granita, the same flavor we'd ordered last time.

"It's good, huh?" Constantine said. "So, how was your first day?"

I ripped off a piece of the brioche and spooned the crystallized fruit over the edge before I popped it into my mouth. "It was okay. Antonio was there and he's always nice, so it wasn't too overwhelming."

"He's a good guy."

"Yeah, I like him."

"If you end up hating it, you don't have to stay, all right?"

"Why would I hate it?" I asked as I kept eating.

"Well, I started to hate it after a while," he said with a laugh. "I'd always smell like food, even after I showered."

"There are worse things."

He gave another chuckle.

And I melted inside.

"I'm sure women love getting railed by a guy who smells like pizza."

"I sure would."

He looked at me again, and he had this smile in his eyes like he thought I was the cutest thing ever. The affection was deep, beyond the flesh, like he loved who I was underneath. "You look fucking adorable in that outfit."

I wore a black Rosticceria Da Cristina T-shirt with black jeans. My hair had been combed back into a loose bun, which wasn't how I usually did my hair. I kept it down and long and mostly curled. "Yeah?"

He moved his hand down to the leg of my chair and effortlessly pulled me closer to him before that hand went to my thigh under the table, giving me a possessive grip that he pulled off so easily.

I tugged my granita closer and continued to eat. There was a nearby table with four pretty girls staring at him hard, but he didn't seem to notice because he was too busy staring at me. "How was your day?"

"Fine. Took Medusa on a walk, and then we watched the game together."

"How'd she do?"

"Good. Kept it short. Didn't want to push her too hard."

"I can't wait until she's better and we can take her places with us."

"Yeah, I'll take her on a hike to Mount Etna."

"The—the active volcano?"

He smirked. "I've been there during an eruption. Not a big deal."

"*Not a big deal?*" I asked.

"The eruptions are small. And even if they weren't, whether we're up there or down here, we're screwed either way."

"It's hard for me to take you seriously when you think getting shot is *no big deal*."

He chuckled and gave my thigh a squeeze. "Just look pretty and eat your granita, sweetheart."

~

His big arms supported my thighs as I sat on his face in bed—and he ate me for dinner. He drew all my folds into his mouth, and then he licked me hard with his powerful tongue, applying as much pressure as hard fingers. He worked me like it was for his enjoyment instead of mine, when I was the one to receive all the benefits.

One of his hands reached up to grip one of my tits, and he squeezed it hard as he continued to devour me whole.

I fisted his hair and rocked into his face, an empress on the throne of his mouth, writhing and riding, pushed over the edge and plunged into a pool of ecstasy. I bucked my hips and gave a cry as I shed tears of pleasure.

He slid his hand up to my neck, and he gripped my throat before he guided me off him. Put me on my back before he moved between my thighs and folded me like I was a strand of human licorice. I'd always been flexible, and I hadn't realized how much I'd need that skill until I met this six-and-a-half-foot behemoth of a man who liked to fuck me like a whore.

He shoved himself inside me without an ounce of gentleness, made himself right at home like my body was his palace, and then nailed me hard like even an eruption from Mount Etna wouldn't stop him. "Fuck, this pussy feels as good as it tastes."

I'd already come on his face so I didn't need another release, and it was so damn hot watching him fuck me like he hadn't had a woman in weeks instead of a day. He gave me so much of his length that it hurt with every thrust, but he'd made love to my pussy with his mouth for twenty minutes, so I could handle it.

He released a growl before he gave his final pumps, filling my pussy with a mound of seed that was so heavy it would register on a scale, and then all the muscles of his core tightened before they released.

He finished, then moved off me, rolling to his back with his head on the pillow.

I gently put my legs back into place, feeling all the stiffness in my joints from being in that position for so long. Then I lay there, fully satisfied and utterly spent.

Constantine closed his eyes and seemed to drift off right away.

I closed my eyes too, tired from my day at work and from the tidal wave of pleasure that had just knocked me off my feet.

Then I heard Medusa give a quiet whine from downstairs.

Constantine's eyes snapped open like a mother with a newborn. "She knows mommy-and-daddy time is over."

I chuckled. "I can't wait until she can come up the stairs on her own."

He left the bed and used the bathroom before he put on his boxers and headed down the stairs. A moment later, he returned carrying Medusa in his arms and put her in her dog bed on the floor next to his side of the bed. He gave her a rubdown before he kissed her on the head. "Good night, baby girl."

He headed back to bed, turned his phone on Do Not Disturb, and then rolled on his side to look at me. "What?"

It must have been the look on my face, the look I couldn't control. "I love the way you love her."

He watched me for a while, the sheets resting at his waist.

"If you become a dad someday, I think you'd be really good at it."

"Only if I had a daughter. If I had a son . . . I'm not so sure."

I could feel the surprise etch into my features because that was not something I expected him to say. "Why do you say that?"

"Sons are complicated. How do you raise them to be strong without being an asshole? How to be assertive but not unnecessarily confrontational? Men are violent, toxic, and rapists, serial killers. It's a fine line, and I'm not sure how to walk it."

"And how would raising a girl be different?"

"Because I'd raise her to be strong and assertive and as confrontational as she wants. Teach her how to handle toxic assholes and how to break their noses and their dicks. I was pretty much raised by a single woman. I understand women. They can be strong and gentle at the same time. But men . . . men are just worthless."

"I'm surprised you feel that way considering . . . you know."

"What?" he asked.

"Considering you're the greatest man I've ever known."

He stared at me endlessly, like he didn't understand if that compliment was genuine . . . or if he deserved it.

"Considering how you've spent your life protecting innocent people, women in particular, how you've treated me . . ."

"Let's not forget that I chop off hands and kill people."

"Men who deserve it. You make the hard decisions that no one else wants to make. You fight crime with crime. It's a fine line to walk, and you do it beautifully."

"I *did* it beautifully. But that's over now."

"Doesn't erase everything you did. How you served the Roman Republic."

He moved onto his back and looked at the high ceiling. "I'm done talking about this, sweetheart."

I noticed the way he used my nickname to lighten the blow, but his dismissal still stung anyway. Like someone had died, he grieved for the person he'd lost—himself. He'd taken so much pride in what he did, said he wouldn't sacrifice it for anything because nothing was more important than his service.

But then he fell in love with me . . . and that all changed.

Chapter 4

Aurelia

I went to Rosticceria Da Cristina the next morning. It was impossible to drive in the little village of Taormina and parking was also a bitch, so Constantine dropped me off at the edge of town before he headed back home to do his morning workout. He wasn't quite himself after last night, but he didn't seem distant with me either.

He was just lost.

The village was empty this early in the morning, so I walked to the restaurant alone. The door was unlocked when I got there, so I let myself inside. No one was in the front kitchen, so I called out, "Anyone here?"

A woman's voice came from somewhere in the rear. "Back here."

I headed farther into the back of the restaurant to the second kitchen. When I rounded the corner, I saw Beatrice, her hair up and flour on the front of her black apron. Her eyes were lively until the moment she saw me, and then they dimmed.

She couldn't even pretend.

In another situation with another person, I'd probably just address it head-on. Cut the shit, rip off the bandage, talk about the issue. But I wanted to marry her brother someday, so I had to play the game by her rules. Needed to give her time to warm up to me, to like me on her own terms instead of forcing her to accept mine. "Good morning." I forced a smile and stepped farther into her workplace, trying to act like I belonged there, when I was definitely encroaching on her turf.

She gave a slight smile, then focused on the dough in the bowl, working to mix it with the flour with her gloved hand. Her eyes were on her hand as she pretended I wasn't still there.

Bitch, we're going to be friends whether you like it or not. "Need a hand?"

"No."

I walked to the sink and looked at the dirty dishes that were piled up. I started to wash them to help her out.

"You don't have to do that," she said from behind me.

"It's no problem. I'd rather be productive while I wait for Antonio." I hadn't done the dishes in weeks, not since I moved in with Constantine. I didn't do anything domestic at all because he had someone do all that for us.

She continued to work on her dough. Didn't try to make conversation. Just let the tension fester.

"You have two boys?" I asked.

"Yeah." Nothing else. She gave me literally nothing to work with.

"What are their names?"

"Amerigo and Edoardo."

God, this feels like an interrogation.

Antonio saved the day when he walked inside and tied an apron around his waist. "Hey, Beatrice."

"Hey." She perked up real nice for him. "How'd it go last night?"

"Pretty good," he said. "We're going out again on Saturday."

"Ooh, nice."

I washed and dried my hands on the towel before I turned to Antonio.

He nodded to the other kitchen. "Let's work in here."

With fucking pleasure.

I walked out, gave Beatrice a smile that wasn't reciprocated, and then joined him in the other kitchen. "God, that was brutal."

He smirked like he knew exactly what I referred to. "Don't let it get to you. Constantine isn't the kind of guy to care what anyone thinks."

If Antonio knew Beatrice didn't like me, that meant she must have talked shit about me when I wasn't around.

A lot of shit.

"What about his mother?" I asked.

"Well, I think she's the one exception. But she loves you, so you're set on that front."

~

Around lunchtime, my alarm went off, so I stepped into the closet where everyone left their purses and belongings and fished my pill pack out of the bottom of my purse. I was about to pop the pill that I took at this time every day, but I realized all the pills were gone.

I'd completely finished the pack.

But . . . I hadn't had a period.

A jolt shook my heart, and then adrenaline made my entire body go numb. I continued to stare at the empty pack as I waited for an explanation to hit me—any explanation other than that.

I'd finished the placebos but didn't bleed, and I hadn't even realized the pack was nearly empty when I'd taken the last pill yesterday. With everything going on, I hadn't really thought much about it. "Oh shit . . . no."

I heard footsteps outside the door.

I quickly shoved the pack back into my purse before anyone saw.

It was Beatrice. She stepped into my line of sight, glanced at her purse and then at me. "Everything okay?"

I was surprised she had enough compassion to address what she'd overheard, but I was too overwhelmed by the earthquake that had just struck me to really care. "Yeah, I'm great. I'm just gonna take my lunch." I pulled the purse over my shoulder and bolted past her, then out the front door.

The sea air struck my face like a breeze because I walked so quickly. "Oh my god, oh my god, oh my god . . ." I felt the heat in my face because the stress was like an inferno in my belly. The possibility that I could be pregnant was horrifying because I wasn't ready to be a mom right now. And I knew Constantine wasn't in that headspace either.

What if he thought I'd done this on purpose?

"Okay, chill." I didn't even know if I was pregnant yet. Maybe I was just late. People were just late sometimes, right?

I booked it to the little grocery store next to the cannoli place we'd been on my first visit here. Loud dance music played overhead, and the store was already packed with local shoppers. I beelined for the aisle in the back and picked up the electronic pregnancy test that explicitly spelled out *pregnant* or *not pregnant* on the screen because I didn't want to be a dumbass and think I read it wrong.

I was so stressed that I could feel the pulse all over my body, right at my neck and wrists and ankles. My bladder wasn't even full, but I felt like I had to pee because of the sheer anxiety. I bought a pack of plastic cups, checked out, and then found the closest public restroom I could.

I peed in the cup, dropped the stick inside, sat on the closed toilet lid, and set a timer for three minutes.

Three long fucking minutes.

The cup was on the floor, and I stared at the stall door as I waited for time to pass.

Longest three minutes of my damn life.

I rubbed my palms together over and over, tried to breathe when I could literally feel my heart beating against my chest, tried not to pass out or throw up. I thought women had morning sickness when they were pregnant, and I hadn't felt any of that . . . so maybe I wasn't pregnant.

Finally, the alarm went off.

I picked up the cup so fast, I spilled it, urine going all over the floor.

I didn't give a damn, and my eyes went straight to the screen on the stick.

Pregnant.

Chapter 5

Constantine

After I finished my workout and showered, I took a day trip to Palermo. Aurelia was at work at Rosticceria Da Cristina, and Medusa was with the dog nanny I'd hired. It took me two hours to get there, and when I arrived outside Villa de la Sirenuse, the guards let me inside without an interrogation.

I greeted the guys outside, caught up with a few others, and then ran into Alfonso.

"What brings you here?" he asked, wearing a pin-striped suit with a cigar in his mouth. He greeted me in the entryway, Tommaso's representative. He was the person who spoke on Tommaso's behalf for diplomatic matters . . . and sometimes threats. Tommaso couldn't be everywhere at once, so he sent Alfonso in his stead. They'd had a great partnership long before I'd joined Cosa Nostra.

"I texted Tommaso. He's expecting me."

He nodded before he breathed a cloud of smoke in my face. "There's been a lot of talk on the street about what went down in Rome."

"Oh, I'm sure."

That seemed to be the confirmation he wanted. "I'll let him know you're here." He walked off and turned into a hallway. The rest of the room was filled with armed guards. Their guns were hidden in their jackets or in the backs of their jeans, but that was their entire purpose. A militia to protect Tommaso, even though he was pretty much untouchable in Sicily. The police were dwarfed by the size of Cosa Nostra, so they didn't interfere with their affairs, and Cosa Nostra mostly did their business in the shadows so no one even knew they were there.

I stood and waited, looking at the guys who all looked at me.

I could feel the change in the room.

The loss of respect.

Alfonso returned moments later. "He's ready for you, Con." He nodded to the double doors that remained open so I could pass through.

I headed down the hallway and heard the double doors shut behind me. I walked past the bulletproof windows that let in the summer sunshine. The rest of his family lived in the villa, but they stayed on the upper floors of the house, where no one was allowed to go except for him.

I entered another set of guarded doors before I stepped into Tommaso's study, an enormous room with several large couches on a rug in front of a hearth. He had a large desk on the other side of the room, like he was a lawyer or a judge instead of a crime kingpin.

He was already on the couch when I walked inside, two drinks on coasters. "Constantine." He rose to his feet to greet me and extended his hand.

I took it, and we made a mutual grip before we both let go. "Tommaso."

He took a seat.

I sat across from him.

We sat together for a while. He gave a long stare, one packed with sympathy but mostly pity.

I sat back against the couch and felt like a lesser man. I'd let my empire fall. Let an inside invader take it from me. Fell for a plan so simple because I solely focused on the complex. "It's been rough."

"I can imagine."

"But I'm a man who can admit my faults. He outsmarted me—and I let him."

Tommaso didn't nod in agreement. Didn't judge me for what I'd lost. He felt more like a friend than a former boss. "Perhaps this is just a battle and not the war."

"No, it's done," I said with finality. "It's the price I paid to save my woman."

"And was that price worth it?" He sat back too, crossing one ankle on the opposite knee.

I felt no doubt in my heart. Felt no resentment toward her. Only love. "Absolutely."

We sat in silence for a while as he processed what I said. He held my gaze as his elbow rested on the armrest, his closed knuckles planted against his cheek. "You know terrible things are about to happen to a lot of people. Not just the Romans, but the president and the Senate and the government as a whole. With everyone at his mercy, who knows what he'll do. He has no love for his country, so he'll make deals with our enemies just to line his pockets. He's reckless and lawless . . . and not stupid."

"I'm aware." Painfully aware of all those things.

"Then I'm sure you'll change your mind. When the time is right."

I shook my head. "I'm a man of my word. He wouldn't have let us go otherwise."

"Then let that be his mistake."

"It's done." I didn't raise my voice, but my tone had an edge to it. I would never forget how it felt to hear from my men that my home had been compromised, that painful realization that Aurelia was the target. By the time I'd made it there, Darius had her on the floor with a gun to her head.

It was Edric all over again.

But this time, I was able to stop it. I was able to save her.

Another cloud of silence passed as he looked at me. "If you're a man of your word, then it's time you keep your word to me."

My eyes narrowed as I failed to understand his meaning.

"My daughter."

When the realization struck me, it was followed by a wave of annoyance. "I just gave up the Roman Empire for a woman. I'm clearly unavailable, Tommaso."

"But are you married?"

"What does that matter?"

"It matters because you're not committed."

"Oh, I'm committed." Very fucking committed. Committed for the rest of my life, whether she was my woman or my wife.

"You said if you weren't married, you would consider my daughter."

I'd come here to be consoled by an old friend, and now I was being propositioned for an arranged marriage. "We both know that was a stupid request—"

"But you agreed to it. And I put my life on the line for your stupid brother."

I suddenly had a kink in my neck, irritation that flooded my entire body.

"Are you a man of your word or not?"

"Why do you even want me for your daughter?" I snapped. "I just handed the keys to the kingdom to a psychopath. I turned my back on my country and my people for a single woman. I'm not a hero."

"And that's why I want you for my daughter, Constantine. I want a man who would turn his back on everyone else before he would turn his back on her. Who would sacrifice the entire world before he'd let anything happen to her. There are so few men like you. A needle in a fucking haystack. That's what she deserves."

"I'm sure she does, Tommaso. But I did those things because I'm in love with this woman, a woman who will someday be my wife. I'm sure your daughter is lovely, but my heart belongs to someone else."

"Con, you said you would *consider* it."

I dropped my head in frustration and rubbed one of my eyes. "You know how insane you sound?"

"I'm just repeating our agreement because you've clearly forgotten."

"And after all these years, you haven't realized how ridiculous of a request it is?"

"No."

"What does your wife think of this?"

"She's on board."

I sat back in the chair and gave a frustrated sigh, unable to believe that this agreement made seven years ago was about to haunt me. "It took me nine years to love someone again. I'm not going to meet your daughter and then suddenly forget Aurelia."

"Just consider it."

"If I consider it, I'm cheating on my woman. That's not who I am, and why the fuck would you want a man like that for your daughter?"

"Why is everything so extreme with you?" Now he raised his voice. "All I ask is you have dinner with her. A bottle of wine with a dinner salad and a nice piece of fish in cream sauce. Just an hour of your time."

"This is ridiculous."

"You gave me your word, Con. I could have been killed that night. Could have left my girls without a father and a husband. I only stick out my neck for men who deserve my spine, and I never would have extended it for that knucklehead brother of yours, especially if I'd known what he'd done—*which you hid from me.*"

My eyes flicked away because I still felt guilty for what I'd done. Compromised my own principles just for the chance to save my brother. Told an intentional lie to get what I wanted, despite the damage to my reputation.

"You owe me."

"Fine."

When Tommaso finally got the answer he wanted, he relaxed in the chair, even wore a smile.

"I still don't fucking understand." I didn't understand any of it.

"Con, God decided I would have daughters instead of sons, which is fine. They're the light of my life, especially now that they're adults and out of the house and not giving me grief every fucking day. But I have to think of the future of Cosa Nostra, how to keep it in the Sirenuse family, and none of my brothers or their kids are up to the task."

Now I understood. "Should have known it was all political."

"It's always political," he said. "You marry my daughter, and I have a good son-in-law who will keep her safe. Who will keep his dick in his pants when she's not around. Who will be a good father instead of a neglectful piece of shit. And I'll have a son to carry on Cosa Nostra when my time comes."

"Why do you assume I would return to Cosa Nostra?"

He gave a shrug. "What else are you going to do? Go back to making those little fucking rice balls?"

"My great-great-grandparents used to make those little fucking rice balls and feed the homeless soldiers after the war—so fuck off."

He tensed before he raised his hands in the form of surrender. "Con—"

"Insult me for abandoning Rome, but don't insult my family or the way we've supported ourselves for generations. Don't for one second think you're better than us because you're the one sitting at the table while we're cooking in the back."

"Con, I didn't mean it that way."

"Yes, you fucking did. Come for me all you want, but come for my family and see what happens." I had a lot of love for the man across from me, but that love could disappear within the snap of a finger when it came to my family. "You think you're better than us since people are afraid of you? Because my mom hosts a big dinner every Sunday night and brings everyone together. Not just family, but friends and neighbors, anyone who needs a place to go, and that's a hell of a lot better of a legacy than threatening and bullying people to get what you want."

"Look, I apologize, all right? I'm sorry for what I said."

I still fumed in my seat, but I had nothing more to say.

"I just meant, What are you going to do now?"

"I have more money than you'll ever see in your fucking life, Tommaso." Darius had taken my home, but he didn't take my billions. Stashed in investment accounts and bonds and in cash at different banks, my money was hidden in all kinds of places.

"I didn't mean for money, but for purpose," he said calmly. "You don't strike me as the kind of man that retires."

I didn't like to sit still for too long. It would drive me mad after a while. Whenever Aurelia went to work, it gave me time to think about what I wanted to do for the rest of my life. I could return to Cosa Nostra . . . or pursue something else.

"You know you always have a place with Cosa Nostra, whether you marry my daughter or not."

I was sick of him acting like there was an actual chance of that happening. "I appreciate that, Tommaso."

He studied me for a while, and when he sensed I'd cooled off from my previous outburst, he changed the subject. "Since you're in town, how about I arrange a lunch meeting for the two of you?"

"Right now?" I asked incredulously.

"Yes."

Fuck that. "Today isn't great, Tommaso."

"Then when?" he pressed.

"I don't know." I had to get him off my back. Maybe if enough time passed, he would drop this and I'd be off the hook. Maybe his daughter would start seeing someone he liked, and he wouldn't need me anymore. I just had to dance around it long enough until that happened. "But I'm still pissed off about the bullshit you said, so I'm not exactly pleasant company right now." It was the only viable excuse I could think of on the spot.

He nodded in understanding, so it seemed to do the trick. "All right, then. Next time."

Over my dead fucking body. "We'll see."

Chapter 6

Constantine

It was almost dark by the time I got home from Palermo.

I didn't tell Aurelia where I was headed that day, and when she didn't text me, I assumed she looked up my location and figured it out. I wouldn't have cared if she'd texted me—she could blow up my phone all she wanted—but I liked the fact that she could just see where I was whenever she wanted.

It was the kind of intimacy I'd never had with anyone before. I shared my entire life with her, where I was every moment of the day, and I could see where she was, like if she went to Bam Bar on her lunch break to eat a granita by herself. I gave her debit and credit cards for my bank accounts and added her to all my other accounts, so she could theoretically walk into the bank and cash out all my holdings if she wanted to.

I shared all of myself with her.

Well, except one thing.

This massive, painful depression that cracked my soul in half. It was on my mind every single day, the loss of purpose, the loss of my identity. Rocco hadn't looked at me the same . . . when I loved him like a brother. I'd never had a high opinion of myself, my entire identity embedded in my service, but now, I hated who I was. Not because I saved Aurelia—but because I needed to save her.

I let everyone down.

I let myself down.

When I came home, I heard the TV in the other room. I walked into the entryway and through the massive arch that led to the main room with the enormous glass windows that showed the sea view outside.

I saw Aurelia on the couch in one of my oversize T-shirts. Normally, she got to her feet whenever I came home and gave me a big kiss while I grabbed her ass, but she didn't look at me right away, as if she somehow didn't hear me enter the room or didn't notice me when I stepped into her presence.

Her eyes found mine, and for a brief second, they were absolutely lifeless. But then she blinked, and there was her smile. "Hey." Medusa was on the couch beside her, using the ramp I'd bought for her so it was easier for her to get on the couch when I wasn't home. Aurelia got to her feet and came over to me, rising on her tiptoes to kiss me.

Something was definitely off. I could feel it, see it, even hear it. "Everything all right?"

"Yeah, just tired," she said quickly as she pulled away. "Medusa and I were just watching TV."

Medusa released a quiet whine from the couch, wanting me to come to her since she couldn't get up and run to me like she used to.

"Hey, baby girl." I moved to her and squatted down so I could pet her and kiss her on the head. When I stood upright and turned back to Aurelia, I caught another glimpse of that dull throb in her eyes, but I didn't question her again. "Have you eaten dinner? Want to go out?"

"Uh, I'm not really that hungry," she said. "So how was your day?"

"Sucked, mostly."

"Oh? What did you do?"

I hesitated as I read her expression, seeing no hint of a lie in the question. "I went to Palermo." And she didn't know that? She didn't look up my location? I had been gone pretty much all day, and she hadn't been curious about where I was?

"No wonder you're home so late." She crossed her arms over her chest, her makeup already off her face like she was ready for bed, even though she normally didn't remove her makeup until right before bed.

"Did something happen at work?" I didn't want to interrogate her for information she didn't want to give, but I knew something was different. I knew it had nothing to do with me because there'd been no conflict between us.

"What?" she asked automatically. "No . . . it was fine."

"Isabella didn't come by or something?"

"No," she said quickly.

"Then what's wrong?" She was pretty forthcoming with me about her thoughts and feelings. I never really had to wonder what she was thinking, and I loved that about her. But now, she wore a mask I couldn't penetrate.

"Um . . ." Her eyes frantically flicked back and forth as the panic set in. "It's pretty clear your sister doesn't like me, and I'm just having a hard time building a connection with her . . . that's all." She gave me a sad smile, then loosened her arms from around her body.

"Don't worry about her, sweetheart."

"I know how important your family is to you."

"You're my family." My hands slid into her hair as I tilted her head back to look at me. "Whatever issue my sister has is her business. Let her deal with it, okay?"

Her eyes were locked on mine, and a softness came through, a softness she showed me nearly all the time.

I was glad to see it again. "Anyone who doesn't like you can fuck right off. Don't prove yourself. Don't play nice. That applies to everyone—including Beatrice. You think I give a damn if someone doesn't like me?"

"No," she said quietly.

"Then don't you dare give a damn about her."

I'd thought we resolved Aurelia's stress, but the very next morning, she was the same. Quiet and distant, she avoided eye contact a lot of the time, which was completely unlike her. The most obvious reason for the avoidance was to hide a lie, but she had nothing to lie about.

I dropped her off at work, then did my morning workout and showered. Had breakfast, took Medusa out on a walk, and then I sat on the patio under the shade of the umbrella and marinated in my thoughts.

I didn't know what the fuck to do with myself.

Didn't know how to stop the pain.

Returning to Rome and defeating Darius was the only way to fix it, but that wasn't an option. Even if I could hide Aurelia in a place where he would never find her, her safety wasn't guaranteed. Because if I lost the battle, Darius would spend the rest of his life hunting for her. And when he found her . . .

There was nothing I could do. I was exiled from my home, and I'd run like a coward. I was a disgrace to my ancestors. I was a disgrace to the empire.

But I'd rather be a disgrace than lose the woman I loved.

Medusa ran around the yard for a while before she came back to me. She stood there in her walker and looked up at me, like she had the intuition to feel my thoughts, my sadness. Her big brown eyes looked into mine as she searched for a solution to my heartache. Then she came closer to me and rubbed her head against my leg, the closest thing to a hug she could give.

I started to pet the top of her head. "I'm okay, baby girl. If I could do it all over again . . . I wouldn't change anything."

I took Aurelia out to dinner, to one of my favorite restaurants, Trattoria Tiramisù. Their family was friends with my family, like pretty much everyone in Taormina, and they had great food.

I ordered a bottle of wine for the table and then looked at the menu.

The waiter poured the glasses of wine, then left us to decide what we wanted.

When I looked up over the menu, I saw Aurelia sitting there, her eyes on a nearby table instead of on her menu. I watched her for a while, noticing the paleness of her cheeks. There was a dullness in her eyes along with an underlying sense of panic.

It'd been this way for a couple days now.

I set the menu aside. "Sweetheart."

Her eyes flicked back to me.

"Did you lie about my sister?"

"What?" she asked, her eyebrows arching.

"When I noticed you were down, you said it was because my sister didn't like you. But that was days ago, and you've been . . . distant ever since. So, was that actually true?"

"Yes. Not only does your sister not like me, but she talks shit about me at work."

I loved my sister and thought we were close, but if that was true, it made me wonder if I really knew her at all. "What does she say?"

"I don't know, but everyone knows she doesn't like me, so she's saying something." Her eyes flicked away again.

"I'll talk to her."

"No," she said quickly. "You'll just piss her off."

"You shouldn't be in a hostile work environment."

"It's fine."

"You don't have to work there, Aurelia. If it's causing you this much distress, it's not worth it."

"It's fine."

"My mother won't be upset—"

"I said it's fine."

I stared at her across the table, seeing the toll this soap opera was taking on her. It was even more idiotic, considering the fact that she had access to more money than everyone on this island combined . . . but she was taking shit from my sister.

I suspected Beatrice had crossed a line and said something to her she shouldn't have. Maybe played a joke on her. Did something to make her life more difficult at the restaurant. But Aurelia, being the person she was, didn't want to cause problems between me and my sister.

She opened the menu and tried to sidestep the tension. "So, what's good here?"

I let the issue slide because there seemed to be no easy solution in sight. "I usually get the sea bass. They cook it in a potato crust. Goes well together."

"I'll try that too."

"Pairs well with the wine too."

"Wish I could have some, but I had a massive migraine earlier and took about twenty pills." She rubbed her temple before she fixed her hair. She turned the menu over and looked at the desserts on the back. "The tiramisu must be good since it's in the name of the restaurant."

"Never had it, but I'm sure it's delicious."

"Well, that's all I need to hear." She set the menu aside and looked me in the eye, seeming to be herself again because she smiled at me. "So how was your day?"

I arrived at my mother's house and knocked on the front door.

It was a big villa, but she opened it right away like she'd been in the entryway, excited for me to get there, peeking through the window every minute to see if my Range Rover was outside.

She greeted me with a big hug and a kiss on the cheek, rising on her tiptoes to reach me. "My boy."

"Hey, Ma." I kissed her on the cheek and walked with her inside.

"Are you hungry?"

"No, I just had lunch." I wouldn't mind her cooking, but she always went overboard and made more than I could possibly eat. A feast for literally one person. Now that I lived nearby, I guessed I could take the leftovers home.

We went into the kitchen, where she had a six-seater table. She had a full dining room, but she used this space as her office when she worked at home, probably because it was closer to the microwave to reheat her coffee. It took her a couple hours just to finish a single cup.

I took a seat and watched her work in the kitchen to make me a latte that I didn't ask for. She brought it to me along with a saucer of biscotti, even though she knew I didn't eat sweets. She made herself a latte and sat across from me, paperwork and her laptop on the table like she was doing the books at home.

"It's been nice having Aurelia at the restaurant."

"Yeah?"

"Yeah, she's great in the kitchen. But she's a better waitress. Easy on the eyes, you know."

"Trust me, I know," I said with a slight smile.

"She'll give you beautiful children, Con," she said. "She has the perfect hips for childbirth."

She had the perfect hips for other stuff too. "Whether we do or whether we don't, I'm very happy." Aurelia wasn't adamant about having children, like most women her age, and I'd never really cared either way. I didn't want to put that pressure on her, because some women couldn't have children and she might be one of those women. The last thing I wanted her to think was that I'd love her less if that were to happen.

"Seeing you happy makes me happy," my mom said with those emotional eyes. "You're a fine young man who deserves a good woman. I'm glad you finally found her. The fact that she doesn't have to work but chooses to get her hands dirty at the restaurant says a lot about her character. That she doesn't mind hard work like washing dishes or doing her best to integrate with your family says even more."

"Yeah, I know." I'd known for a long time. Even when I'd been pissed at her and walked out, I still knew. I just needed to wait for my anger to pass like a gray storm cloud to see the sun again. "I wish Beatrice felt the same way."

"She doesn't?" she asked in genuine surprise.

I didn't want to throw Aurelia under the bus after she'd confided in me. "That's my perception."

"Well, I think your perception is wrong, Con. She's just overwhelmed with work and the kids and all that. She asked me to babysit so she can work, but I'm running two restaurants—what makes her think I can babysit?"

"True." She wouldn't need a babysitter if that piece-of-shit ex of hers hadn't run from his responsibilities. Didn't abandon his family like worthless scum.

She tapped her fingers on the rim of her mug as we fell into silence.

The few times in my life when I felt overwhelmed, I'd come to her and she always made me feel better. But now I didn't know how to start, how to confide in her when she didn't want to know about my life in Rome in the first place.

She took a drink of her coffee before she studied me across the table. "Something's on your mind."

"Yeah."

"You know I'm always here to listen."

My eyes drifted elsewhere, to the open window that let in the sunlight, to the colored plate that hung on the wall. It was something I'd made when I was little, but she still had it up, even in her new villa. "Been feeling lost . . ." I swallowed, feeling a swell of emotion that seemed to come from nowhere. I'd barely said a few words, and I was already drowning in my misery. I questioned who I was as a man, something I'd never done before.

She didn't ask questions. Didn't pry for more. Just listened.

"I left Rome because I had to—not because I wanted to." I swallowed again, feeling guilty for destroying my mother's fantasy, that I'd come home because I wanted to be close to her and the rest of the family. "I was outsmarted by my enemy, and I had to choose between my world and Aurelia. I chose her. Obviously." I kept my eyes on the window because it would be too hard to look at her. "I let everyone down. My men, my friends . . ." The thought of Rocco made my throat tighten, remembering our final conversation with bone-splitting pain. "My people, my country. Aurelia . . ." I didn't look at my mother, because I knew I would succumb to the sadness that I carried like a bag of bricks in my chest.

I could feel her eyes on me, feel her pain waft across the room like smoke.

"I fucked up . . . and I can't fix it." I felt the distant rim of moisture at the bottom of my eyes, but I took a breath, held it for a couple seconds, and then I felt the tears drain back into my head like they'd never been there.

My mother didn't ask for specifics or clarification. She just listened to me. Was present with me. "I'm proud of you."

My eyes flicked back to hers quickly, surprised by what she'd said.

"You put her before yourself. You put her before everyone else. And that's exactly what a man does. I wish your father had done that for me. I wish Beatrice's husband had done that for her. You're exactly the man that I raised you to be, that I dreamed you would be." Her eyes started to water. "I'm very proud to call you my son." Her hand moved to the center of the table, her palm slightly turned up.

"Ma . . ." My hand moved to hers, and I grabbed it, felt her squeeze me. It was the deepest, most heartfelt thing she'd ever said to me, and I didn't know how to accept such a beautiful love. "Everything I am . . . is because of you."

Her eyes watered further, like receiving the credit meant the world to her. "I wish there was something I could do to absolve your guilt, take it for you, carry it for you. But only you can let it go. And I think you deserve to let it go, son."

I gave a slight shake of my head. "A lot of people will suffer. The consequences of this will last for decades."

"And nothing can be done?"

I gave another shake of my head. "If I didn't have Aurelia, I would try. But I can't risk her."

She nodded in agreement before she pulled her hand away.

"It's done. And I have to find a way to move on. Just not sure how."

"Cosa Nostra?" she asked.

"I was there last week. I've considered it. Just seems like a step down, a much slower pace than what I'm used to. Not to mention, it's a two-hour drive, so I'd have to be there days at a time and leave Aurelia here."

"She can always stay with me or Antonio."

"I mean I don't want the kind of relationship where we're apart like that." I wanted to be home with her every night. I'd just asked her to move in with me, just told her I loved her, but I already felt like we were married. Or maybe that was just how committed my heart was. "She'd move to Palermo with me, but I know her heart is here."

A small smile moved over her lips. "I'm glad this place is already home to her."

"I know a big part of that is you. You've been so good to her, and I really appreciate it, Ma."

"You love her, so I love her." She shook her head. "No questions asked."

No one had my back like my mother did. None of my men. Not even Rocco. She was the first one to show me the meaning of loyalty. It marked my skin like a tattoo, and I'd carried it with me ever since.

"Every man needs a purpose. Perhaps you should consider opening a restaurant here in Taormina. Could be an addition to Rosticceria Da Cristina, or perhaps you could do something else. Aurelia is smart and learns quickly, so I'm sure she could help you run it. I know you'd attract a lot of customers with her as a waitress."

"No doubt," I said with a smile.

"And if you're thinking about the future, about having a wife and maybe a family, perhaps that's the better fit than returning to Cosa Nostra."

"I suppose." I remembered when I'd left Taormina when I was a young man, excited for something new, to get out of the kitchen and do something more professional. But the older I got, the more I realized how special my family and our restaurant were, the kind of impact we had on people through our love of cooking. Now I was proud of it. "Just thought I'd do something more exciting."

"What's more exciting than a family of your own?"

"Ma, I told you kids may or may not happen for us. Please don't put that pressure on us, especially Aurelia."

"You misunderstand me, honey. When you marry her, you'll become a family of two. Or I guess three, if you include Medusa," she said with a smile. "Whether you have kids or not, she'll take your last name and be a part of you forever. And that's more exciting than anything you could do with Cosa Nostra."

Chapter 7

Constantine

We had dinner together on the terrace, the sunset making the sky burn in an array of beautiful colors. Fresh sea bass with white rice and slow-roasted asparagus. That was the one thing Rome lacked, fresh seafood prepared in the Sicilian style. The capital was close to the sea, but it didn't compare to island living, when the boats left the ports before dawn and brought back the catch to the village before restaurants even opened. I started to eat a lot of steak once I moved to Rome because the seafood was always disappointing in comparison. Now that I was back, it was what we ate every night.

Better for my health anyway.

Aurelia sat across from me in a dark-green T-shirt and cutoff denim shorts. As the sunlight left, the temperature started to drop, but she didn't go inside and grab a sweater. Her hair was straight, her makeup done, and she looked as beautiful as always—except for the trepidation in her eyes.

It seemed to be there almost all the time now.

I had no fucking idea why.

"How was your day?"

"Good," she said. "Antonio is a really nice guy."

"He is."

"I fucked up the dough this morning, but he didn't give me shit about it."

"He knows I'll kill him if he does."

She smirked slightly.

"How are you liking it?"

"It's stressful and I don't love having to be there so early in the morning, and you're right, my hair smells like tomatoes all day, but I do like it. I like being a part of the . . . tribe. Plus, all the free food."

I smiled. "You'll get over that pretty quickly."

"I don't know. Fresh pizza right out of the oven . . . can't beat that."

"I used to go out for lunch every day because I got so tired of it." I grabbed the bottle of wine and filled my glass before I moved to hers.

"Oh, none for me, thanks," she said quickly. "Antonio and I shared a bottle over lunch."

"At the restaurant?" I asked in surprise.

"Well, we ate together at the restaurant, and he said the wine was free, so . . ." She grabbed her fork and scooped it through the rice before she placed it in her mouth, her eyes on her plate.

"That's interesting," I said. "Antonio usually hates wine."

She sliced her fork into her fish and took a bite. "Said it went with the food," she said with a shrug.

Or maybe he was just trying to be polite around Aurelia. He'd always been a gentleman, ever since we were young men. Always accommodating to others, especially women. She must have said how much she liked it, and he sucked it up so she wouldn't feel uncomfortable.

"How was it with your mom?" she asked quickly as she continued to eat.

I didn't confide my feelings to Aurelia. Not because she'd done anything wrong or I didn't trust her. I just didn't want her to feel guilty, to make her wonder if I wished I'd made a different decision. If she knew just how deep this depression went, it would break her heart. And I didn't want that either. So I told the one person I knew could handle it—my mother. "Good. We discussed my options."

"Your options?"

"Whether I should return to Cosa Nostra or keep my focus here in Taormina."

"Oh." Her plate was clean, but she continued to scrape up every grain of rice like she was starving. "What do you want to do?"

"Not sure, honestly." I couldn't deny that my mother was right, that Aurelia was my priority now and I needed to revolve my life around her. Cosa Nostra didn't fit the bill. But I wasn't sure if I'd be fulfilled running a restaurant.

"Well, you know I support whatever you decide."

"I know, sweetheart." I finished my plate and focused on my wine, a white wine from Mount Etna. The wineries at that elevation were some of the best on the island.

"So . . . how have you been feeling . . . in general?" There was so much hesitancy in her voice, like she knew she wouldn't get an answer even as she asked the question. But she probably asked it anyway just so I'd know she cared.

I couldn't share any of it with her. Couldn't burden her with that. "Fine."

"You can always talk to me about it. I'm here."

"There's nothing to say." Maybe one day, all this guilt would drain out of my body, but I suspected it was a permanent part of me now. I used to be proud of who I was, and now I was mostly ashamed.

She looked at me for a moment, still holding her fork even though her plate was empty at that point. The plates were blue and yellow, striking colors from a local artist in a traditional Sicilian style. There wasn't a single aspect of this house that reminded me of my home in Rome, and maybe that was a good thing. "Have you . . . talked to Rocco?"

The sound of his name nearly made me spiral in a mixture of rage and sorrow. I used to not dream because my sleep schedule was so unpredictable and I was too exhausted to dream, but now, I experienced them. And Rocco was in my dreams most of the time. It was either an alternate version of our final argument or distorted memories. Three weeks had passed since I'd been exiled from Rome, and his name never appeared on my phone—and mine never appeared on his.

She continued to stare at me as she waited for an answer.

"No."

The disappointment was heavy in her gaze, and she curled her fingers underneath her chin. "Maybe you should—"

"That friendship is over." I didn't want her to mention him again. Didn't want to talk about a friendship that couldn't be resurrected. He was the closest thing I'd had to a brother after Edric died, but now he was dead to me too.

"Why?" she asked gently. "What happened?"

She deserved to know, but I didn't have the heart to tell her. Didn't have the strength to relive that conversation where he'd ripped my fucking heart out of my chest. "He said some things to me that . . . can never be unsaid."

~

A week passed, and Aurelia still wasn't the same as she used to be. There was no way my sister could be causing her this much stress, and according to my mother, she was a great addition to the restaurant, so I knew she was welcome there. All I could assume was that the weight and trauma of what had happened had permanently scarred her.

And that trauma had happened because of me. Because I hadn't been there to prevent it. Trapped on the third floor behind that fortress of a wall, she'd had no other choice but to sit there and wait for him to come for her.

This whole time, I'd assumed I was the only one who suffered, but I wasn't.

When I came home from Francesco's place, she was outside on the terrace with Medusa. She slouched on one of the couches and looked out at the sea. Medusa lay on her side on the tile at her feet. I could only see the side of Aurelia's face from where I stood, but her eyes appeared wet, like she'd been crying.

Just when I thought I couldn't despise myself even more . . . I did.

A tear slipped from her lid and streaked down her cheek but stopped at her chin.

She absentmindedly reached for it, her eyes still on the sea, and she wiped it away with her fingertips before she crossed her arms over her chest. I saw her entire body rise when she took a deep breath, when she calmed herself and returned to her center.

Medusa lifted her head as if she sensed Aurelia's sadness. She slowly got to her feet, putting some weight on her leg because it seemed to have improved enough for her to do so, and then she moved her chin to Aurelia's lap.

Aurelia smiled and dug her fingers deep into Medusa's fur. Her lips moved like she said something. Together, they looked at each other, comforting each other . . . both survivors of my incompetence.

The next evening, we had dinner together on the terrace. It was the only meal we shared together. She went to work and skipped breakfast, and I hit the gym before I had an egg-white omelet alone in my study. Sometimes I went to the restaurant for lunch just to watch her wait on me, her tits incredible in the tight little shirt, but we didn't actually eat together. Dinner was the only time we dined with each other.

I opened a bottle of wine and filled our glasses. I removed the silver lids Elio had placed over the food to keep it warm and revealed the grilled fish and prawns over a bed of mashed potatoes and wilted greens.

"So I guess I can expect fish every night for the rest of our lives," she teased.

"I'll tell Elio to change it up."

"I'm kidding," she said. "I mean, you can't beat it, that's for sure."

There were little moments like this when she was herself again, but they were brief and fleeting. It was just yesterday when I saw her crying on the terrace. I pretended I hadn't seen and didn't question her about it, because she dismissed me every time I tried.

I'd brought us to Taormina in the hope we could find happiness in each other, but it seemed like what had happened had affected us too deeply. Maybe we'd never be able to recover. Maybe we were doomed to this sadness forever.

We ate quietly, neither of us having much to say. Our sex life hadn't been that great either. She never seemed interested, and to be honest, knowing your woman was depressed because of you wasn't the biggest turn-on. I already felt like a failure, and knowing she probably agreed with that sentiment made it so much worse.

"I wish you would confide in me." I didn't realize the words were on my tongue until they were out of my mouth. The urge couldn't be suppressed, not when I drowned in this suffocating silence. It was hard to remember our lives before, even though it had been just a few weeks ago.

She stiffened when she not only heard my words but felt them. Her eyes were on her plate, but instead of taking a bite, she pushed a red prawn away from the mashed potatoes. There was no hesitancy or bewilderment, like she knew exactly what I referred to. But she didn't say anything, just held her silence, like she actually considered coming clean.

But she didn't. "You don't confide in me either, Constantine."

It felt like a slap in the face, but it was true. I hadn't shared any of myself with her at all. Whenever she asked, I sidestepped the question or rejected her entirely. I barely said a few words at all.

I grabbed the bottle of wine and refilled my glass. I was about to tip the bottle toward hers, but I realized she hadn't touched it at all, even though I was on my third glass. I set the bottle aside, then sat there, not interested in the food on my plate. "I've struggled to let it go. Struggled to move on and accept this new identity. Don't misunderstand me, I have no regrets about the decision I made. But I feel lost every day, like I don't know who I am anymore."

Her eyes lifted to meet mine with a sadness that somehow rivaled my own.

"I wait for it to get better, but I suspect it'll never get better. The world sees me as a coward who chose exile . . . instead of as a man who did everything he could to protect his woman. I used to be respected, but now people despise me. Like all the good things I did in my life never happened. It was all erased the moment Darius defeated me in a game of checkers because he was playing chess." I didn't want to share any of this with her. It was so fucking painful to say out loud. But I knew if I wanted her to confide in me, I had to do the same. "I vowed to kill Darius and avenge my brother, but instead, I let him take the Roman Republic and my home. And now, he sleeps in my bed while my brother continues to float in an oil drum at his bedside." I felt so fucking worthless. I didn't just let down my brother, but my mother as well, who deserved to have the bones she'd grown in her own fucking body.

"Constantine . . ." Her eyes welled up with overwhelming sadness, and in that moment, she reminded me of my mother. The love she had for me was beautiful and genuine and endless. Without actually saying it, she showed me that she didn't think all the horrible things I'd just said.

She was just heartbroken for me.

"There has to be something that can be done—"

"No." It was not worth the risk. I'd already watched Darius put a gun to her head, and I couldn't do it again. I knew if he got his hands on her, he would do something infinitely worse. Would break all of Medusa's bones and force me to listen to her cry. There was nothing he could do to me physically that scared me, but just a single scratch on either of them could bring me to tears. "Giving it all up for you was the easiest decision I've ever made. But living with the consequences . . . that's another beast."

"I'm sorry this happened. I wish it had turned out differently. I hate seeing you like this."

"I know, sweetheart," I said. "And I hate seeing you like this too."

She held my gaze for another second before her eyes darted away, avoiding the question I didn't ask.

I'd shared with her, so I expected her to share with me, no matter how painful or difficult.

But she either looked at the house or the sky or her plate . . . and never at me.

Because she didn't want to tell me how Darius had hurt her. Didn't want me to know she had nightmares about it. That she hadn't really been herself since he'd laid a hand on her. That she didn't trust she would ever feel safe again. That she didn't trust me to protect her after I failed her.

Was it one of those . . . or all of those?

But she held her silence and looked progressively more uncomfortable, paler in the face, colder in the lips.

"Talk to me, sweetheart."

"I—I can't." She inhaled a deep breath, turmoil bright in her eyes.

"Yes, you can. I can handle it."

"I'm just not ready." She suddenly rose to her feet, the chair moving backward over the tile from her momentum. Then she walked back to the house and left me to sit there alone with dinner that neither of us would finish.

I didn't go after her. Wouldn't force her to confide in me. Wouldn't force her to do anything she didn't want to do. But I felt even more worthless, knowing I was the reason she suffered . . . and she wouldn't even let me fix her. Wouldn't let me do anything to help her.

The sun was completely gone now, and only the lights from the city and the coastline were visible. A summer breeze moved through my hair as I sat there alone, Medusa lying on one of the nearby couches.

I grabbed my full glass of wine and downed it in a single gulp. Then I reached for hers, which hadn't been touched all night, but I stopped before my fingers made contact. I stared at the glass of white wine as hard as I'd stared at her face. Then I slowly pulled my hand back as the realization hit me. Hit me like a bolt of lightning on a cloudless day and triggered an earthquake below my feet.

But a second later, the world went still.

And I smiled. Smiled wider and harder than I had in a very long time. I felt an inexplicable joy that brought me to the clouds. My heart suddenly doubled in size as my love reached new heights. In an instant, my whole world changed—for the better. "Oh, sweetheart . . ."

Chapter 8

Aurelia

My anxiety was through the roof, and if I didn't get it under control, I was worried how it would affect our baby. The only time I felt a sense of calm was when I was at work—because I knew Constantine wouldn't be there. Wouldn't be able to ask me what was wrong.

I didn't want to lie or evade his questions anymore, but I was scared as hell to tell him the truth. I took a few more pregnancy tests as time went on, just to be sure it wasn't a false positive, but they all said the same thing and my period never came . . . so this was real.

Fuck, I was gonna have a baby.

I'd known Constantine for less than three months, and he was in a depression so deep that I feared this news would just launch him into a spiral. He'd given up his entire life for me, and he was struggling to adjust. If he found out he was going to be a father too, it might push him over the edge.

He might think I did it on purpose, and he wouldn't trust me ever again. I'd never skipped a pill and I'd been on the same contraceptive for years and years, so I couldn't believe it failed me.

But if it was gonna fail, thank god it was with Constantine.

What if it had been with Enzo . . . fuck that.

I worked in the kitchen through the morning, thinking about all those things incessantly, feeling plunges of anxiety in my stomach and then tremors in my fingertips. I had to tell Constantine soon because I couldn't carry this lie much longer. And I couldn't carry this truth alone—because I was fucking terrified. Terrified to be a mom when I wasn't ready. Scared that I would have to do it alone, the way my mother had to. Scared to push a baby out of my vagina and not die.

Scared of everything.

There was only one man I'd ever met who made me feel safe, but I was even afraid to tell him.

Once everything was prepped for the day and we opened our doors, I headed to the other side of the building where the main restaurant was located. People came in for lunch, and I seated them at tables and took their orders. Waitressing was a lot easier than prepping in the morning because I got to write everything down and give it to one of the cooks to prepare. The rest of the time, I just tried to stay busy.

The lunch rush ended and the tables cleared out, so I wiped them down for the dinner crew that came in before five. We were open for another forty-five minutes, but people hardly ever came in for lunch past one.

But then the door opened, and Constantine walked inside. Dressed in a black T-shirt and dark jeans, he helped himself to one of the tables—with the biggest smile on his face. "Hey, sweetheart." A six-foot-five, tremendous hunk with arms that nearly split his sleeves, he was the juiciest piece of man meat ever.

I was a little taken aback by the sight of him, particularly his mood. I'd gone to bed last night and pretended to be asleep when he came in. So we didn't talk, and I left earlier than usual this morning and took a cab to work. This was our first interaction since that tense conversation over dinner, but it was as if it had never happened. "Hey." I approached the table, unsure what I missed, why he was a whole different person, but I didn't dare ask. "What are you doing here?"

"I was in town and decided to stop by for lunch." He dropped his arm over the other chair, completely relaxed, like he didn't have a care in the world. "And I thought I could watch your ass shake while you hustle."

I was still shocked by all of this. It took me a couple seconds to accept this reality. When I'd first seen him, I felt that jolt of anxiety, like he was here to confront me about last night. But that didn't seem like his intention.

"Come here." His hand moved to my hip, and he guided me to his lap.

"I'm at work—"

He slid his hand into my hair and kissed me, kissed me like we were at home with no one around. Like he didn't give a damn if anyone saw us.

The second I felt the command of his mouth and the softness of his kiss, I lost all restraint. I didn't care if his own mother walked in and saw us together, my ass on his lap in the middle of the restaurant.

When he pulled away, he gently brushed his nose against mine before he kissed the corner of my mouth. "All right, now you can get back to work." His grin was big, beautiful, and infectious. It brought a twinkle to his eyes, a warmth hotter than the Sicilian sun.

I got off his lap and felt his big hand give my ass a playful smack.

"I'll take the Palermo-style cutlet," he said. "And a glass of red wine."

"Sure thing."

He winked at me. "Attagirl."

I turned away and headed back to the kitchen to put in the order, but I felt his eyes drill into my back, hot and possessive, like we'd just met all over again. I glanced over my shoulder and saw exactly what I predicted—but there was also a smile.

I got him a glass of wine and returned to the table.

He kicked out the chair across from him. "Sit."

"Well, I'm at work."

"Doing what, exactly?" He looked around the dining room. "No one's here, all the tables are clean. Now sit that fine ass down."

"Fine ass, huh?" In a couple months, my fine ass would be a big ass. I took a seat across from him and crossed my legs, my arms on the table.

He took a drink of his wine and relaxed in the chair.

"Constantine!" Antonio shouted from the kitchen. "I'm making this for you?"

"Yeah, and it better be damn good," Constantine yelled back.

"Only the best for you, man."

"That's what I like to hear." He turned back to me, still smiling like it was permanently carved into his face. "You're fucking beautiful, you know that?" He cocked his head slightly as he looked at me, his smile slowly fading from his mouth but remaining in his gaze, looking at me like he'd never really looked at me before.

"Okay, what's gotten into you?"

"Gotten into me?" he asked, eyebrows cocked.

I should probably have just left it alone, but now I needed to know why he'd woken this morning in a whole different mode. "Last night was rough, and now . . . it's like it never happened."

He gave a shrug. "Guess I remembered what I have, and how lucky I am to be here with you. That there's so much more to life, and I'm excited to live it—with you." Affection and happiness still burned in his gaze, a shadow of a smile on his lips. "I'm here to talk whenever you're ready. But no rush. Take all the time you need."

Another burst of adrenaline filled me, but it dissipated quickly when he removed the pressure. It seemed like he was done asking me about it. Finally gave me the space to decide how and when I would tell him the truth . . . that I was pregnant.

The bell in the kitchen rang, so I headed into the back to retrieve his lunch. A breaded piece of chicken with a side of pasta. I returned to the table and placed it in front of him before I sat down.

He dug into it right away, then called into the back. "Thanks, Antonio."

"You got it, Con."

He cut into the meat, took big bites, and smiled at me with his eyes while he continued to eat—the happiest I'd ever seen him. Last night, he'd confessed how lost he was, but now, he'd never looked more sure of himself.

My mind continued to question it, but I decided to let it go.

I always took a shower when I got home from work. I wore a shower cap to protect my hair, but I washed away the smell of tomatoes, eggplant, and fried rice balls. There were worse things to smell like, but I didn't want to stink up the beautiful house.

I walked out of the bathroom in just my towel and found him on the bed—completely naked. And he was hard as hell. Like just thinking about what he wanted to do to me was enough to make his balls turn blue.

I stilled, feeling like prey that had been caught walking through the grass by an enormous lion.

He didn't pat the bed or order me to come to him. He left the bed, rose to his full six and a half feet, and then came behind me, gone from my view. His hand reached for the towel that covered me, and he tugged the edge where it was tucked in to make it come free.

It fell to the floor at my feet, and I felt the bumps form on my arms.

He hooked one arm over my chest while the other moved over my stomach. He gently tugged me into him and kissed my neck and then my shoulder, kissing me but doing it in a way that felt like he was eating me alive.

Then he moved in front of me and took a knee, his eyes level with my tits because of how tall he was. He hooked one of my legs over his shoulder then brought me close, pressing kisses to my stomach and licking my belly button ring that I hadn't taken out yet. My stomach was still flat because I wasn't more than a month pregnant, and there was no way he or anyone else could tell. And when I'd had my period, our sex lives hadn't changed because he didn't care about the bleeding. He probably didn't notice that it hadn't come this month. So I wasn't afraid he would figure it out for a while. I had at least another month before it might catch his attention.

He kissed my hips before he lifted me slightly and pressed a kiss to my entrance. I hadn't shaved in the last two weeks because I'd been too overwhelmed by the news, but he kissed me like he couldn't care less I wasn't groomed. He devoured me harder than he devoured my mouth, balancing me above him while his big hands gripped me like he couldn't squeeze me hard enough.

I dug my hand into his short hair, and I got swept up in his touch, in the fact that this gorgeous man was on his knees for me, that he wanted me when he could have anyone else he wanted.

And something about it made me a little less scared. Actually turned me on a bit, knowing about the life we'd made together inside me that very moment. Something made out of love and passion, something that would outlive us both.

When he rose to his feet, he took me with him, carrying me to the bed and rolling back with me as he remained on top. His eyes took in mine as he adjusted me underneath him, his lips just inches from mine. When he was nestled between my thighs and his hand was deep in my hair, he sank into me, releasing a quiet moan under his breath when he filled me deep. He paused as he felt me, as he took in my eyes and savored the moment like it was the first time our souls touched. Then he started to move inside me, slow and easy. "I love you, sweetheart."

"I'm gonna be late." I slapped his hand away as I moved for my purse on the counter.

But he was all over me anyway, pushing up against my back before he guided me to the couch.

When my alarm had gone off that morning, he was buried inside me in record time. It happened so fast, and I got swept up in how damn fine he was that I forgot how little time I had to get out the door. I hopped in the shower and got dressed before I headed downstairs, but he was all over me as if he hadn't already come inside me once.

"Constantine."

He got me on my back on the couch and slipped my shoes from my feet. Then he tugged off my jeans and my panties before he bent me into place in the corner of the couch.

"Jesus, what has gotten into you—"

He gave a hard thrust inside me and nailed me like a piston in a car engine. A rough quickie like I was a booty call on a timetable. His sweats were pulled down below his hips, and he pounded into me like I was a whore rather than the woman he loved. "Fuck." He took me the hardest he ever had, his arms pinning my legs far back. "Yes." Within thirty seconds, he was finished, blowing his load like it'd been a week rather than thirty minutes since his last lay. He filled me with another load that would soak into my panties at some point while I was at work.

He pulled out of me as soon as he was finished. "All right, now you can go."

I relaxed my stiff joints, then scrambled for my clothes and shoes. When I looked at the time on my phone, I realized I was already fifteen minutes late. "Shit."

"Relax, sweetheart." He smiled like this was all a joke, pulling up his sweatpants and putting on his T-shirt. "It's not like you can get fired or anything."

~

Constantine said he wanted to go out for dinner, so we went into Taormina and stopped by one of his favorite spots, La Napoletana, a restaurant hidden off the main path, up a couple flights of stairs and in a secluded courtyard. He'd taken me there once before, when we were in the throes of our white-hot fling.

We took our seats and looked at the menus. "No fish tonight." He said it with a smile, teasing me for the comment I'd made a couple nights ago.

I got lost in that smile every time I saw it. He was so unbelievably handsome all the time, but something about his happiness really pulled me in. The light in his eyes, the way his arms and shoulders were relaxed, all the ways he teased me. I'd seen him in a good mood before, but he'd never been this consistently happy.

He was practically bursting at the seams.

"What?" he asked.

"What?" I blurted back, unsure of what he'd said.

"You're staring." He continued to smile like it wasn't an intrusion.

"Oh, sorry."

"Don't be sorry. I stare at you all the time. Just wasn't sure if you had something to say."

"I'm glad you've been so happy . . . just not sure why you're so happy." We had just been in our darkest place, him struggling with his depression and me struggling with the fact that I might blow up our relationship when I told him the truth. I guessed the second thing was still an issue, but it didn't stress me out as much. With every passing day, I accepted the circumstances, and seeing him love me so deeply made me a little scared to tell him.

He gave a shrug. "I guess I just got over it."

"But overnight?"

"Just doesn't seem important anymore," he said matter-of-factly. "Here I am in the most beautiful place in the world with the woman I love, and my family is right down the street. That's what life is all about. I feel nothing but gratitude."

The tension in the muscles around my chest relaxed a bit. Knowing he was happy with our lives brought me a sense of calm. It made me feel like everything would be okay . . . when I finally found the courage to tell him. That he wouldn't be resentful that he'd lost everything, and now what little piece of independence he had left would be gone too. If this had been a year in the future or some other time, I wouldn't be worried about Constantine's reaction to the news. He said he could go either way, could have kids or not. But the timing was just awful. This relationship was still new, even though it didn't feel that way.

"I feel like the luckiest man in the world."

I released a quiet scoff because it sounded ridiculous. "I'm the lucky one, Constantine." This gorgeous, smart, six-and-a-half-foot hunk of a man was mine. And his eyes didn't stray and he didn't lie and he didn't cheat. He took care of me, and for the first time in my life, I felt like I had someone I could rely on. It wasn't just me on my own anymore, trying to keep my head above water. For a time, I'd felt safe and secure with Enzo, but most of that relationship was spent with me begging him to make it work.

I was still ashamed I'd done that.

He looked at the menu. "So, what are you going to order, sweetheart?"

I scanned the menu. "The La Napoletana." It came with mozzarella, garlic . . . and *anchovies*.

He quickly picked up on the joke. "You're becoming more Sicilian by the day."

The waitress came over, and we each ordered our own pizza. He got the mortadella, which had mozzarella and ricotta cheese along with mortadella and pistachio sauce. I noticed he ordered mortadella on pretty much everything when he wasn't eating seafood. I got the bufala pizza, which was basically a margherita pizza but with big chunks of buffalo mozzarella. I hadn't had any unusual cravings yet, nor had I been sick at all. If this was how the pregnancy was the entire time, then I'd consider myself lucky.

Constantine ordered two glasses of wine without asking me what I wanted and sat with his arms folded on the table, sitting forward toward me. "I've done some thinking. Don't think Cosa Nostra is right for me anymore. It just feels like a major step down, and I'm not commuting two hours each way."

"You could stay there for a couple days."

"My place is here with you."

I didn't want him to give up even more for me, but truth be told, the idea of sleeping alone for several nights while he was hours away made me uncomfortable. And when there was a baby in the house, I'd be terrified, even with Medusa there. I knew Darius wouldn't come for me in Taormina after he'd let us go, but now that fear of being ambushed without Constantine around was a part of me. I would never tell him that, of course. Not when it would make him feel like shit. "I could come with you."

"I don't want the job. Have something else in mind."

"Oh, what is it?"

"I think we should open a third Rosticceria Da Cristina. But offer a completely different menu. No takeaway food, only a sit-down restaurant. I have a couple ideas for what we can offer. Include some Roman elements as well."

The very last thing I'd expected him to suggest was getting back into the restaurant business. It seemed like that was behind him and he had other interests. "I didn't know you were still interested in that."

"I'm not going to be the one back there cooking, but it'll be part of the family business and a great way to stay connected to the community. And we can pass it down to our kids one day if they want it."

"Our—our kids?" He'd said he was open to the idea of having a family, but never once had he talked about it with any sort of certainty. But now, it was almost presumptuous, like we'd already discussed it but I'd somehow forgotten. "You want to have kids?"

He leaned a little farther over the small table, a slight smile on his lips, raw intensity in his eyes. "Fuck yes, I do."

Chapter 9

Aurelia

Constantine seemed to be a whole new man, happy and carefree the way he'd been when we first met. He didn't seem to care about the empire anymore, didn't care about everything he'd left behind. Now, he was present with me, making love to me before bed but fucking me viciously first thing in the morning. Always had a smile on his face, always had a skip in his step.

I wished I could feel the same way, but I carried a secret heavier than the world. Now I knew I was at least a month along, and I continued to check pregnancy tests like they would somehow give me a different answer.

I needed to tell Constantine, but what if he wasn't happy? What if I destroyed this good mood he was in, and he never got it back? What if he'd finally gotten himself to a good place and I destroyed it with this life-changing news?

I went to work at Rosticceria Da Cristina in the morning, prepped the arancini in the kitchen while the music played over the speakers. My mind was elsewhere, barely on the task at hand, thinking about how and when I would tell him. I probably needed to see an obstetrician soon, go to a checkup and make sure everything was okay.

The door opened, and Sofia walked inside with her leather satchel over her shoulder. She didn't wear the uniforms we had on, the black

T-shirts with the logo on the front. I'd never seen her in the kitchen, and it seemed like she only focused on running the business.

She beamed when she saw me at the counter. "Good morning, honey." She came to me and gave me a one-armed hug because my gloved hands were covered in tomato sauce. "How are things going?"

"Good. Think I'm getting the hang of it."

"Antonio said you're doing great." She took off her satchel and placed it on the steel counter in front of the credit card reader used during business hours. "And it's nice to have another hand around here."

Especially if it was a free hand. "I'm glad I'm not making your life more difficult."

"More difficult?" she asked incredulously.

"You know, because it takes time and resources to train someone. Kinda slows everyone down."

"You are not a burden, Aurelia. You're family."

A smile kicked onto my lips, but it was a painful one. The more I spent time with Sofia, the more I realized how much Constantine was like her. His attitude and his warmth and his work ethic—it all came from her. He could be the kindest man I'd ever met, but he wasn't a pushover either, or if you crossed him, there would be hell to pay. Sofia had never shown that side to me, but she wouldn't be able to run these businesses on her own if she weren't tough. She wouldn't have raised Constantine into the man he was if she didn't have a steel spine.

I wanted to be a part of this family so much, but I worried I'd put that in jeopardy with this pregnancy. Would his mother think the worst of me? That I'd planned it maliciously because her son was rich? That I was just after his money? That I was forcing him to settle down?

"Honey." She seemed to see the pain flicker across my face, because her eyes were full of pity. "Everything okay?"

"Yeah," I said a little too quickly. "That's—that's just nice of you to say."

"I mean it, Aurelia. You're a part of this family now."

I didn't know if it was just her words or the pregnancy hormones, but my eyes started to water out of my control. I sucked in a sudden breath to calm myself, feeling loved . . . but also feeling alone.

"Oh honey." She came to me and gave me a big hug, not caring about the dirty gloves on my hands.

I couldn't hug her back, so I just stood there, trying not to cry, trying to keep it together even though I'd already been emotionally wrecked.

She pulled away and helped me pull off the gloves and toss them in the trash. "Talk to me. Something's bothering you."

She reminded me so much of my mother sometimes. When my mom would force me to cut through the bullshit and talk to her about my problems. Most of my memories of her were of her being sick, because she was ill for so long and it had been such a traumatic time. Those sort of replaced all the good ones, but right now, Sofia made them come back.

"Honey." She started to rub my arms, tried to bring me back to calm. "There's nothing you can't share with me." Her kind eyes continued to bore into mine, desperate to take on the heartache I carried alone.

"Um . . ." There was something about her I inherently trusted, something that made me feel safe, made me feel at home. "I'm pregnant." I said the words out loud, and suddenly, the burden felt so much lighter. When I got it off my chest, the weight on my shoulders decreased.

Her entire body went still as she paused to process that information. The shock moved in and out of her eyes quickly . . . and then there was joy. A smile came and widened to full capacity, and she squeezed my arms. "That is so wonderful, Aurelia. What a blessing." She pulled me in for a hug and squeezed me tight, embraced me like she meant it, like there wasn't a hint of disappointment.

She stepped back and looked at me again. "It's okay to be scared. Your life has completely changed, even though nothing has actually changed yet. It's normal."

"He doesn't know."

She gave a nod in understanding. "I assumed."

"I'm so scared to tell him."

Her hands left my arms. "Why?"

Now I felt like I was speaking to my own mother instead of his. "I'm afraid he'll think I did it on purpose. Like I did it to trap him or something. We've only been together for three months. It's so soon, and he just went through so much in Rome . . ."

"It'll be okay, Aurelia."

"I don't know what happened. I've never missed a pill. I've been on this stuff forever."

"It happened because it was meant to happen." When she smiled at me, her eyes watered. "It happened because you're meant for each other. You're meant to grow your love into a son or daughter. I know it's scary right now, but trust me when I tell you this is the greatest blessing of your life."

I nodded even though I didn't fully agree. Wouldn't be able to agree until Constantine knew the truth. Until we got through this.

"Don't be afraid to tell him, Aurelia. I know my son, and I promise you he'll be nothing but happy. He thinks the world of you, and he would never think the horrible things you're afraid he will."

I nodded, clinging to her words. "Please don't tell him. I'm just not ready yet."

"Your secret is safe with me, honey. The moment you tell him, he'll feel the greatest joy he's ever known. And I would never take that away from my son."

~

When I got home, Constantine wasn't there.

Which was a relief because I needed some time to take everything in. I'd had a beautiful moment with his mother and I would treasure that forever, but it was hard to appreciate it with all the stress.

I needed to tell him.

It was better for him to hear it from me than to figure it out another way, like when he noticed my stomach was more swollen than usual or when I didn't have another period. "Fuck, I gotta do it."

When I came inside, I greeted Medusa with a good rubdown. She still used her walker, but she was so much better. She didn't need pain meds anymore, and when we'd had her checkup with the vet, he said her leg was healing nicely. She could put some weight on her leg, but to make sure she didn't halt her progress, we made her continue to use the walker.

I showered upstairs and reapplied my makeup before I returned to the main sitting room.

My heart was in shambles, the adrenaline making me so tense that all my joints ached. I wasn't sure where he was, so I pulled up his location, which was something I hardly ever did. Felt like I was spying on him or invading his privacy.

He was at Daiquiri, the vibrant cocktail lounge he'd taken me to before. He was probably there with some of his friends, catching up after work. It was nice to be in a relationship where I didn't have to wonder what he was doing or who he was with. I could call or text him at any time, and he'd answer right away. Wouldn't leave me on read . . . like Enzo used to do.

I helped Medusa out of her walker, and she walked up the ramp Constantine had made for her so she could get on the couch easily. She curled up beside me and placed her chin on my thigh.

I petted her gently as I looked down at her. "You're going to be the best big sister, Medusa."

Constantine came home before dinnertime. Dressed in dark jeans and a gray T-shirt, he filled out his clothes with all that muscle. With the dark ink all over his skin, he looked even stronger. Any woman who looked at him fell under his spell, and any guy who looked at him was fucking terrified.

I watched him through the glass from the patio as he walked through the house. With a straight spine and an aura of confidence, he pulled out his phone and fired off a text before he moved to the bottom of the stairs and called up, like he was looking for me.

I raised my hand and waved at him to catch his attention.

He caught the movement in his peripheral and looked at me. Instantly, there was a smile, a man happy to come home to his family, his joy breaking through the glass and hitting my skin.

He opened the back door and walked across the terrace toward me.

Medusa got to him first, moving up to him in her walker, her tail wagging harder than it wagged for anyone.

Of course he stopped and kneeled down to give Medusa his attention, petting her cheeks and giving her a kiss on the head. "Hey, baby girl." He rose to his full height, then finished the walk toward where I sat at the table.

I was happy to see him . . . but never more scared.

He leaned down and kissed me. "Hey, sweetheart." He sucked my bottom lip into his mouth before he sat down across from me. "How was your day?"

"It was good." When the tumultuous moment was upon us, I felt all my fiery nerves burning my body. So tense I felt hard as a rock. My defenses were up, my expectations were low. Men had let me down my entire life, and I was afraid Constantine might do the same. "What about you?"

"I took a quick tour of this open spot in town. A little small, think we need something bigger."

"For what?" I asked.

"The restaurant."

"Oh, you were serious about that."

He grinned. "When I say I'm going to do something, I do it."

I just felt like it was rushed. Maybe not to him, because the restaurant business was in his blood, but for someone like me, it felt like a lot. And maybe my mind was on the baby that he didn't know about . . . and all the stuff we still had to do.

He pulled out his phone and sent a text. "Told Elio we're ready for dinner. I'm starving."

"I get hungry when I drink a lot too."

He grinned at me again. "You saw I was at Daiquiri."

I didn't realize what I'd said until it was over. I'd just shoved my foot into my mouth, and now, I couldn't pull it out. "Sorry. You're usually home—"

"Don't be sorry. I like knowing that you check. I check yours all the time."

"You do?"

"Yeah," he said. "I like to know where you go for lunch, like to see your little dot move around the restaurant. Makes me feel like I'm a part of your day. I met with the real estate agent, and then I met Francesco and Aldo for drinks afterward. Didn't tell them about the restaurant. I'll tell my mom first. Technically, I have to get her permission first if I want to use the same name. I know she's been thinking about another location."

"Yeah." The second he mentioned his mom, I mentally left the conversation. His mind was in a whole different place from mine. He was thinking about buildings and recipes, and I was thinking about how I could tell him this unbelievable news.

He studied me for a moment, his eyes shifting back and forth between mine like he was reading my mood, but he didn't ask what troubled me. Just left it alone.

Now I wished he would ask, because I wasn't sure if I could tell him this on my own.

Elio appeared on the terrace with the cart he brought up on the elevator. It was spread with a white tablecloth with a pitcher of water and a bottle of wine, along with two plates covered in silver lids.

I got more anxious at the sight of him, knowing I would tell Constantine after he left.

Elio greeted us with a smile, served our dinner, and opened the bottle of wine. He left the cart there so we could put everything inside the lockbox when we were done so we wouldn't attract the birds. He usually cleaned it up sometime in the morning when we were at work or Constantine was in the gym.

Elio said good night and left.

Now it was just the two of us, the summer breeze welcoming, now that the sun was mostly gone. The string of lights over the terrace started to get brighter as the sunlight disappeared.

Constantine removed the lids from our dishes and started to eat, elbows on the table. A large filet of fish in white sauce and capers, along with a side of greens and roasted potatoes. It was an appetizing sight, but I felt no hunger at all. In fact, I felt like I might throw up my lunch.

He ate a couple bites as he glanced at me here and there.

I didn't even reach for my fork, just watched him eat, feeling sicker and sicker as time ticked by.

He wiped his mouth with the linen, then stopped eating his dinner. He took a drink of his wine, then gave me his full attention, arms on the table, eyes locked with laser focus. A small breeze moved through his hair.

Oh my god, I wasn't sure if I could do this . . .

He continued his stare, eyes demanding and desperate, like he wanted me to answer the question he never asked out loud.

My heart was like a drum in my chest. The pace compounded every few seconds. I felt like I was on the verge of collapse, I was so anxious.

"Sweetheart." He extended his hand across the table, palm up, eyes still on me. "Come on, tell me."

If I didn't do it within the next few seconds, I thought I might pass out. I couldn't handle this stress anymore. Needed to be free of this anxiety. My hand moved to his, and I took a deep breath.

He squeezed it before he enveloped it with his other hand. Then he sat and patiently waited, looking at me with confident eyes tinted with emotion. "It's okay," he said gently. "It's okay . . ."

My eyes started to water in fear and catharsis. "I'm—I'm pregnant."

He inhaled a deep breath and squeezed my hand simultaneously. Then a slow smile moved over his lips and reached his eyes . . . and they filled with unshed tears. His espresso-colored eyes turned into mirrors because they became so wet and reflective. He inhaled another deep breath as his smile widened, and he squeezed my hand even harder. Two tears streaked down his cheeks.

I'd run through so many possibilities of how this conversation would go, but I'd never suspected this could be one of them. I felt my own tears burn my eyes from relief and happiness . . . and love.

He released my hand to wipe away his tears. He sniffed and blinked and swallowed back the emotion he'd let escape to the surface. "I've never felt this happy in my whole life." His hand went back to mine, and he looked at me again.

All that fear about telling him . . . was for nothing. I felt stupid keeping this secret. Felt stupid for keeping it for weeks, for stressing myself out until my hair started to fall out, afraid that I was going to lose him over this. "That's what's been on my mind all this time. I was just too afraid to tell you."

"Why?"

"I didn't want you to think I did it on purpose. I've never missed a pill. I don't know what happened. I don't want you to think I'm trying to trap you or something."

"Why would I think that?" His eyes remained emotional, but his voice sounded calm, as usual.

"I—I don't know. We've only been together for a couple months."

"But we have a lot of sex." Then he grinned widely. *"A lot."*

A laugh escaped my chest, a laugh I hadn't felt in a long time.

"And even if you did, I couldn't care less."

"What?"

"Trap me, I don't care," he said. "I've wanted to be trapped by you since the moment we met. Fine by me." His signature smile came through and reached his eyes, so confident in his happiness, so calm in his aura. His fingers started to caress mine, being the gentlest with me he'd ever been. "I don't care if it was unplanned, I don't care if it's been just a few months, this feels right. It feels right because it's you—*because it's us.*"

~

Constantine undressed me slowly before he guided me to the bed. Stripped off his T-shirt and jeans and his boxers before he moved on top of me. Instead of bending me into place and taking me with enthusiasm, he kissed my belly.

Kissed it like it was distended and swollen with life.

Kissed my belly button and my hips, right at the bottom of my rib cage, everywhere. His hands felt me, his rough fingertips brushing over the smooth skin. He moved down between my thighs and kissed the flesh before he kissed the area where I wanted to feel his lips most. He gave me his full attention and his tongue, and he sucked my body into his mouth to taste.

Then he moved back over me, back to my stomach, worshipping it once again like it was what turned him on the most. I hadn't changed at all anatomically, but it made him a whole different lover.

My fingers dug into his hair, and I watched him kiss me, like he wanted to feel a heartbeat against his lips. I'd thought this would make him love me less, but it seemed to make him love me more.

When he finally had his fill, he moved up my body until our eyes were level. His eyes smoldered for me like I was the hottest woman in the bar whom he'd taken home for the night. He started to separate my thighs as he nestled between the soft flesh, eyes on me all the while, sliding his hand into my hair before he kissed me. Once and then twice, kissing different parts of my mouth before my jawline.

Then he guided himself inside me and started to sink, releasing a quiet moan when he felt me for at least the hundredth time. He didn't pin my legs back like he normally did, letting my knees hug his torso while my ankles locked together at the small of his back.

He thrust within me, long and sure strokes, an even pace that wasn't quick or slow. With his hand deep in my hair, he kissed me, our breaths growing together as we felt each other, as my nails dragged down his back and his tongue delved into my mouth.

I had no doubt that Constantine was honest with me, that he was happy rather than disappointed. Because he might be able to put on a show during a conversation, but he wouldn't have been able to make love like this. To come so close to me I could feel our souls touch, to look me in the eye like that with an endless sea of love. To touch me so gently because he thought I might break.

I loved this man long before I'd said it aloud, swept off my feet and lost in his arms the moment we met. But now, our love had deepened into something I could hardly describe. I didn't feel broken after my relationship with Enzo died, not when Constantine healed me before I could shatter on the floor. It felt like God had given him to me as payment for what I'd suffered, for not having a father, for losing my mother so young, for giving my heart to someone who wasn't man enough to take care of it.

And now, he'd given me the life that grew inside me.

I was scared to be a mother, wasn't ready for such a big responsibility. But all of a sudden, it didn't feel scary anymore. Now it felt like we'd wanted this all along, that we'd been trying to make this blessing since we met.

Now I felt confident to take this on.

I felt brave . . . because Constantine made me feel brave.

Chapter 10

Aurelia

I woke up to the obnoxious sound of my alarm the next morning.

I rolled over in bed and jabbed my finger down on the screen to make it stop.

It woke up Constantine too, and he turned over toward me, his chest against my back. "Don't even think about it, sweetheart." His dick was hard like every morning, and it was pressed hard against me, warm to the touch but solid like a steel pole.

We had been up late last night, making love and fucking and then making love again. I'd never been this sore in my life, but I didn't dare complain. "I have to."

"No, you don't." He tugged me into his body, his arm pulling me by the chest instead of my hips or stomach. "You aren't working anymore."

"Why?"

"Because your full-time job is growing my son or daughter."

"You know I can do both—"

"But you don't *need* to do both."

"If you really want to open our own restaurant, I need the experience."

"I'll teach you."

"Your mom was nice enough to give me this job, and I'm not going to let her down."

"You're giving her another grandchild. Trust me, she doesn't give a damn about the restaurant."

I released a quiet sigh. "Constantine." I felt like a mother who admonished her son with just his name.

He dipped his head and pressed a kiss to my shoulder, seeming to understand he'd reached the limits of my patience. "All right, we'll talk about it later." He kissed my shoulder again.

I pulled the sheets back and got out of bed.

Of course, his palm gave my ass a playful smack before I walked away. Then his eyes followed me the whole way, watching me cross the room to the bathroom until I shut the door.

He drove me down the mountainside to the village, pulling aside when enormous tour buses needed to get by, understanding the narrow roads carved into the mountainside.

Driving on the streets of Rome was chaos, but this was a whole other level. I wasn't sure if I'd ever feel comfortable driving around here.

"We should tell my mom before this weekend."

"Why this weekend?" I asked, looking out the window at the sea in the morning light.

"We're going to a wedding."

"We are?" I asked in surprise.

"Yeah, my third cousin Cassandra is getting married."

"Well, this is news to me."

He drove with one hand on the wheel, slowing down when he came around a sharp curve, and continued down the mountain. "I declined her invitation because we were in Rome at the time, but when she realized I'd moved back to town, she extended the invitation again.

And everyone is going to notice you aren't drinking, so we should tell my mom first."

The guilt washed over me when I realized what I'd done. I'd taken this moment away from him, the moment when he'd get to tell his mother about his first child. When I'd confided in her, I didn't really think about the big picture. "I'm so sorry, Constantine . . ."

He took his eyes off the road just for a second to look at me, eyebrows raised. Then his focus was back on the road as we came to the outskirts of the village.

"I kinda already told her."

"You did?" The road leveled out, and he took a couple streets to get to the entrance of the village. "When?"

"The other day."

He came to a stop on the side of the road. There weren't many cars or pedestrians yet, not this early in the morning when most of the shops weren't open yet.

"I was having a hard day. I was scared how you would react when I told you. The stress was getting to me, and she walked in and knew I was upset. It was one of those moments when I wanted to talk to my mom . . . but I talked to yours instead." I looked down at my lap and felt his stare on the side of my face.

He leaned over the center console between us, and his big hand went to my thigh. "Sweetheart, I'm not mad." The smile was in his voice.

"You aren't?" I whispered, my hand moving to his on my thigh.

"Look at me," he said gently.

I swallowed before I followed his command.

A slight smile was on his lips, and there was nothing but affection in his eyes. "I'm happy that my mom feels like your mom. I'm happy to share her with you. She's the best."

"Yeah. She's pretty great."

"I'm just sorry that you were that worried about my reaction." His smile faltered, like that was the part that wounded him.

"When I found out, I was kinda a wreck. It was too soon, thought I'd have at least five more years before I had to think about this. Thought we'd have more time together. I feel bad for saying it, but I wasn't happy or excited at all. Just terrified, honestly. So I expected you to react the same way."

He was quiet for a little bit. "Do you still feel that way?"

"No. After I told you, I was happy."

"I think you're misinterpreting your fear as unhappiness. I wish you had told me sooner so you wouldn't have had to carry this stress around by yourself for so long."

"I just remember you said you could or could not have kids . . . could go either way."

"And then I found my soulmate, and all that changed." His big hand enveloped mine the way his strength enveloped my fear.

My heart did a little dance when I heard his words. I felt joy that I couldn't put into words. I'd lost my home when my mom died, but I'd found it again in Constantine.

"If someone else I'd been seeing told me she was pregnant . . ." He released a quiet chuckle. "Yeah, I would have had a very different reaction, to say the least. But the moment I knew . . ." He gave a slight shake of his head. "All I felt was joy. All the emotional baggage I've been carrying just disappeared. I realized none of that matters anymore. The two of you and Medusa are all that matters now—and I've never been more excited for anything in my life."

~

We pulled up to Sofia's villa and parked outside.

I was nervous, even though I had no reason to be. Sofia already knew the truth, so there was no news to break. I'd already been accepted into their family. But my heart was in my throat anyway as we walked up to the front door.

Constantine knocked and stepped back.

Sofia opened the door a moment later, and as with any time she saw Constantine, she drowned him in maternal affection. A kiss on the cheek, a long embrace, calling him her boy rather than using his name.

I loved seeing them together.

Then she greeted me just as warmly, with a hug and a kiss on the cheek. She didn't give away that she knew something she shouldn't. She might suspect we were there to tell her the news, but she didn't show her hand.

"I hope you're hungry," she said. "Because—"

"You cooked for thirteen instead of three?" Constantine teased. "I didn't eat anything all day because I knew we were coming here."

We sat outside on the patio with the string of white lights hanging overhead. A couple of wine bottles were already sitting there along with some glasses. While Sofia went inside to retrieve the platters of food, Constantine opened a bottle of wine and poured himself a glass.

"I'm glad I don't have to pretend anymore."

He grinned before he took a drink.

His mother returned with a casserole dish that contained eggplant lasagna along with a bowl of salad and a basket of bread. The casserole could easily feed twenty people. "I know it's a lot for the three of us, but I know Con loves leftovers."

"You got me there, Ma." He held up the bottle of wine and silently asked her if she wanted some.

She nodded.

He filled her glass before he corked the bottle again.

Sofia glanced at me, a smile on her lips when she noticed my empty glass, like she was still thrilled by the news days later.

Constantine broke the ice without preamble. "Aurelia told me she's pregnant."

Her eyes lit up instantly, and moisture coated the surface. Her hands came together and moved over her heart. "Oh thank god. I wasn't sure if I'd be able to get through this dinner otherwise." She got to her feet and came around the table to hug her son. "My boy, I'm so happy for you."

He stood up to embrace her, a skyscraper compared to her small size. He held her against him and pressed a kiss to her forehead. "Thank you, Ma. And thank you for always being there for her. I really appreciate it."

"You know I love her like a daughter."

They talked to each other like I wasn't in the room. I watched them together, loving the fact that Constantine was always good to his mother. That he was a man in every way, but still a mama's boy at heart.

Constantine pulled away and gently rubbed her back. "Congratulations."

"Congratulations to you," she said. "Now it's time we celebrate."

"Will you stay here in Taormina?" Sofia asked hopefully.

"Definitely," Constantine said. "It's a great place to grow up. A small village with a tight-knit community close to family. Can't think of a better place."

Sofia beamed, an internal light glowing from her skin. "I hope it's a girl. Already have two grandsons."

"Me too," Constantine said. "Hard to imagine raising a son."

"Yes, they're a handful." She sliced her fork through her lasagna. "The two of you almost gave me heart attacks on a daily basis. All the girls you would sneak into the house and late nights out on the boat, that Virgin Mary statue you two knocked over . . . I don't miss those days."

Constantine chuckled. "Sorry about that."

"Beatrice was easy. Always a nice girl. Doesn't make the best decisions, but still a breeze compared to you two."

"If that's the case, then why am I your favorite?" Constantine teased.

She rolled her eyes. "I don't have a favorite."

"Right, right." He grinned before he took a drink of his wine.

I noticed the way they talked about Edric indirectly. He was part of the conversation but never mentioned by name. It seemed like the loss was still devastating, even after all this time.

"If you have a daughter, she'll be magnificent," Sofia said. "Beautiful like Aurelia and tall like the two of you. She'll be a model in Milan by the time she's eighteen."

"I'm sure that's true—except the model part," Constantine said. "She'll be too smart to stand still for pictures. She'll be doing something more worthwhile with her time. Running a business or being an athlete or traveling the world."

I liked that Constantine wanted more for a daughter we didn't even know that we were having. That he wanted the same for her that he'd want for a son.

"And if it's not a girl, just keep going until you get one," Sofia said.

Constantine gave a quiet chuckle. "That's hard to picture, honestly. I like having siblings, but it's hard to imagine having more than one. I selfishly just want to love one kid and give them all of me."

Sofia smiled. "You already sound like a father, honey."

He gave a slight nod. "The second I knew, my whole world shifted. I became a parent without a kid. My perspective on everything was altered dramatically. I became a different person even though my life hasn't changed at all yet. Strangest thing . . ."

The second we were home, he buried me in the corner of the couch, just my bottoms off because he was in too much of a rush to remove my top and bra. I was still sore from last night, but I didn't dare interrupt him. That was like taking food away from a starving bear.

He bent me like a pretzel in the corner of the couch and nailed me hard, like he'd wanted to fuck me the last few hours, and now he finally could. He didn't even undress himself, just tugged his bottoms down far enough to get his cock out. He left his shirt on and gave me the hardest quickie, made me come fast like he'd kissed my sex for the last twenty minutes. Then he released inside me with a satisfied moan, like he'd finally scratched the itch that had been gnawing at him all night.

He left me there when he was done and walked over to the bar cart to make himself a drink.

Medusa stayed in her dog bed until we were finished, able to pick up on the mood before anything physical had even happened yet. But when she knew it was over, she pranced over to Constantine, able to put some weight on her leg.

"Sorry, baby girl." He took a drink before he kneeled down and gave her a rubdown. Now that she was feeling better, she turned her body and rubbed her flank against him, being playful when she got his attention.

A part of me felt bad about how much her life had changed since I'd come around. She used to be the only woman in his life, but now she came second . . . and soon she would be third.

After she got her fill of Constantine, she came over to me on the couch, walked up the ramp, and sat beside me.

I pulled my panties back on and left the jeans on the floor.

Constantine looked out the window and admired the city lights before he came to the couch. He handed me a glass of water that I didn't ask for, then sat beside me. "Want to get married next Saturday?"

I heard what he said, but it took me a moment to accept the words in the air. I turned to look at him, the glass of water in my hand. "What?"

"There are a couple nice churches around here. I'm sure we could make any of them work."

"Are you serious right now?"

"Of course I am." He looked me dead in the eye, his dark eyes back to their usual intensity when we were alone together.

"I don't think we should get married just because I'm pregnant."

"It's not *just* because you're pregnant."

"Yes, it is. Otherwise, you would have proposed to me. But you just said it like . . . an obligation."

"Definitely not an obligation."

"This isn't the early nineteen hundreds, where we can't have a child out of wedlock."

"Never said it was. And that's not why."

"Yes, it is. And that's not how I want us to get married. When the time is right . . . someday . . . we'll do it."

"Someday?" His voice rose in the quiet house. "Let me make this clear. I don't want to get married because you're having our baby—at least not in the way you think. Not because it's an obligation. Not because it's the right thing to do. None of that bullshit. But because we're a family now and I'm fucking in love with you and I want you to be my wife. Because we're going to be together for the rest of our lives, and I'd rather do that as husband and wife instead of man and woman. I just told you earlier today you're my fucking soulmate, and you think I want to marry you out of obligation?"

"It just . . . the way you said it—"

"I said let's get married next Saturday because I want to be your husband by next Saturday. I didn't think I could fall more in love with you, until I realized you were pregnant. And now, it's become a full-blown infatuation. I can't keep my hands off you. I've never been more fucking turned on in my life. I was obsessed with you before, but now it's on a different level. So, when I ask if you want to get married next Saturday, I'm not really asking you. *I'm fucking telling you.*"

My eyes shifted away, and I remained quiet, suddenly uneasy.

He continued to watch me. "Talk to me, sweetheart." His voice turned softer once again, like he hadn't been ruthless a moment ago.

"That's just . . . not how I want to get married."

He was quiet for a bit, absorbing my rejection in silence. "Then tell me exactly how, and I'll bend over backward to make it happen."

"I understand your intentions and it's romantic, but I wanted you to ask me. I wanted a ring and a proposal that I didn't see coming. I wanted you to ask because you decided I was the one you wanted for the rest of your life."

"I've felt that way since the moment I asked you to move in with me. I wouldn't have asked if I didn't think you'd be my wife. I told you weeks ago that you would be my wife. I've never doubted that."

"Well, I want to be your wife on that timetable, not because I'm pregnant."

He took a breath, like he had a lot to say, but he restrained himself. "We're getting married before our baby comes, sweetheart. We aren't doing this any other way."

I should just be happy that he wanted to commit to me so badly, but I didn't like the way it had come out. I didn't like his lack of sensitivity. He was usually thoughtful and open minded, but in this instance, it was as if my feelings didn't matter at all. "So you're just going to force me to marry you?"

"That's not what I said—"

"It sounds like I don't get a say in this at all. I don't want to get hitched at a church in two weeks. I don't want to rush the most special moment of my life because you're in a hurry—"

"I'm not in a hurry."

"Don't interrupt me again."

"You literally just interrupted me—"

"Because you aren't listening to me, Constantine. I'm telling you I want a proposal when it's right for us. I don't want it to happen before the baby simply out of principle. We have our whole lives together, but one wedding."

There was a pause, like he deliberately waited to make sure I had nothing else to say before he continued. "Again, that's not how I feel. I love you, and I want us to be married. That's it."

"And what if I lost the baby tomorrow? Would you still want to get married?"

He gave a wince like I'd sliced him with a steak knife. "Let's not even put that out into the universe, all right? And yes, I'd still want to get married. That wouldn't change."

"Well, my answer is still no."

He released an irritated sigh, like he wanted me to know exactly how frustrated that made him feel.

"I want a ring and a proposal and a wedding—and I'm not sorry for wanting that."

He looked across the room toward the open window, sitting perfectly straight with a strong spine, and said nothing.

I didn't want it to be tense between us, not when we were so happy an hour ago. But I had to stand up for what I wanted. I'd dreamed of the moment Constantine would ask me to be his wife—and it was never like that.

After several minutes of silence, he looked at me again. He seemed to release his anger, because there wasn't a hint of it in his gaze. His hand went to my thigh, and he gave it a gentle squeeze. "Let's get to bed. I'll take care of Medusa."

"All right."

He gave my thigh a pat before he stood up and took Medusa out the back door so she could do her business in the garden.

I sat there and watched his silhouette darken as he disappeared from the light. I felt a wad of guilt in my stomach for denying what he wanted, but also a sense of pride for standing up to him. I knew he meant well and his intentions were pure, but a wedding meant a lot more to me than it ever would to him.

Chapter 11

Aurelia

The ceremony was held at a church, with at least five hundred people crowded into the aisles. We sat next to his mom and his sister Beatrice. It seemed to be a child-free wedding, because her two boys weren't there. Then we all drove to the hotel where the reception took place, on a private terrace with beautiful views of the Ionian Sea.

We sat at a round table with a white tablecloth and a tall centerpiece in the center. So many people were there, and of course a ton of guests came over to say hello to Constantine. He was warm and charming, all smiles and good vibes.

Sometimes it was hard to believe he'd been the emperor of Rome.

If I hadn't seen his barbarism with my own two eyes, I might not have believed it.

Constantine and I had returned to our normal routine after our little fight about marriage. He didn't seem to hold any resentment toward me, because his eyes lit up at the sight of me. He kissed me every morning and every night. Still wanted to fuck my brains out constantly. He was always in a good mood, no matter the time of day or the company in his presence.

He introduced me to a lot of people.

The one person I didn't want to see and hoped wasn't there was Isabella. She didn't seem to be in attendance, but with five hundred people on that terrace, I couldn't really be sure. Beatrice stayed at the table with us, so if her friend was there, she seemed to be ignoring her.

Beatrice did nothing more than say hello to me with the fakest smile I'd ever seen.

If Constantine didn't care what his sister thought of me, then I guess I shouldn't either.

After dinner toasts, the dance floor opened up, and it was a madhouse. Everyone was excited to jump up and party, drinks still in their hands, raucous bursts of laughter somehow overcoming the loud music.

"Con!" Constantine had his arm over my chair as he looked at one of his many, many cousins, who was waving him to join in the festivities.

"Come on, sweetheart."

"I'm not the best dancer."

"Does it look like a competition out there?" he teased. "Come on, have fun. In a couple months, you aren't going to want to move much, so enjoy it while you can." He stood up first and helped me to my feet before he took my hand and guided me onto the dance floor.

He and his friends and family jumped around and seemed to be having the time of their lives. It wasn't about the best dance moves but just joking around and having a good time. When Constantine danced with me, he grabbed my hand and spun me around before he circled me, being the most playful I'd ever seen him.

He snapped me out of my fear of embarrassment, and I just went with it.

He wasn't the best dancer traditionally, but he had so much confidence in the way he moved, the way he looked at me, that he pulled it off so well. He made me live in the moment with him and his friends, dancing and laughing, the night passing in the blink of an eye.

~

Constantine drank all the time, every day, but I'd never seen him drunk—and that was a testament to how much booze he drank at the wedding. One of his cousins gave us a ride home after the wedding because Constantine was too drunk to drive, and I didn't feel comfortable driving around all the cliffs, especially in the dark.

When we made it to the house, he unlocked the door and got us inside. Our dog sitter had already left for the night, and Medusa was asleep on the couch. It was so late, she didn't even want to get up and greet us.

"You know what?" He started to unbutton his shirt in the living room even though he'd normally get undressed upstairs. "You're right." His eyes were glazed over, and he had a bit of a sway to his steps. "I want a big-ass wedding with all my family, friends, my seventy-five cousins, and, of course, you." He turned to me, looking at me with a pure, beaming stare of love. He showed me his love in a lot of ways, but this was something new. "In a white dress with a belly. Or in a white dress with our daughter there. I can hold her when you walk down the aisle."

"We don't know what we're having, Constantine."

"I know, but I just have a feeling." He tapped his temple with his fingertips. "A hunch."

"We'll see."

"And I want her to look just like you." His hand moved over his heart. "See you in her eyes every time I look at her. Fuck, that would make me so happy." He dropped his shirt in the middle of the floor and headed upstairs. "I'd name her Julia, for the empress my great-great-great-great . . . however many greats . . . grandmother never got to be." He continued up the stairs until his footsteps turned quiet.

I smiled to myself when he was gone, loving this vulnerable and transparent version of him. It was also a relief to know that there truly was no animosity on his part. That he wasn't angry with my stubbornness.

I sat beside Medusa, petted her, and said good night.

Constantine called from upstairs. "Sweetheart, get your ass up here."

On Monday, I went to work at Rosticceria Da Cristina. I'd had enough training now that I could do a lot of the prep work myself. Antonio still came in, but now, it was an hour later than usual. I prepared most of the dough for him and the rice for the arancini, acting as his assistant in a lot of ways.

It was nice having that time with him, because it allowed us to build our own friendship—exactly what I wanted. To be a part of Constantine's family as if I'd been born and raised in Taormina like everyone else. I wanted the same with his sister Beatrice, who was there a lot of the time, but she was still ice cold. Even at the wedding, she didn't give me the time of day—and her mother was *right* there. She obviously didn't give a fuck.

I was in the front kitchen alone that morning when Beatrice walked inside. Like always, she pretended I wasn't there and headed into the back. Ever since Constantine told me not to worry about it, I'd stopped making an effort with her. Didn't say good morning or look at her either. If I did something wrong and her wrath was appropriate, that would be a different story. But I hadn't done a single thing wrong to earn this potent despisal, so she could fuck right off.

I continued to work, and then fifteen minutes later, someone else walked in the door.

It wasn't Antonio or another member of the crew. Wasn't Constantine either.

It was Isabella.

I froze at the counter, my gloved fingers covered in tomato sauce with rice and chunks of eggplant. I took in her dark features and hazelnut eyes as a rock rolled down my throat and dropped into the pit of my stomach. I'd only seen her in the flesh once before, months ago, when Constantine had taken me to a family dinner. She hadn't looked at me. But she certainly looked at me now.

There was no question that she hated my fucking guts.

To someone other than the two of us, the standoff probably only lasted a second or two, but it felt like minutes for me.

I was certain, beyond a shadow of a doubt, that she knew I was pregnant.

She was a beautiful woman who carried herself with confidence. A single look told me exactly why Constantine had wanted to marry her. Her long, thick hair was up in a high ponytail, showing the sharp and feminine angles of her face. She was petite, much shorter than me, but with an hourglass frame. The kind of beautiful woman that could have any man she wanted.

Well, except mine.

After she gave me the look of murder, she moved inside and headed toward the back.

I wasn't sure what made me do it, if I actually believed it would make some kind of difference, but I opened my mouth and words came rolling out. "I don't want it to be like this." I shot my shot, hoped the ball would pass right through her net.

She stopped to stare me down again, but she seemed to hate me more.

"I don't expect us to be friends by any means, but I don't want it to be this tense either. Constantine said you're a part of his family, so I'd like it if we could, you know, be in the same room together. Say hello. Make small talk—"

"I have no desire to share a single sentence with you."

Damn. All right, then. "So you'd rather just stare me down like I murdered your whole family every time we're in a room together?" I knew I should keep my composure and be the bigger person here, but I was sick of this mean-girl shit. "Let's remember I'm not the one who kissed his twin and then lied about it. That relationship ended because of you—not because of me."

Her eyes widened like she couldn't believe I just said that.

I couldn't believe I said it either.

"I'm just some girl Constantine met nine years later. A girl who doesn't want any conflict or drama. A girl who wants everyone to get along. And you're marking me as your enemy when I didn't do anything to deserve it. So why don't we give this another try? *Hello.*"

She was either still in shock at what I said or distracted by her rage, because she didn't speak for a second or two. "I was supposed to spend the last nine years with that man. Supposed to have children with that man. And you think I can say *hello* to the woman who has my soulmate?"

I could be really petty and tell her that Constantine referred to me as his soulmate, but that felt so cruel. "If Constantine were any other man, I would question why you're still hung up on him, but I totally get it. I get why this is hard for you, and believe it or not, I feel for you. Because if our situations were reversed, I'm sure I'd feel the same way—"

"I don't need your pity, bitch." She marched off to the back to look for Beatrice, cutting me down like I'd personally wronged her.

I almost didn't hold my tongue. Almost went after her and gave her a piece of my mind. But I took a deep breath and let it out slowly. Constantine was the man I would spend my life with, and my stomach might not look any different, but the life we'd made together was growing deep inside and had changed us both irrevocably. I had his present and she had his memory. I had his heart and she had his regret. She wasn't worth my time, so I got back to work and tried to forget the conversation had even happened.

I took a taxi home and found Constantine playing with Medusa. She couldn't chase down tennis balls anymore, but she could stand still while Constantine bounced a ball off the ground and she caught it in her mouth. He held a handful of green tennis balls and threw them one at a time, and she'd snatch them in her jaw, squeak it once, and then drop it to catch the next one.

When Constantine finished the balls in his hand, he rubbed her on the head. "Attagirl." He stood up and looked at me, and as always, his eyes lit up like I was his whole world and the universe that surrounded it. He walked over to me and pulled me close, kissed me like he'd missed me all day.

I couldn't believe I got to come home to this every day. And I got to do it for the rest of my life.

"How was work?"

The confrontation with Isabella flashed across my mind, but I didn't want to ruin our moment together. I decided to keep it to myself. "It was good. Just a bunch of arancini and pizza."

"I know." He leaned in and kissed me on the temple. "I can smell it in your hair." When he pulled away, he had a smirk on his lips. "A smell that's permanently tattooed inside my nose at this point."

"And you think our new restaurant will smell any different?"

"We won't be the ones cooking, so who knows what it'll smell like."

Medusa came over to me in her walker and let me give her a rubdown. "I love how well you're doing, honey." In the last month, she'd progressed so much. Soon, she'd be able to take off her cast and do more physical activity. I was excited to see her run around the terrace on her own, to go on hikes to Mount Etna with Constantine, to be a dog again.

We headed back inside the house. "Want to go out or stay in?" he asked.

"I could go for some Roman pizza, but I know we won't be able to find any of that."

"The chef can make it."

"That's not really a dinner, though, right?" Normally, we had a piece of fish or chicken with vegetables and rice or potatoes. It was pretty boring because Constantine eyed his macros all the time. He still lifted twice a day like he had gangs to police every night, not that I minded.

"Sweetheart, we can have whatever you want. It's your house."

"My house?" I asked with a smile. "If it's anyone's house, it's Medusa's—and she just lets us live here."

"Can't argue with that." Constantine pulled out his phone and sent a text to his chef downstairs. He made himself a drink at the bar while

I went upstairs to shower and change. I tried to cover the aroma of the kitchen with perfume, but only a deep scrub could get the smell out.

I changed into little cutoff jean shorts and a blouse, enjoying my wardrobe as long as I could before I couldn't fit into it anymore. When I stepped onto the terrace, Constantine lounged in the dining chair and stared at the sea, relaxed in his T-shirt and jeans, his hand absentmindedly rubbing Medusa's head beside him.

He had a glass of water sitting there for me because all the good stuff was off limits.

Constantine turned his focus to me across the table, his stiff drink on the table before him.

"I've never seen you drunk before," I said as I remembered the wedding.

He smirked. "Kinda lost it, didn't I? I haven't been drunk like that in over ten years. Hope I didn't take anything too far."

"No, you were fine." Just named our unborn daughter if we had a girl.

"You're still here, so I guess that's true."

"I like drunk Constantine," I said with a smile. "And it would take *a lot* to chase me away."

"Well, you won't see me like that again."

"What about at our wedding?"

"No," he said quickly. "I want to remember it all. I don't remember much after the dancing started. It's just uncommon for all my cousins to be in the same room together like that, so it got wild quick."

"How many cousins do you have?"

"Fuck, I don't know," he said as he rubbed the back of his neck. "Both of my parents each have five siblings . . . so probably like fifty first cousins. Something like that."

"And they're all here in Taormina?"

"They're a bit spread out across the island, but all local."

I was envious. I didn't have a single sibling. Never felt like I had a tribe, even when my mother was still alive.

Elio appeared a moment later and brought out two Roman pizzas with a set of plates so we could share. He also presented a green salad with seared prawns on top, probably because Constantine wouldn't eat much of the pizza.

After Elio left, I took a bite of the margherita pizza and felt the crunch of the dough, the crispiness I hadn't had since we were in the city. I hadn't thought about Rome much since we'd left. That part of my life suddenly felt like a dream, and this life in Taormina was my only reality. "Have you told Rocco I'm pregnant?"

The second I said Rocco's name, the entire energy at the table shifted. He didn't say a word and his expression didn't change whatsoever, but the anger was so palpable it felt like someone lit a fire.

I waited for him to answer me, but it seemed like he never would.

He stabbed his fork harder than necessary into the salad and took a few bites, elbows on the table, eyes down on his food.

I didn't eat another slice of pizza, just looked at him across from me.

When he felt my stare, he finally addressed what I'd said. "That friendship is over. Already told you that."

I loved the friendship the two of them had, the way they could be serious one moment and then joke around the next. From what I'd observed, they were both good men and great friends, and it broke my heart to see it spoil. "What happened—"

"He's dead to me, and I never want to speak of this again." He didn't raise his voice at me, but his hostility was so powerful I felt like he'd struck me down with his bare hand. Like a wolf that growled when I came too close to his den, he was prepared to bite my face off if I tried again. The territory was off limits.

"I just think . . . he might want to know we're having a baby."

The ice-cold stare Constantine gave me was utterly terrifying.

He'd never once looked at me that way—like he might kill me.

"What part of *I never want to speak of this again* did you not understand?" Again, he didn't raise his voice, but he was scary.

My appetite for the pizza vanished, and I boiled in his anger. I didn't know how to sidestep it or change the subject. So I just looked down at the pizza slice I'd previously put on my plate and forced myself to take a bite . . . to hope this painful discomfort would evaporate on its own.

~

It was one of the exceptionally few times when we didn't make love before bed. Constantine was still mad as hell about my line of questioning, and I wasn't sure if even an apology would defuse his rage. I wasn't sorry for what I'd asked, because I believed Rocco couldn't have done anything that egregious. They were just two stubborn men playing a game of emotional chicken.

When Constantine took his nightly shower, I grabbed my phone off the nightstand and quickly found Rocco's number. I typed a message to him from where I lay in bed. Hey, it's Aurelia. I know you and Constantine aren't talking right now . . . but I wanted to let you know we're having a baby.

I expected to see three dots pop up right away when he saw my message come through, but there was nothing. I put my phone on the nightstand and waited for it to vibrate with a response, but that didn't happen either.

And when I woke up the next morning, there was still nothing.

~

Constantine was in a better mood the next morning, but not quite himself just yet.

I got ready for the day and headed downstairs to grab my purse. I released a heavy sigh because it was the first time I actually didn't want to go to the restaurant. Isabella was a piece of work, and I wasn't sure if I could look at her face and be kind. That made me dislike Beatrice even more too.

"What's on your mind?" Constantine asked when he heard me sigh.

"Oh, just not excited to go to work."

"Then don't go."

"I have to."

He came to my side, his hand gently grabbing my elbow. "You *never* have to do anything. Don't go."

"No. I should be there." It would make me look weak if I stopped showing up after that confrontation. And how would I explain to Sofia that her daughter's best friend was a damn cunt?

His eyes shifted back and forth between mine like he spotted something in my gaze. "Something happen yesterday?"

"No."

His eyes narrowed as if whatever he found became more obvious. "Don't lie to me."

I didn't know how he could read me so well, didn't know what he saw to make him so confident in his assessment. "When I was there yesterday . . . Isabella came by."

His fingertips released my elbow, and the accusation in his eyes started to fade. His anger faded and was quickly replaced by unspoken frustration, like he already assumed that the interaction had been a shit show. "What did she say to you?"

"It was unpleasant. Let's just leave it at that."

"Aurelia." He pressed me just by using my name, a name he hardly ever said.

"I tried to be kind to her, and she was hostile to me. Told her I'd love it if we could get along, and she basically called me a bitch and the other woman. I called her out on her nastiness, and that made it worse."

"Good. I'm glad you put her in her place."

"Well, at this point, it's infinitely more hostile than it was before . . . and your sister will never like me now."

"Beatrice needs to be put in her place too," he said. "Fucking brat."

"Don't confront her about it. It's not going to improve the situation, and it's just—"

"You don't come into my family's restaurant and insult my future wife and the mother of my child. I don't know who the fuck she thinks she is, but I'm going to tell her exactly *what* she is."

"I don't want to make this worse."

"She can give me shit all she wants, but she crossed a line when she insulted you. There are consequences to our actions, and she's about to feel the flames of my wrath."

"I really don't want this—"

"Then you can thank her for that. She came into my fucking restaurant and insulted my family, and she thinks she can get away with that. Nope. I don't fucking think so."

Chapter 12

Constantine

After I dropped Aurelia off at work, I headed to Isabella's apartment. She lived in the same place as far as I knew, and when I got to the front door, I pounded on it so hard I felt the hinges strain from the force.

She might be at work right now, and if she was, then I'd head there next. Put her on blast in the back room just the way she put Aurelia on blast in the middle of the fucking kitchen.

But then she unlocked the door and stepped aside, wearing athleisure with her hair in a high ponytail, like it was her day off. Her family ran a couple of gelato places in the village, and she intended to take over when they were ready to retire.

Looking at her face somehow pissed me off even more.

Her eyes were wider than usual, like she felt sheer panic at the sight of me. She showed no confusion about why I was there, so she knew exactly what she'd fucking done.

I let myself inside and stepped into her living room. *"Who the fuck do you think you are?"* I didn't intend to yell at her when I got here, but holy hell, I was fucking mad. I'd never yelled at her like this, ever. Never yelled at a woman like this in my life.

She flinched when I raised my voice, like she was fucking scared.

Good.

"You come into *my* family's restaurant. *Mine.*" I slammed my hand into my chest. "And you have the nerve to insult my family. So, let me ask you this again—*who the fuck do you think you are?*"

She was paralyzed in fear, like a cornered deer that was too scared to try to run. Her eyes were frantic like she wanted to find an escape from this terror, but there was no way out of this. Out of this fucking hole she'd dug with her own shovel. "Hearing the news from other people was a shitty way to find out—"

"So that justifies you coming into my family's restaurant and insulting the mother of my child? Please, explain that to me. Explain to me why that justifies calling my future wife a bitch." I crossed my arms over my chest and waited.

"I—I didn't mean for it to go that way."

"I think you fucking did. Aurelia tried to make peace with you, tried to break bread, extend a goddamn olive branch, because she's twice the woman you'll ever be, and you tear her down and call her a bitch. She's known about our twisted, never-ending drama since the beginning, and she's never once cared about it because she actually feels sorry for you. She thinks I overreacted to the whole thing. She was able to humanize you and see the good in you, and you can't even be polite to her. *So what the fuck is wrong with you?*"

Her eyes started to water.

I didn't give a damn. "I'm actually asking you, Isabella. Because you're clearly irrevocably fucked in the head."

Tears immediately streaked down her cheeks, and she started to sob.

Okay . . . maybe I took it too far. "Look, I don't owe you anything. I don't owe you an explanation. I'm not going to text you about my personal life like you're still a part of it, because you aren't. And if that really pisses you off, then you take it out on me and not her."

She continued to sob in front of me, covering her face with her hands and turning toward the wall.

I should have felt worse about what I'd done, but I was still ripe with anger from how she'd treated Aurelia. Cross my girl, and I was the least compassionate motherfucker in the world.

"I'm—I'm sorry. Okay?" She breathed between her sobs. "This has just been really hard for me. Life didn't work out the way I wanted, and I always believed at some point we would find our way back to each other. But knowing you're going to have a baby . . . when I always thought we would have kids together . . . it just hurts. It hurts more than I can even describe." She kept her back to me as she cried. She tried to calm herself a couple times, but after a short pause, she would just cry hard again.

I listened to her and continued to feel nothing. "I hope you can find peace. I hope you can move on. Because our families are very much united, and I don't want to change that. I don't want to cut you out of my life. But treat Aurelia with anything other than respect, and I'm done with you—and my mother will stand with me on that." I would hate to put my mother in that situation, but she'd taught me the meaning of loyalty, and if I told her how Isabella had treated Aurelia, she'd cut Isabella out of our lives with a pair of meat scissors. Would burn that bridge with her best friend because blood was thicker than wine.

She took several deep breaths as she brought herself to a sense of calm.

"I wish we hadn't slept together—biggest mistake of my life." I didn't mean to hurt her more, just wanted to take responsibility for my error in judgment. "I'm sorry I let that happen. Maybe all of this wouldn't have gone down the way it did otherwise."

She slowly turned to face me, her face red and puffy and splotchy. "Then why did it happen in the first place?"

I felt my heart drop in unease.

"If there wasn't something here, then why did it happen at all?"

My arms remained tight over my chest, and I could feel the beat of my heart against my flesh. I felt the discomfort of the pending conversation, but also felt the relief of the closure I was about to obtain. "For a long time, I'd wondered if I made the right choice with us. Years passed, and I didn't meet anyone who meant anything to me. There was nothing wrong with the women in my life, so I started to wonder if there was something wrong with me. If I'd been too harsh with you, if maybe you were the person I was supposed to be with and I was too stubborn to admit that."

Her glossy eyes stared at me, her arms tightening around her body like armor.

"But I knew . . ." I swallowed in guilt, afraid to put this weight on her shoulders. "I knew the real reason I couldn't be with you again was because . . . of how much I resented you. Resented you for what happened with Edric. Because if that had been handled differently, I wouldn't have cut him out of my life, and he wouldn't have joined Cosa Nostra in Palermo and then the Skull King in Florence . . . and he'd still be alive."

Her eyes started to water again.

"I know it's unfair, but that's how I felt."

She dropped her chin and placed her hand over her mouth as she sucked in a harsh breath through her nose.

"It was wrong to feel that way, and I'm sorry I blamed you all these years. Truth is, that kiss happened because Edric tricked you. That's how it all started. And then he was killed for having an affair, because he was still the same asshole. He was a fuckup his whole life, and he died a fuckup. I've cleaned up his messes and taken the fall for him so many fucking times—and it still got him nowhere."

She dropped her hand and inhaled another breath, her eyes still watery.

"I'm sorry." I'd come here to rip her into a million pieces, but instead, I found the closure I'd been searching for all my adult life. Not closure for our relationship, but closure for my brother's death. My life's purpose had been to get revenge against Darius for murdering him, but I realized now that would accomplish nothing.

My whole life, I'd been looking after my brother and making excuses for him. Vouching for him to Tommaso, covering his tracks to my parents, letting him copy my homework, everything you could think of.

But he wasn't my responsibility.

He'd never been my responsibility.

And I was finally ready to accept that. To move on with my life. To focus on Aurelia and the family we were going to have together. To let the past go . . . and embrace the life I should have had all along. "I'm sorry."

Her eyes flicked away and stayed focused on the wall instead of me. "I would do anything to go back in time and change what happened. For us to still be together, for your brother to still be here. Anything."

I gave a slight nod in understanding, even though she couldn't see me. "I know."

I headed to Palermo after my conversation with Isabella. I had to go through the security checks like any other visitor since I was no longer part of Cosa Nostra. I made it to Tommaso's study, where he spent most of his time if he wasn't out on the town.

"You're back." Tommaso greeted me with a smile and a stiff handshake before he clapped me on the shoulder. "Sit and have a drink." He moved to the couch and motioned for one of his men to make a couple drinks at the bar. He sat in the corner of the leather couch and crossed his legs.

I sat across from him.

He pulled a cigar out of the front pocket of his vest and lit up. He held up another, silently offering it to me.

I shook my head. I hadn't smoked much since I'd been home. Stopped altogether when I realized Aurelia was pregnant. When I got back home, I'd have to undress in the garage so I wouldn't bring the secondhand smoke into the house.

He smoked on his own and watched the men bring the two old-fashioneds. "How's Taormina?"

I skipped the question he didn't even want an answer to. "I decided to open a restaurant in Taormina. That's how I'll fill my time from now on."

He took in a deep drag before he released the cloud between us. "A restaurant."

"Yes." I waited for him to mock me so I could lunge at his throat.

"And that will keep you entertained more than Cosa Nostra?"

"The restaurant itself, no. But I just found out I'm going to be a father." I hadn't been thinking about fatherhood before I'd noticed Aurelia hadn't touched her wine. Hadn't had any distinct plans for the future, because I was living in the past. But the second I heard the news, I was happier than I ever could have expected. A smile moved over my lips at the memory.

Tommaso hesitated as if he needed a moment to process what I revealed. "An accident? In this day and age?"

"Wasn't an accident. More of a surprise."

"And you're doing okay?"

"More than okay. I'm really excited." My smile was genuine, and the clouds in my chest were light and fluffy. "Which is why I think a quiet life in Taormina is the right choice. I had a great childhood there and learned a lot of values that have stuck with me all this time."

"And leave Rome to its fate?"

"Rome isn't my responsibility anymore." I said it and meant it. "My whole life changed the moment I knew I was going to be a father. Everything else . . . just lost its importance. I feel no guilt or shame for it."

He took another puff on his cigar before he released the cloud of smoke. "And our deal?"

"You can't be serious, Tommaso."

"And our deal?" he repeated.

"I just told you I'm having a baby."

"But you aren't married."

"But I'm getting married."

"So, you're engaged?"

I'd wanted to have our wedding this weekend, but Aurelia denied me. I wanted to be husband and wife and start our lives together, but she wanted to slow everything down. I had been frustrated at the time but conceded that she was right. If she weren't pregnant, I wouldn't have suggested rushing into a marriage. "No, not yet."

"Then you're fair game as far as I'm concerned."

"*I'm having a baby,*" I repeated like he hadn't heard me before. "And I just told you I'm not interested in Cosa Nostra."

"I understand that."

I fished my phone out of my pocket and opened the photo I'd taken. "This is sitting in my nightstand as we speak." I turned the screen toward him to reveal the enormous engagement ring I'd already bought for Aurelia. I didn't have a plan for how I'd propose, but I wanted to be ready when the moment was right, when I thought she would say yes to me.

"But she's not wearing it."

I released a frustrated sigh and returned the phone to my pocket. "I've always considered us good friends, Tommaso. I came here under the assumption you would be happy for me. That we'd have a drink together and you would tell me about all the joys of fatherhood and the wonderful years ahead. My father was never around, and you somehow filled that void when I first came to Palermo."

"You know that affection is reciprocated, Con. I've always loved you like a son."

"Really? Because it doesn't feel like it."

"Why else would I want you to marry my daughter?"

"*Force* is the word I would use."

He released a quiet chuckle. "You know how I force people, Con. I'm definitely not forcing you."

There wasn't the barrel of a gun against the back of my neck or in the center of my spine. There wasn't a promise that he'd kill my entire family if I didn't comply with his demands. So, yes, I had free will.

"I'm asking you to have a meal with her. How about now?"

"Now?" I asked blankly.

"I was just about to have lunch with her on the terrace, but you can take my place."

Fuck me. "Tommaso—"

"It's a meal, Con."

"I'm in a loving and committed relationship."

"Then don't fuck her on the table, all right?"

Who the fuck talks about their daughter like that?

He rose to his feet. "Let's go. Come with me."

I rose to my feet. "I told you I'm unavailable."

"And you promised me you would meet my daughter before I risked my life to help you. When you lied to my face and told me falsehoods about the shit Edric got himself into. I risked not only my life, but the future of Cosa Nostra and my family for you. And now you can't uphold your end of the deal? That's the kind of man you are? It's one fucking meal, Con."

I felt like I was about to betray Aurelia. It was just a meal that I didn't want to attend, meant literally nothing, but I still felt like shit about it. However, it was the only way I would get Tommaso off my back. "One meal and this is done?"

"Yes."

"All right . . . fine."

~

The outdoor terrace was under the shade of white umbrellas, fantastic views of the city and the mountainous terrain in the distance. I pulled out one of the chairs and took a seat, my heart so heavy in shame it felt like an anchor that struck the rocks at the bottom of the ocean.

"Have fun." Tommaso walked off, cigar still in his mouth, and headed back to whatever the fuck he was doing.

A seagull landed on the stone ledge, and I watched it for a while, doing anything to distract myself from the guilt that gnawed at my stomach. I knew the lunch was meaningless with no chance of leading anywhere. Just a business meeting, really. But I felt like an asshole anyway.

Gina approached the double doors that led to the terrace and stepped out in a white linen dress with ties on the sleeves. The material had a yellow-and-blue pattern, a distinctly Sicilian dress, perfect for summer. She had long dark hair, a heavy gloss to her lips, and she was thin and tall like her mother.

I'd never interacted with his daughters before. I'd seen them in person at events over the years, but I only spoke to Tommaso's wife. So this was the first time I'd actually met Gina. "Constantine." I rose to my feet and greeted her with a handshake instead of a hug or a kiss on the cheek. I pulled out her chair for her to be a gentleman, but it was nothing I wouldn't do for my sister or my mother.

"Gina." She sat across from me, a little bit timid and shy.

Fuck, this was awkward. She was twenty-five years old, so almost ten years younger than me, and that made me uncomfortable. It was way too big of an age gap for me. Aurelia was turning thirty this year, so that was close enough.

"My father said you wanted to have lunch with me?"

More like *forced.* "He just thought it would be nice if we met each other." I was careful with what I said, because if I said the wrong thing, Tommaso might get angry. I didn't want to do this once, let alone twice, so I had to get through it and move on. "So, are you in school or anything?"

"Um, I'm twenty-five."

"Oh yeah, right. So what do you do with your time?" How long did I have to sit here for?

"Well, I'm really into fashion. My mom and I go shopping a lot. And we spend a lot of time on the boat. It's better than the crowded beaches . . ." She went on for a while, talking about the little details of her life.

I tried not to zone out too much.

When she was done, she asked me about working with her father.

That was something I could talk about all day, so I told her how I got started with Cosa Nostra and then became the emperor of Rome . . . and then the downfall that came afterward.

"Wow, that's a lot."

"I was in a dark place for a while, but I'm better now."

"That's good."

Tommaso really believed I'd have one lunch with his daughter and turn into a pile of mush? That was all it took for me to ditch my pregnant woman? The man was fucking delusional. Even if I weren't committed, nothing would ever happen with this girl. Not because anything was wrong with her, but she was just too young for me. I knew most men were into that, but I never had been. I wanted a partner, someone to grow old with, and even if I wanted to fuck someone for the night, I wouldn't pick Tommaso's daughter.

We chatted over the three-course meal, and I grasped at straws to make conversation with her. If I wasn't invested in a person, I naturally didn't have much to say. So I was forcing myself to keep the conversation going, reaching for anything to talk about to make it to the end.

And then it took a turn for the worse.

"You're really hot," she said with a hint of shyness.

I didn't smile, felt really sick. The self-loathing felt toxic in my bloodstream. I'd hoped that if I kept the conversation cordial and boring, it wouldn't lead in this direction, but it happened anyway. I didn't accept the compliment because that felt like treason, and obviously, I didn't issue a compliment in return because that felt deceitful. But I'd been there for an hour and I fulfilled my end of the bargain, so it was time to bail. "I should get going. I have somewhere to be."

Chapter 13

Constantine

When I came home from Palermo, I took a shower to wash off the smell of smoke and perfume—like a scumbag who'd just had an affair. I knew I had to tell Aurelia what happened, but I wasn't in the mood to do it today. Too much bullshit had happened in eight hours, and I was dead tired.

I was downstairs with Medusa on the couch when Aurelia came home from work. She was in a much better mood than when she'd left that morning, so Isabella obviously hadn't stopped by after I'd yelled at her.

She put her purse on the counter. "Hey."

Medusa walked down the ramp off the couch and headed over to her, just the way she did with me. Aurelia had been a stranger to her just a few months ago, but she accepted her as part of the family unconditionally. And Medusa didn't like just anybody. She had great instincts when it came to people.

Aurelia smothered her in affection and attention before she turned to me. "How was your day?"

I came over to her in nothing but my sweatpants, ready for bed when it wasn't even four in the afternoon yet. "Pretty shitty." My arm circled her lower back, and I pulled her in for a quick kiss.

"How'd it go with Isabella?"

"I screamed at her . . . *a lot.*"

"Con . . ."

"Probably took it too far, honestly. But I don't feel bad about it. She had it coming."

"I don't know if that's actually productive."

"I think calling someone on their bullshit is more productive than you realize. The effects may not be immediate, but they're like seeds that slowly grow after they've been planted. Told her that if the bullshit continues, then I'm not afraid to cut her out of my life. I think she got the message."

"Are you okay?" she asked.

"I told her the reason I couldn't forgive her was because I resented her for everything that happened with my brother. Told her it was wrong, and that's on me. But it was nice to get it off my chest."

"I thought you said that to her already?"

"Not quite as explicitly, though. We didn't leave on a good note or a bad note. And maybe that neutrality is a good thing."

She started to rub my arm, the touch of her fingertips so subtle but loving at the same time. "Why don't you go out with your friends tonight? Get some drinks and blow off some steam?"

"Why would I want to do that when I can be home with you?"

Her eyes deepened in affection before a gentle smile shone through. "That's sweet. But I can tell you've had a long day. Might be nice to do something fun."

"Then come with us."

"It's okay, Constantine. We don't have to do everything together."

"I know we don't. But I'd like to."

She moved past me and pressed a kiss to my chest on the way. "I'll be fine. It's not like I can drink anyway."

I sent a group text to the boys to meet me at Daiquiri, and Antonio was the first one to arrive. I'd already had two drinks since I got there, needing the booze to take the edge off the shit day I'd had.

Antonio clapped my hand in his when he got there and took a seat. "Still drunk from the wedding?" he teased.

"That hangover was the worst, man."

He chuckled before he looked at the menu. "Aurelia still around?"

"Yeah. Good thing I didn't throw up."

"That you remember . . ." He waved for the waiter's attention and ordered his drink. "Why isn't Aurelia here?"

"She told me to go out without her. She can't drink anymore, so I kinda feel bad doing it around her."

"Yeah, I get that."

"I also had a day from hell."

"Isabella?" he asked.

"Yeah, how'd you know?"

"Beatrice told me. She heard the two of them going at it in the restaurant."

"And she didn't do anything?" I asked, mildly hurt.

He shrugged.

Why did my mother understand loyalty so well, but my sister was oblivious to it?

"To be fair, Beatrice said Isabella was a little over the top."

But my sister didn't do anything, and that's what mattered. "That's actually not on my mind. I went to Palermo today to talk to Tommaso." I told him the whole thing and the shitty predicament I'd gotten caught in.

"Is she cute?"

I shot him a glare.

"I mean for someone else . . . or maybe me."

I continued the glare.

"All right, never mind."

"He forced me to keep my end of the deal, and I feel like shit about the whole thing."

"Why?"

"Because it was inappropriate. I shouldn't have been there."

"But you didn't *want* to be there. You just did your time and left. You really think Aurelia will be mad about that? You're like the most loyal guy on the planet."

"I don't think I'll lose her or anything, but she might be a bit ticked."

"If she's so reasonable about Isabella, I really doubt she'll be unreasonable about this."

"Yeah, fair point."

"I wouldn't worry about it. I mean, you don't even need to tell her since there isn't much to tell."

"No, I'll tell her." If it was something I wanted to hide, then that meant I needed to come clean. I preferred honesty and full transparency. I was an honest person because it was the right way to be, but I also couldn't handle the guilt of deceit. So my honesty didn't come from strength . . . but weakness. "Just not today. I'm so fucking tired." I sank into the chair and took a drink.

"Yeah, that's fair." Antonio looked toward the stairs. "Francesco and Aldo are here."

"Great, let's get the party started."

~

We sat together for an hour or two, ordering more drinks and eating the appetizers they continued to bring out. Being with the boys made me forget all the bullshit that happened that day, so I finally let it go.

The guys shot the shit about some of the girls they were talking to, we argued about football for a while, talked about heading to the beach next weekend to jump off the cliffs. I'd been jumping from the rock since I was a boy, and it was the first time I felt hesitant to do it.

Because people depended on me.

Aurelia, Medusa, and now someone I hadn't met yet.

My whole perspective on life had changed ever since Aurelia told me about the little one growing inside her. Everything was easier but also more complicated. My life seemed to have more value, not because of my importance, but because of the impending responsibility of fatherhood.

"Oh no . . ." Antonio's eyes followed someone who'd stepped onto the terrace.

That caught my attention, so I followed his gaze.

Isabella had appeared on the terrace with some of her friends, my sister among them. All in dresses and flats. It seemed to be a girls' night out. I never cared about Beatrice maintaining her friendship with Isabella, but now I was ticked that she couldn't even bother to try with the woman I was going to marry because of some misplaced loyalty.

"Con can't catch a break, can he?" Francesco said.

I grabbed my glass and finished my drink. "I'm sure they're gathered to talk about what happened this morning." And I would probably look like the asshole—and so would Aurelia. Because nothing we did made any fucking difference. "Let's bounce before she sees me." I got the attention of the waitress and motioned her over.

"Too late," Antonio said as he quickly looked back at our table. "Yeah, she definitely saw you."

"Then let's find another spot." I kept my focus away from Isabella's direction, trying to blend into the background, praying that she didn't want to revisit our previous conversation because she had too many drinks.

I continued to wait for the waitress to bring the tab, but it felt like a fucking lifetime.

"She keeps looking," Francesco said.

"Then stop giving her something to look at," I said quietly. I couldn't believe I was in my fucking thirties but my life still felt like a teenage soap opera.

The waitress finally came over with the tab on a tray.

The guys pulled out their wallets to split the bill, but I threw my card into the tray. "Put it all on this."

She could tell I was in a hurry, so she left again.

"I'll get the next round," Antonio said.

"You know I don't give a shit. I just want to get out of here."

The waitress took the tab to the stand to process it.

Fuck, I wished I had cash.

I rubbed my palms together as we waited. No one made conversation, all anxious to leave so I'd be myself again.

She finally came back, and I signed the check and we got to our feet. "Just head for the stairs and don't look."

"All right," Francesco said.

The four of us beelined for the exit to get the fuck out of there. There was a set of stairs and then a platform halfway up. Once we made it to the main street, we'd be free of the dilemma.

But I only made it halfway up before I heard her voice from behind me.

"Con?"

Jesus fucking Christ, why is this happening to me?

The guys stopped on the stairs to look at me.

"Can't talk, Issy," I said as normally as I could. "We're meeting some people."

The guys made it to the street and turned back to me.

But Isabella caught up to me on the platform halfway. "Wait, wait." She grabbed me by the forearm.

I spun out of that touch so fast. "I think we've talked enough for the day."

The guys turned the corner to give us our privacy.

I'd gone out with the guys to let off some steam, but now I was in a secluded alleyway with my ex, a position I didn't want to be in, while my pregnant woman was at home waiting for me. I felt like a dick just for being there.

Issy had this glaze to her eyes, like she was already drunk before she'd even arrived at the cocktail lounge. "Con, I'm sorry about all of this. I told Beatrice to make more of an effort with . . . *her*."

She should have wanted to do that on her own, and the fact that she didn't pissed me off even more. Made me angry at both of them. "I've gotta go, Issy."

"Wait." She reached for my arm again.

This time, I made sure I was out of her reach. "What?"

"Why are you so angry right now?"

"Because I don't want to spend another second in your presence, Issy. That's fucking why." I wanted this part of my life to be over, a relationship nine years dead to finally be buried in the cemetery with my ancestors. "If you need help getting home, I'm happy to get you there safely, but if that's not what you need, leave me the fuck alone."

Her eyes started to water. "How is this so easy for you?"

"Because I'm in love with someone, Isabella. Because I'm happy. Because I'm going to be a father. It's time you move on too."

Her eyes continued to water. "Con, what we had was special—"

"Stop."

"Con—"

"You're drunk. Probably not even going to remember this in the morning."

She moved into me, some kind of insane last-ditch effort, and tried to kiss me.

She didn't come close. Probably because a part of me expected it to happen. "Isabella, fuck off. *Just fucking fuck off.* I used to love you and I've always cared for you, but now, I just fucking hate you." I headed to the stairs to put more distance between us.

I heard her gasp before she choked.

Halfway up the stairs, I looked back at her.

She drowned in a wave of tears, music coming from the terrace of the cocktail lounge, people passing on the main street above, oblivious to the fucking soap opera. "It's not fair. It should have been us. *It should have been us . . .*"

~

The restaurant was closing down, but they didn't ask me to leave.

Antonio stayed with me while the others headed out. He didn't say much, just silently supported me.

I wanted another drink, but I'd cut myself off a while ago. Now I slouched at the table and rubbed my temple like I could feel a stress migraine approaching over the horizon.

Antonio continued to drink his wine as he glanced at me from time to time.

It was midnight. I knew I should head home because Aurelia couldn't sleep unless I was there. She hadn't been that way before, but after what happened with Darius, I knew she was irrevocably changed. "At least this day is officially fucking over."

Antonio smirked slightly. "Sorry, man. But Aurelia will understand."

"Understand that I'm out drinking with the boys and talking to my ex in an alleyway, and she tries to kiss me? Yeah, she'll just love that."

"That's not how it happened."

"That's *exactly* how it happened."

"You're being way too hard on yourself."

"I was afraid Isabella was going to fuck this up in the beginning, and now I'm afraid she's still going to fuck this up for me. Honestly, I wonder if that's what she's trying to do. Thinks if she can get rid of Aurelia, then maybe we can work it out."

"Why would she think that?"

"Well, I told her that the reason I couldn't make it work with us is because I resented her for what happened to Edric. But I don't know. I've had some closure with that and know it was wrong to blame her for any of it. Maybe that gave her a glimmer of hope, which isn't what I wanted."

Antonio gave a slight nod. "Yeah, maybe."

"Am I twenty-three or thirty-three?" I snapped. "I can't tell the difference anymore." I finally paid the tab and left the table, and the two of us walked down the deserted walkway out of the heart of the village.

We parted ways on one of the roads because Antonio lived in an apartment in the center. He clapped me on the shoulder. "You'll be all right, man."

"Yeah, thanks." I walked to where my Range Rover was parked and headed up the mountainside to my villa. As the crow flies, my home was actually really close to the heart of Taormina, but with the winding roads up the cliff face, it took at least twenty minutes, maybe a little less if no one else was on the road.

It was the first time I'd come home and didn't want to be there.

The first time I didn't want to see Aurelia.

I parked in the garage and headed through the door. The lights were still on, like she was wide awake. When I stepped into the living room, Aurelia and Medusa were asleep on the couch together, side by side, Aurelia spooning Medusa from behind.

I stopped and stared at them for a while, the smirk that moved onto my lips unstoppable. Medusa must have been dead tired if she didn't wake up at the sound of my footsteps. I could hear her snore a little bit when I came closer.

Aurelia was wrapped in a blanket she'd pulled off the back of the couch, wearing one of my T-shirts, the TV still on but the volume off, like she'd turned it down before she fell asleep.

I took a seat by her head and gently ran my fingers through her soft hair, watching her sleep like a fucking angel.

Medusa must have smelled me, because her eyes opened, and she turned her head to look at me. Then she released an excited whine, her tail wagging and smacking Aurelia on the hip. Unable to contain her excitement, she got up and moved into my lap.

I chuckled quietly. "Oh baby girl." I held her in my arms and gave her a rubdown while her tail continued to go crazy. "Thanks for looking after her while I was gone."

Aurelia sighed before she got up, moving the hair out of her face. "What time is it?" she asked in a strained voice.

"After midnight."

"Oh wow." She moved her back against the couch and pulled her knees to her chest. "Guess that means you had fun."

If only that were true.

I dropped my arm around her shoulders and pulled her in close to Medusa and me, brushing a kiss to her hairline. "I love you."

She turned into me, sliding her arm over my torso as she snuggled into me, half asleep. "I love you too."

With both of my girls on me, I didn't want to get up. Didn't want to ruin the special moment by talking about someone I truly had begun to hate. So, I watched them instead, watched Medusa fall back asleep on me while Aurelia's breaths deepened as she drifted off.

Chapter 14

Constantine

I didn't tell Aurelia.

She got up when her alarm went off and readied herself for work like every morning. I didn't think it was the right time to tell her that my obnoxious ex had tried to kiss me on the stairs, so I decided to tell her later.

I dropped her off at the entrance to the village, and shortly after I pulled away, a text from my mom popped up on the screen. **Come to the restaurant. I want to talk to you.**

"Fuck." I already knew what this was about. I almost decided to ignore it and head home anyway. But if it was about the shit with Isabella last night, this was not how I wanted Aurelia to find out about it.

So I turned around and headed back.

I walked along the side of the building before I unlocked the glass door and stepped inside.

Aurelia was at the counter in her black T-shirt with her hair in a high ponytail. Her eyes went wide with surprise like she didn't expect me, but once the surprise faded, she looked happy to see me, like she hadn't just seen me a couple minutes ago. "Hey, what brings you here?"

I came to the counter and gave her a kiss as if eight hours had passed since I'd dropped her off. "Mom wants to talk to me."

"Con, is that you?" she shouted from her office down the hallway in the rear.

"Yeah!" I shouted back. "Be there in a second."

Aurelia's eyes studied my face with trepidation. "Everything okay?" Now she knew me well enough to know when something was off. She picked up on my energy, my body language.

"Yeah. But there's something I've got to tell you—"

"Con." My mom came from the back, walking with an angry strut like she had heard about last night. "Lucia called me at *dawn* this morning to tell me you brought Issy to tears at Daiquiri last night."

So she was the victim in all this?

"I understand that things have been difficult between you two, but yelling at a woman like that is never okay—"

"Ma, listen to me." I held up my hand to silence her before she verbally eviscerated me.

"You two need to find a way to coexist with each other if you're going to be living here—"

"Ma."

Both of her hands went to her hips, and her eyes were savage.

"Look, I wanted to tell Aurelia this last night, but it wasn't the right time. So, I guess I'll tell you both." I looked at Aurelia. "I'm sorry you have to find out like this."

Her eyes quickly flicked to my mother and back to me, and I could see the signs of stress all over her face.

"Issy tried to kiss me." I looked at my mother instead of Aurelia, not wanting to face her disappointment. "I tried to leave Daiquiri with the guys, and she followed me. I tried to get her to leave me the fuck alone, but she wouldn't stop. She grabbed me twice, and I stepped away. And then she tried to kiss me, and that's when I snapped. Don't expect an apology, because I'm not sorry about it. I spoke to Isabella earlier in the day since she disrespected Aurelia, and I *thought* we'd finally worked it out, but she was fucking wasted and belligerent."

Within the snap of a finger, my mother's rage disappeared. "What do you mean, she disrespected Aurelia?"

Aurelia didn't say anything, but she looked at me and shook her head.

Nope, I was not covering for that cunt. "When she came into the restaurant the other day, Aurelia extended an olive branch, and Isabella continued to be hostile and called Aurelia a bitch. So I went to her apartment and told her she can't come into my house and insult my family. I'm not sorry for anything I've said or done." I used to hang assholes from the Pantheon, and now I was in the midst of some secondary school drama.

My mother continued to look at me without the sassy rage she'd worn a moment ago. Her arms crossed over her chest, and she released a heavy sigh. "Well, she left out that part . . ."

"I'm sure Isabella left it out when she told her mother. I can give her the benefit of the doubt that she doesn't remember, but I'm pretty fucking sure she does." Made me out to be the asshole when she was trying to sabotage my life.

"I'm sorry, Con," my mother said. "I should have known better."

"It's okay, Ma."

"I was glad you two didn't work it out nine years ago, and now I'm even more grateful nine years later. I see her true colors now, and she was never good enough for you. I'll give her and her mother a piece of my mind."

"I don't want you to do that, Ma. I just want peace."

"That's too fucking bad. She crossed a boundary, drunk or not, when she was very aware of the fact that you've settled down, with a child on the way. She disrespected you, and she walked in here and disrespected Aurelia—and that shit isn't gonna fly in my house." She turned around and walked back down the hallway to her office, probably to finish up whatever she needed to do before she drove straight to Lucia's house.

When we were alone again, I looked at Aurelia, afraid to see her hurt and disappointment.

But she seemed to feel neither. In fact, I could see only sympathy.

"I'm sorry I didn't tell you yesterday. But it was late, and you were already asleep on the couch . . ."

"I'm not upset, Constantine."

"You aren't?" I asked as I felt a rush of relief through my body, afraid I'd fucked up the one relationship that mattered the most.

"Of course not." She stepped closer to me, her hand moving to my arm, her fingertips slipping slightly underneath the sleeve. "Why would I be angry?"

"Well, if some asshole tried to kiss you, I'd punch him down a flight of stairs."

She smiled slightly. "Lucky for Isabella that I'm not the violent type."

"Let me explain what happened. I was already at Daiquiri—"

"I don't need you to explain anything, Constantine," she said calmly.

"I just want you to understand I wasn't with her—"

"Constantine." She gave my arm a gentle squeeze to snap me out of my anxiety. "I trust you more than anyone. I don't need an explanation. I don't need details. Frankly, I don't think the situation needs further attention."

I believed that Isabella was trying to sabotage everything, and after Aurelia's last relationship ended with lies and deceit and infidelity, I was afraid that this would be a trigger for her. That it would make her anxious and paranoid and chase her off, but that didn't seem to be the case.

"To be honest, I just feel bad for her."

"Are you serious?" I asked in both shock and awe. "She's disrespected you twice now. The first in here, and the second time when she tried to kiss me."

"But she doesn't owe me anything. I'm a stranger to her."

"You're the woman I love, Aurelia. You're the mother of my child. You've had my last name since the moment I met you, even if you aren't my wife yet."

"That's sweet of you to say," she said quietly, her eyes shifting away, probably in guilt because she'd declined my marriage proposal.

"But she's lost in her grief, and people do unusual things when they're depressed."

"Grief? It's been *nine* years."

"I don't expect you to understand this, but having a child means something different to a woman than it does to a man, okay? She's probably always pictured the two of you finding your way back to each other and having all the things she's always wanted. So to know that I'm having your child means that dream is never going to come to pass. It's grief, Constantine. It's grief for a life she desperately wants . . . but will never have. I'm not excusing her behavior, because she should apologize for all the shit she's done, but I understand it."

I never expected her to be calm and logical about this. It made me realize I was the more emotional one of the two of us. My fuse was shorter and my temper was grander. I cared for others, but I didn't have the empathy that she possessed.

"If I lost you . . ." She shook her head. "I would never get over it. Even if I were married with kids, I would hate knowing someone else was having your child instead of me. It's one of those wounds that doesn't heal in time. If I didn't love it here so much, I'd say we should move just to give her space to move on, but this place is home now."

"I'm not moving to make someone else comfortable. This is where I want to raise our child. It's a great place to grow up."

"I don't want it to be this way. I want everyone to get along. I want peace."

"I do too."

"So, let's hope she comes around and apologizes. And if she does, let's give her a clean slate."

I rolled my eyes and shook my head. "I'm not doing a damn thing—"

"Constantine."

I released a sigh.

"Forgive and forget. That's how you move on."

"I know she's trying to sabotage our relationship."

"Well, I'm sure she's done now. I'm not worried about someone coming between us. You make me feel like the center of your universe every day. You make me feel secure. I fell asleep on the couch last night because I'm never worried about what you're doing or who you're doing it with. Maybe that's why I'm not upset about any of it."

Knowing I did my job and did it well took away a layer of rage.

"So let's not worry about her anymore. I'm sure she's embarrassed about the whole thing now."

"She should be." This made me realize that Aurelia wouldn't care about my predicament with Tommaso and the lunch date I'd had with his daughter Gina. She wasn't the jealous type. Wasn't insecure. Trusted me even though her last relationship had been a dumpster fire of lies and deceit. I wanted to put it off for another day, but since today was already shitty, I decided I'd like to start off tomorrow on a different foot. "Since we're on this subject, there's something else I've got to tell you."

"All right," she said calmly, the beautiful angles of her face on display with her hair up in a tight ponytail like that. There was no fear in her eyes, like she wasn't afraid of what I might say.

"It's a really long fucking story, but I made a deal with Tommaso years ago . . . and I had to fulfill my end of the bargain recently."

"Okay. What does that mean?"

"Basically, he said he would only help me save my brother from Darius if I agreed to *consider* marrying his eldest daughter Gina."

Her reaction wasn't the same as it'd been with Isabella. Now, she stiffened, focused her hard eyes on my face. "I don't understand."

"When I went to Palermo to visit and inform him of my retirement, he asked me to join Cosa Nostra and asked me to keep my end of the deal. Because he wants me to run Cosa Nostra when he's killed or lives long enough to step aside, and I'd be the perfect partner for his daughter."

Her eyebrow arched, and she looked as irritated by this as I felt.

"Yes, I know it's the most ridiculous thing you've ever heard. I felt the same way."

"Where is this going, Constantine?"

"He asked me to have dinner with Gina—"

"And did you?"

"No. I told him I was in a committed relationship. Then I told him we're having a baby. Told him we're getting married. But since I'm not engaged, that wasn't good enough. He continued to push and I pushed back, but then he made me feel like shit because he risked his life to help me . . . and I lied to him."

"How did you lie?"

I lowered my voice so my mother wouldn't overhear. "I'd told him I didn't know why Darius wanted Edric dead, but I knew exactly why. So Tommaso and his men could all have been killed that night. He probably wouldn't have helped me if he'd known the truth. So, he had me by the balls."

Aurelia continued to stare at me, her arms tight over her chest.

"No matter how many times I told him I've settled down, he said he wanted me to meet her. So the last time I went up there to tell him that we're going to open a restaurant here and I wouldn't be returning to Cosa Nostra, he asked me to have lunch with her."

"And did you?" Her tone was different, on the edge of hysteria.

I knew I was fucked, but I told the truth. "Yes."

"What?"

"It was an hour long on the terrace at headquarters. I could tell she was bewildered by the whole thing too—"

"You went?" She shifted her weight, looking a lot like my mother when she was this mad.

"It was literally just a lunch. Basically a business meeting. I only did it to get Tommaso off my back and keep my word—"

"You went on a date with another woman, Constantine."

"It was *not* a date. It was awkward as fuck."

She stepped away from me and moved to the counter on the other side of the kitchen, arms still crossed, putting distance between us.

I'd never seen her react this way before. "Sweetheart, Isabella telling me she loves me and kissing me is a hell of a lot worse."

"When did this happen?"

"Yesterday."

She raised her voice like she didn't care if my mother heard all of this. "How would you feel if I went on a date with some guy because my old boss made me promise to do so? That even if it meant nothing to me, I still went?"

I wouldn't like it one fucking bit, but I didn't dare say that.

"That to keep my word, I had to *consider* marrying him . . ."

"I didn't *actually* consider it. I just did it to pay my debt, and it's done now. I'll never see her again. She doesn't have my number, and I don't have hers. I'm telling you, it was just an awkward and weird lunch."

"Did you tell her about me?"

"Well . . . no."

Her eyes were furious.

"Because if she told Tommaso, he might make me see her again or some nonsense. I just wanted to get it over with so it would be done."

"So this woman thinks she was on a date with you and you're fully available?"

"I'm not sure what she thought it was, honestly. He sprung it on her just like he did with me."

"How old is she?"

"Twenty-five."

"Oh, a younger woman."

I almost rolled my eyes. "Too young. I've never been into that. And even if I were, it wouldn't matter, because I'm in love with you. Sweetheart, you're letting this get to you when it shouldn't."

"How would you feel if this were reversed?" she pressed, knowing what my answer would be even if I didn't give it. "Constantine?"

I sighed as I dragged my hands down my face. "Look, I didn't have a choice."

"So there was a gun pointed at your head the entire time?"

"Aurelia—"

"Answer my question."

I sighed.

"Answer. It."

"No. I wouldn't like it."

That seemed to settle the argument, because she turned her back to me, putting on a pair of gloves like she was ready to get to work. The silence was somehow louder than her shouts. She grabbed the washed tomatoes from the sink and tossed them into a steel bowl before she brought them to the counter.

I stood there and waited for her to say more. To at least look at me.

But she ignored me.

"Sweetheart—"

"Go, Constantine. I don't want to hear you or fucking look at you right now."

Chapter 15

Aurelia

I sat at the dining table in Sofia's home, still in my work clothes that smelled like a kitchen. The tightness of the scrunchie holding up my ponytail started to make my temples throb, so I pulled it through my long hair until the strands came free. It relieved the tension in my scalp—but not the stress in my heart.

Sofia stepped into the room with a pile of clothes over her arm. "Good thing we're the same size." She gave me a warm smile before she laid the pile of clothes over one of the dining chairs. Then she moved to the barista-level coffee maker and brewed me a fresh cup of coffee before she brought it to me, along with a little jug of milk. "It's decaf."

"Thank you." I brought the mug close, the smell of coffee always welcome, regardless of the hour. "And thanks for letting me stay with you." I stared into the cup and saw the lighter-brown foam sitting on top . . . and immediately thought of Constantine's eyes. "I know this must be awkward for you."

"Not at all." She pulled out the other chair and took a seat. "You're my family, Aurelia—and not just because you carry my grandchild." Her hand moved to mine and rested there for a moment before she pulled away.

The watery sensation started in the back of my eyes, but I quickly looked down at my coffee and waited for it to wane. "You remind me of my mother."

She paused.

I continued to look at the foam, watching the small bubbles start to pop and dissipate.

"I take that as a great compliment, honey."

When I recovered from the emotion that nearly took me down, I looked at her again. "I love him with all my heart, and we'll work it out. I'm just so angry right now." I grabbed the milk and poured it into my coffee, letting it rise just below the top.

"I don't blame you."

"You don't?" I whispered.

She shook her head. "I heard the whole thing. Con didn't come off very well."

At least I wasn't overreacting. "I know it didn't mean anything. I believe everything he says. I just . . . feel disrespected."

"I know."

"He could have told me beforehand, but he didn't."

"To be fair, it sounds like he tried to avoid it as much as he could. And from what I know of Cosa Nostra, you have to be a man of your word or you aren't a man at all. He made this deal long before you, Aurelia. It's complicated, I understand that. Love isn't jealous, but it is jealous when a line is crossed—and that line was crossed."

I didn't expect his mother, of all people, to be on my side with this. "I just picture him with this hot twenty-five-year-old, while I'm caked in tomato sauce at work, looking like hell."

She gave a quiet chuckle. "You do not look like hell, Aurelia. And she's only a few years younger than you. You're still so young and so beautiful."

"Thank you, Sofia."

Our moment was interrupted by a loud knock on the door. Loud, distinct, angry . . .

The corner of her lip upturned in a smile. "Ready for this?"

"I really don't want to see him right now."

"Well, if I don't open that door, he's gonna break it down." As she rose from the chair, he pounded on the door again, this time harder, shaking the whole house. She walked out of the kitchen and disappeared from sight.

From the other side of the house, I heard the door open and shut, but no conversation. Constantine's footsteps could be heard down the hallway before he rounded the corner and stepped into the kitchen.

I kept my eyes on my coffee, even though I could feel his stare pierce me like bullets.

He stood there for a while, staring at the side of my face, before he pulled out the chair his mother had occupied a moment ago.

My heart raced with adrenaline. My fingers felt numb and sweaty the second he was in my space.

"Sweetheart."

My eyes stayed on the coffee.

"Look at me."

"I just want some space, okay?"

"Well, that's too fucking bad, isn't it?" He didn't raise his voice, but his tone was sharper than broken glass. "Because you're my woman and you're carrying my baby and I'm not letting the two of you sleep under someone else's roof."

"It's your mother's—" I raised my chin and looked at him.

"You're my responsibility. Not hers."

"She said she doesn't mind."

"Of course she doesn't mind, but that's not the point," he snapped. "We resolve our issues at home. We don't run from each other."

"I said I need some space," I said calmly. "Just a day. You really can't give that to me?"

His furious eyes burned white hot into my face. "Just a day." He repeated the words, clinging to them like life rafts filled with hope.

"I understand nothing happened. I believe everything you say. But I'm still disappointed . . . and I need time."

He sank into the chair and stared at the painting on the wall for a beat. "You do realize that I used to sleep with Isabella every day? Used to tell her I loved her every day? That I wanted to marry that woman. Bought a fucking ring. None of that bothers you at all, but Gina, *a woman I don't even know*, is enough to push you over the edge."

"You obviously don't get it, Constantine."

"Then explain it to me."

"It hurts me because it's the last thing I expected you to do. You aren't a pushover, you don't concede a fight, but you spent time with this woman and let her believe you were available. She's sitting there thinking she just won the fucking lottery and that you might be hers, but you're supposed to be mine. It feels like a betrayal."

It was the first time he winced, like my words had actually cut him.

"And you knew this was a situation beforehand and didn't tell me."

"Because I assumed it would go away if I dodged it enough. And then the lunch was literally on the spot, and Tommaso guilt-tripped me hard. Believe me when I say I felt like shit for being there, but it was just a means to an end. Sweetheart, you know you're the only one for me. You said yourself that I make you feel loved every single day."

"I know that, Constantine."

"Then forgive me and let's go home."

My eyes moved back to the coffee.

He released an irritated sigh at my reaction.

"I forgive you and I love you and I want to spend my life with you." I stared at the coffee for another moment before I raised my chin and looked at him again. "But I'm still so angry with you."

His eyes hardened like armor, wanting to protect his heart from the bite of my words.

"I just need some time."

He inhaled a deep breath, his chest rising and expanding, and then he let it out in a painful whoosh. He didn't say a word before he left the chair and walked out of the dining room. A moment later, I heard the door open and close—and then he was gone.

~

His mother cooked us dinner, cacio e pepe with a side salad and fresh garlic bread. I offered to help, but she was practically indignant at the request. I watched her as I sat at the dining table, in the change of clothes she'd given me. I'd washed my face, but since I didn't have any makeup, I wasn't able to doll myself up again. I would have to go to work like this in the morning, not that I cared all that much.

Sofia set the table. "Thought you'd like a taste of home."

I smiled when I looked at the Roman pasta, something I used to eat all the time. "I will always have a fondness for Rome, but Taormina became my home the second I met Constantine."

She took a seat and smiled. "I'm glad to hear that. Love the fact that the two of you will always be here. Nothing makes me happier than seeing Constantine leave behind a dangerous life and settle down. It's not as exciting as guns and drugs . . . and whatever else he used to do. But it's far more meaningful."

"Yeah, definitely."

She opened a bottle of wine and poured herself a glass. We ate together at the table, talking about the restaurant and her fellow restaurant owners and neighbors.

"So, did you talk with Lucia and Isabella?"

"I sure did," she said. "Gave that brat a piece of my mind."

"Oh no."

"Lucia is my best friend. I've known her since we were kids. I'm not worried about our friendship. She kept her silence out of loyalty to her daughter, but her eyes told me she knew Isabella was wrong. How could anyone argue otherwise."

"I don't want the dust to be kicked up like this."

"Well, that's how life is," she said simply. "The skies will be clear one moment, and then a cloud of dust will approach the next. It's always changing, never the same, not even for a day sometimes."

"Yeah." That was how my relationship with Constantine suddenly felt.

We finished our dinner, and she left the room and returned with a photo album. She sat beside me and opened to the first page. "Would you like to see pictures of Constantine when he was a boy?" she asked with a smile, as if nothing would make her happier than to show her collection.

"Absolutely."

"He was just as handsome then as he is now, just much less testosterone," she said with a chuckle.

We flipped through the pictures together, seeing him as a baby and then as a toddler, and then he was a young boy at the beach. There were pictures of him with his hands dirty, helping out at the restaurant. Pictures of him with his father in the living room. I studied his life in pictures, watched him grow into a teenager and then a young man, every part of him growing bigger and stronger. The only thing that didn't change was his eyes. He wasn't the muscular man I knew now in any of the pictures, as if he didn't bulk up until he left Taormina.

"You raised a wonderful man, Sofia," I said. "I know how lucky I am." Even now, when I was pissed off at him, I still loved him with all my heart. My jealousy burned me alive, and I was wounded by the way he'd caught me off guard. But my feelings for him had not changed, and they would never change.

Her hand moved over mine. "And I'm lucky my son brought home such a wonderful woman to be my daughter."

Chapter 16

Constantine

I woke up the next morning with Medusa beside me. Opened my eyes and saw her head on the pillow next to me, snoring quietly right in my face. I'd slept like shit last night. Kept checking my phone to see Aurelia's location. She remained at my mother's house, not that I expected her to go anywhere. They were in the kitchen a long time, so I assumed my mother had cooked a feast that my woman could never possibly finish.

I reached for my phone and immediately checked her location. She was already at the restaurant, prepping in the kitchen for the throng of tourists that would burst through the door the second they opened.

She hadn't texted me last night or this morning.

I knew we'd get through this, but it still fucking sucked.

I knew I deserved this too. I'd always been secure in who I was, but I quickly learned, with Aurelia, I was an extremely possessive man. I'd barked at Enzo when he'd come to her apartment, even though I never felt threatened by him. It was just the principle of the matter, that he stepped on my turf, that he came close to my woman.

So if this situation had been reversed and she'd gone on a date with some guy even though it meant nothing to her, I would have reacted worse than she did. There would be a pile of bones in my wake.

Medusa stirred when I moved around, and she opened her eyes to look at me. She inched a little closer, wanting to cuddle the way we used to when it was just the two of us.

I rubbed the back of her ear. "I miss her too, baby girl."

I hit the gym but couldn't really focus. Music blared through my headphones, and I watched myself lift in the mirror, but both my mind and body weren't invested. I eventually ditched the attempt and hopped in the shower instead.

I headed downstairs in my sweats and had a cup of coffee. I would normally turn on the TV, but I continued to glance at my phone, like she might text me during her shift. I checked her location over and over, seeing her move around the restaurant.

She'd better come home today. Otherwise, I'd lose my fucking mind.

A message from Tommaso popped up on my phone as I was staring at the screen. Gina said she enjoyed your company.

I released an irritated sigh and closed out of the message. A wave of guilt hit me when I read those words. If Aurelia saw that pop up on my screen, she'd stay at my mother's for another week.

Guess I was an asshole.

Guess I really did fuck this up.

I opened the message and quickly typed a reply. Didn't feel it. Wish her the best. Then I went to delete the message but stopped before I wiped it from my phone. If I had to delete something, that meant I had something to hide, and if I had something to hide, then I'd done something wrong.

I felt like shit.

I'd betrayed my woman for a debt I owed.

I didn't delete the message. Instead, I went to Aurelia's message thread and texted her. I'm really fucking sorry, and I really fucking love you. I sent it off without thinking twice about it. I didn't expect a reply, not just because she was at work, but because she probably still didn't want to talk to me.

But then the dots appeared right away, like she'd taken off her gloves to pull her phone out of her pocket to see if I had texted her. I fucking love you too, Constantine.

I read her words and felt a wave of reassurance I didn't know I needed so badly. I put the phone to my chest and sighed. "Oh, sweetheart." *Please come home today so I can breathe again.* It was just a fight, but it killed me as if it'd been a breakup. Killed me as if she'd packed her bags and headed back to Rome.

I waited for the three dots to appear.

But they didn't.

I sat on the couch with Medusa and waited for the hours to pass. I was tempted to have lunch at the restaurant so I could watch her work until her shift was over and then beg her to come home. I had no self-control or restraint. I should just give her the space she asked for and be patient, but patient wasn't in my vocabulary.

Elio texted me. President Barsetti is outside the gate. Should I let him in?

I had to read that message two different times because I didn't understand it. My mind had been on my woman at work, and then I was snapped back into a world I'd left behind for good. It took me a second to compose my thoughts before I pulled up the camera feed on my phone.

I could see a short line of black vehicles outside the gate, two Range Rovers with a car between them.

It was definitely him. Yeah, let him in. I felt a flush of irritation and unease when I watched the gates open and the vehicle enter my property. He wouldn't have come all the way here if it weren't absolutely dire.

So whatever news he had . . . it was bad.

I got to my feet and slid my phone into my pocket. I was barefoot and in just my black sweatpants when I walked to the front door to let him inside. I unlocked one side of the double doors and opened it.

Crow stepped out of the back seat of the car and buttoned the front of his suit. Tom Ford sunglasses sat on the bridge of his nose, and he looked like a billionaire CEO from Manhattan. His private security moved with him as he walked toward my house, but he raised his hand when he approached my front door. "I'll be done in fifteen minutes."

Private security would normally search me and my residence for weapons and threats to the president's life, but because it was my home, it was a guarantee they would find all the things that shouldn't be there. So, it was pointless.

President Barsetti entered my home as he removed his sunglasses and dropped them into the front pocket of his midnight-black suit. Designer quality, perfectly tailored to his build.

I shut the door behind him, and we were alone.

Medusa approached, taking her time because her leg was still sensitive to her weight.

I made a fist to my chest, telling her to heel, that he was a friend and not an attacker.

Crow slid his hands into his pockets as he looked at Medusa. "Beautiful dog."

"Beautiful? She'll bite your fucking face off." I took the lead and walked to the rear of the house with the spectacular view and the terrace. "Want anything to drink?" I treated him like a guest I'd invited rather than the nuisance he actually was.

"Wine, if you have it."

I uncorked a bottle and poured two glasses before I nodded toward the terrace. We headed outside and sat under the large open umbrellas, submerged in the cool shade. I sat across from him in fucking sweats while he stared at me in a suit. I didn't apologize for my attire because he was the rude one who'd shown up uninvited.

He stared at me for a while, like he didn't know where to start.

I still couldn't believe he was here. I'd become so absorbed in my new life that I'd forgotten my old one. Shed my previous identity like dead skin from a snake. Let my scales change colors.

He took a deep breath before he began. "It's bad, Con."

"What?"

He cocked an eyebrow. "You haven't watched the news?"

"Nope." I never turned it on and had disabled notifications on my phone. I'd buried my head in the Mediterranean sand, focused on my woman and impending fatherhood.

"Well, it's bad."

"Yeah, you said that."

Irritation flashed across his eyes. "This isn't a joke."

"Did I laugh?" I snapped. "Whatever state Rome is in is not my responsibility."

"You're the emperor—"

"Not anymore." I felt no obligation to the place I used to call home. Home was now a person and not a place.

"Then let me enlighten you as to the changes Darius has made." He straightened in the chair, moved to the edge of his seat. "He's reinstated the black market for organs and expanded its distribution. Not only is he trafficking people for resources, but he's also selling them as a product to third parties. The number of missing persons reports has skyrocketed—and it's mainly women, but even children. All the graffiti you removed? It's back and worse than ever before. You should see what they've written, Constantine. *Death to the Emperor, Flames to the Empire.* It's everywhere. All the criminal organizations rejoice in your exile as they flood the streets with drugs, terror, and crime."

I kept a straight face as I listened to my worst nightmare. But inside, I felt my heart be crushed under an invisible weight. I felt a wave of guilt and nausea . . . and shame. Under my rulership, the Roman Empire flourished in every way imaginable, and now it was just rubble.

"And it's only been six weeks," Crow continued. "Darius is egregiously violating the laws of the EU and selling weapons to enemies as well as allies, with absolutely no discretion or loyalty. Putting guns into the hands of people who want to burn us to the ground. Pope Zephyrinus has tried to speak with him, but Darius refuses a conversation. Vatican City and the papacy seem to be the only things that Darius respects, because he's left both untouched."

"Because the only man he fears is God."

Crow stared at me hard, eyes dark like mine, full of irritation and hostility. "Constantine."

"I'm sorry to hear all of this. Truly, I am. But I'm not the emperor anymore."

"As long as you live, you're the emperor."

"No."

"You came to the council at the Pantheon and convinced us to give you this power. Promised to protect the Republic and the empire. Vowed to give your life for the Eternal City and its people—"

"Yes, I remember all of this."

"Then honor your vows."

"You know I can't."

"Yes, you can."

"You wasted your time coming here, Crow," I said simply. "I've made my choice, and that decision can't be changed. I may have been the emperor, but many men also served me. You still have Rocco and those men who were loyal to the empire. This is their problem now—not mine."

"Rocco was not the emperor, so men are not as loyal to him as they were to you. When you fled, everyone else did the same. They stopped believing in the empire the moment you did. Everything has come crashing down in an avalanche of stone. Rocco continues to fight alongside those who remain, but we're greatly outnumbered. Only the return of the emperor will give people hope again."

"The day I came to the Pantheon, I told you we needed to remove Darius from power. Did I not?"

He sat back in the chair and crossed his legs.

"And you told me it would be foolish to start a war."

He stared.

"We both know you remember that. And you chose momentary peace over the discomfort of war. You chose to ignore the problem, despite its exponential growth with every passing year. All of this has happened because you were too much of a coward to take the first swing when we had the chance. Don't blame the fall of the Roman Empire on me when you're just as responsible for its destruction. Don't call me a coward for choosing exile when you were a coward long before I was. Don't give me a history lesson when you omit the facts from your lecture."

Crow said nothing as he stared me down like his enemy instead of his former ally.

"It kills me to hear all this, but my place is here in Taormina. My woman is pregnant with our first child, and there's no way in hell that I would risk either of them by returning to Rome. I sacrificed the empire for her life, so you'd be foolish to think I would risk her life by trying to save it."

"Perhaps she would feel differently if she knew what had become of her home."

"Wouldn't make a difference. She could beg me to go, and I wouldn't even get out of this chair. We both know what Darius is capable of. He wouldn't fight me head on but go around me to her like he has before. He would grab her by the neck and choke her while he cut my child out of her belly. This time, my pleas wouldn't stop him, because he let me go once, but he wouldn't let me go again. So there's no fucking way I would ever go back. Call me a coward and an asshole and whatever else you want, but I won't change my mind."

A veil of frustration had lowered across his irritated eyes, but he didn't give voice to it. Just stared me down like he wanted to strangle me but knew I'd snap his neck the second he tried. He eventually looked away and stared out at the sea as he tried to regroup his thoughts. He probably didn't expect to fail so spectacularly.

I heard Medusa get up from where she lay on the tile and move to the door. My eyes followed her to see Aurelia standing there in the open doorway, still in her work clothes, her face free of makeup because she hadn't had anything at my mother's house.

My heart gave a jolt at the sight of her, a V12 engine that came to life in a shipping semi. I was on my feet instantly and headed toward her like I hadn't seen her just yesterday, like she hadn't told me she loved me only a few hours ago. I wished President Barsetti hadn't stopped by at the worst possible time, but I moved right to her like I didn't care.

Her eyes glanced at President Barsetti before they flicked back to me. "Is that the president—"

I slid my hand straight into her hair, and I kissed her like he wasn't there.

Her lips hesitated before she gripped my wrist, her head back to accommodate the angle of my mouth.

My back blocked our embrace from his sight, but I highly doubted he wanted to watch anyway. I kissed her hard before I let her go, before I looked into eyes that appeared glazed by my passion. "You're right, I fucked up. I'm sorry." I never apologized to be diplomatic. Only apologized when I meant it. So this apology was sincere and blossomed from deep within my heart.

Whatever tendrils of anger she held on to seemed to slide between her fingertips. "It's okay, Constantine. I'm sorry I interrupted your conversation."

"You can interrupt any conversation you want."

"But . . ." Her eyes glanced back to Crow behind me. "But he's the president."

"Like I give a damn." I was just happy she was home, that she was back with me and Medusa, that this stupid fight was over. When she'd pissed me off, I'd turned my back on her and ignored her calls. She never once did that to me through this, and now I felt guilty for how I'd acted in the past.

"I'm going to shower," she said. "We'll talk after he's gone."

I'd rather join her in the shower than talk to that prick. "All right." My arm circled her lower back, and I pulled her in for a kiss and an ass grab before I let her go. I returned to Crow, where he remained seated at the table, drinking his wine and watching the sea stretch out over the horizon to the mainland in the distance. "Are we done here?"

He swirled the rest of his wine in the bottom of the glass before he finished it off. "We both know you're the only one who can stop Darius."

"Really? Because we're in this situation because he outsmarted and outmaneuvered me in the first place. He's an irrational psychopath, but make no mistake, he's smarter than you give him credit for."

"And you understand that better than anyone, Constantine." He rose to his feet and buttoned the front of his suit. "Think it over."

"Told you I already made my decision."

He started to walk away. "I'm sure if you turned on the news, you'd feel differently."

Chapter 17

Constantine

I joined her in the shower, bounced her up and down on my length while she gripped my shoulders for support, thrust my hips from underneath and made up for the workout I'd skipped that morning. Even with the water that streamed down our bodies, I could feel her cream around my length and building up around my base. Her body hadn't changed to the naked eye, but my perception of her figure was completely different now. She'd always been a fine woman whom I wanted to fuck in every way imaginable, but knowing she was pregnant was the biggest turn-on. I dreaded the day she wasn't pregnant anymore because I would miss this time.

After the fun was over, we stood in the shower together, and I rubbed soap into her soft skin, watched the water run down her beautiful body, making her hair stick to the back of her neck. Not much was said, but our eyes feasted on each other like we hadn't really looked at each other in a long time.

"I'm sorry for my treason," I said, apologizing again because the guilt was still there.

"It's okay," she said. "I said I forgive you."

"I know, but I see now why it was fucked up."

She touched my arms, traced the big muscles like they were mountains. "It's in the past now. I'm not one to hold a grudge, especially against someone this fucking hot." She smiled up at me, her eyes turning playful like she wanted to lift my mood.

I wasn't so easily swayed. "Tommaso texted me and asked what I thought of her, and it really hit me then that I'd crossed a line."

Her playfulness flickered slightly, but she maintained her calm. "It's over now. Just let it go."

She let me off the hook quicker than I deserved, but I was happy to find peace again. Happy to be a family under one roof again, the three of us and Medusa. My hand moved down her body and cupped her flat stomach, a tummy that looked and felt exactly the same as it always had.

"I liked spending time with your mom."

"Yeah?"

"She showed me one of your family photo albums."

"Of course she did."

"You look a lot like your dad."

I nodded, having heard that assessment before.

"But spiritually, you're the spitting image of your mother."

I smirked. "I'll take that compliment. What else did you guys do?"

"She made dinner and we talked. I told her how much I love you, that she reminds me of my own mother. I love you for you, even if she'd hated me like Beatrice does, but it's nice to have her."

"I know." I pulled her into me, holding her close and resting my chin on the top of her head as I cradled her into me. We stood together under the warm shower, listening to the water fall like rain on a winter night.

After a while, she broke the silence. "What did President Barsetti want?"

I hadn't thought about him since the moment he'd left my sight. My whole world revolved around Aurelia the second she returned to me. "Was in town and just wanted to catch up."

We sat together at the dining table on the terrace, Medusa lying in her dog bed under the string of white lights that hung overhead, listening to the silence when the birds stopped chirping at sunset.

We'd only been apart for a day, but it felt like a lifetime since we'd had dinner together like this. The chef prepared sautéed fish with vegetables and a side of rice, a dinner that Aurelia probably found boring but I found essential. I was a little more flexible with my diet throughout the day, but in the evening, I tried to keep my nutrition as basic as possible. Besides, it was a healthy meal for both her and our baby.

She took a few bites but seemed mostly distracted.

"Something on your mind?"

She pushed pieces of her fish around as she considered what she'd say next.

Maybe she was still mad after all.

"When I saw you two together, it didn't seem like old friends catching up." She set down her fork and looked at me. "I know how you are when you're with your friends or your family, and you aren't like that."

Damn.

"So, what did he really want?"

I wanted to spare her the guilt and obligation. Her only concern should be the life growing inside her. "He asked me to return to Rome and remove Darius from power." I told her the truth since she wanted to hear it. "I declined."

She gave a slight nod. "I've heard things are bad."

"From where?"

She shrugged. "Just headlines and stuff. Haven't looked into it too much."

"I told him it's not my problem. Don't worry about it."

"Then whose problem is it?" she asked.

"His." He was the president of Italy. Not me.

"But he's a politician, and Darius . . . is not."

"He has the military and the police at his disposal. He'll figure it out."

"But if he could figure it out, he wouldn't have come here."

I cocked my head slightly, unsure of what she was trying to imply. "What are you saying, sweetheart?"

"That it must be really bad if he came all the way here to ask for your help."

I wouldn't tell her about the changes that had taken place. The destruction to the streets, the crimes against the good people who lived there. I needed to make sure she knew only peace. "Even if it is, it doesn't matter."

"I think it does." She stopped eating altogether.

So did I. My appetite dropped out of my stomach like a stone. "No."

"No, what?"

"You know what," I said with a warning in my tone.

"I just . . . that place means a lot to both of us."

"You mean more to me than anything else ever could."

"I know, but . . . I could hide. You could hide me somewhere, and you could go—"

"No."

"You act like you don't care, but I know you, Constantine. I know how much this must be bothering you."

"Do I look bothered?" I challenged, not wanting to have a fight the second she got home, but my temper got the best of me. "We're having a baby, Aurelia. The single most important thing to both of us is our child. I'm sorry about what's happening back in Rome, but it can burn to the ground for all I care. I'm not risking you or her or Medusa. Everything is different now, and I've moved on."

"Just because you've moved on doesn't change reality, Constantine."

"You want me to go back and risk my neck?" I snapped.

"No. But I know it's what you want."

"It's not."

"You say that, but deep down, I know you want both—"

"I'm not going to tell you what Darius will do to you if I set foot in Rome. But trust me when I say you wouldn't be able to sleep for three weeks if I did."

She paused, her eyes dropping down to her food. "You forget that I was there, Constantine. I've seen what he's like. I know what he did to your brother. I'm very aware of the monster that he is. But I believe you're the only one who can take him down."

I ignored the rush of pride I felt at her words. Ignored the way it made me feel to know she believed in me. That she didn't think I was weak after sitting on my ass these last six weeks in Taormina. That she believed I was still the man she met. "I won't change my answer, so let's drop it."

"I'm sure Rocco would help you."

"Couldn't care less." I was relieved when Crow mentioned him. That meant he was still alive . . . not that I should care.

"Constantine—"

My temper finally blew. "You just got home and I don't want to fight, but you're pushing me there." I abruptly shoved back in my chair and got to my feet before I stormed off. I wanted to leave the house and check in to a hotel, but the idea of leaving her here alone didn't sit right, not when she was pregnant, not when Medusa was still hurt.

So I went into the office that I didn't use anymore and shut the door behind me. Sat in the hard chair behind the desk and stared at the wall across the room. There were paintings on the walls that I hadn't picked out. An interior designer had made this place into a home after it was renovated. It was nothing like my home in Rome, and I missed it sometimes.

I tried not to think about the fact that Darius was sleeping, eating, and shitting in it.

I propped my elbow on the armrest and focused my stare, trying to mitigate all the anger that pounded in every vein. I could feel the throb in my muscles, even my face. Choosing Aurelia over the Republic was the easiest decision I'd ever made—but that didn't mean the consequences didn't kill me. They burned me alive from flesh to bone.

My phone vibrated in my pocket, and I pulled it out to glance at the screen, to see if Aurelia had sent me a text.

But it was Rocco.

Out of nowhere, without preamble or explanation, he said something that meant the world to me.

Congrats on the kid.

I inhaled a sharp breath when I read that message, hearing his voice in my head as I absorbed every word. I'd never expected to speak to him again, and if he reached out, it would be to tell me how much he despised me.

My eyes read the message over and over. Stared at the screen until it turned black. My finger tapped the front to get the message back before I swiped and typed a reply. Thanks, man. I sent it so fast I wouldn't be able to second-guess the decision. Put it out into the ether. Took his olive branch and extended my own.

I'd fallen asleep in the chair at some point, slouched with my head resting in the corner. There were guest rooms in the house, but this was the one space that felt like it belonged solely to me.

The sound of the door cracking open registered in my mind instantly. I didn't move, but my eyes opened to see Aurelia step into the room, her shadow Medusa with her.

I took a breath before I straightened in the chair and wiped the sleep from my eyes. My fingers tapped the screen of my phone where it lay on the desk, and I watched it light up with the time. It was almost two in the morning.

"You'll get a kink in your neck if you stay there." She was dressed for bed, in one of my T-shirts with the makeup gone from her face, her long hair brushed out. "Come to bed."

I remained seated, not because I was mad at her, but because I was mad at the world right now.

She watched me for a while before she approached the desk and sat in one of the armchairs that faced me, for guests who never came, business meetings that never took place. It was all part of the stylistic choices of the interior designer I'd hired. My T-shirt fit her like a dress, half of the neckline down her shoulder because it was far too big for her. Her eyes were heavy with fatigue, but they were mostly filled with stress. "I didn't mean to upset you."

"I know you didn't, sweetheart."

"I just . . . want you to know you always have my support." She chose her words carefully this time.

"You know how lost I was when we came here."

Her eyes softened as she watched me.

"I turned my back on everyone, and I fucking know it. Wasn't sure I'd ever be able to bounce back. And then you told me something that put everything in perspective, and I got my life back. Got my joy back. And now . . ." I shook my head. "It's gone again. I wish President Barsetti hadn't come here. I wish Rome weren't falling to an asshole dictator. But there's nothing I can do about it."

Her eyes dropped down to her hands in her lap.

"It kills me, but I can't risk the alternative."

"Can I say something?" she asked quietly.

I drew in a slow breath and tempered my anger.

"Wouldn't you be able to catch him by surprise?"

"If he's smart, he'll be keeping tabs on me."

"Like, having men follow you?"

"Not necessarily. There are other ways to watch someone's movements. Their phone records, financial transactions, utility usage, flight records."

"But if you left right now and hopped on a flight or a ferry, he wouldn't have much time. You could coordinate with Rocco—"

"Sweetheart, let it go." I kept my tone even because I didn't want to push her away, not when I already felt like a mountain stood between us at that very moment. "Darius is petty and spiteful. Even if I hid you away somewhere, he'd spend the rest of his life searching for you. Keep me alive until he found you and then do unspeakable things to you and force me to watch. Just let it go."

A flash of fear moved across her eyes before she swallowed. "But if you were to defeat him, you would have both. You would have us and the Roman Republic again."

"Even if that happened, I wouldn't want it."

"You wouldn't?" she asked quietly.

I shook my head. "I've been fueled by revenge these seven years. Wanted to defend the Republic, but what my heart truly desired was justice for my brother. But I realize now . . . it's time to move on. I cleaned up his messes his entire life, and now that he's dead, I'm *still* cleaning up after him. He didn't deserve to die for what he did, but he also knew it would get him killed and he did it anyway, so . . ."

She stared at me, hanging on every word. "What if you helped Rocco reclaim the Republic . . . and then walked off into the sunset?"

"You know why."

"But if I say it's okay—"

"You think your consent is what's holding me back?" I asked incredulously, unsure how she could ask that after we'd discussed this for so long.

"I know in your heart this is what you want—and I want it too."

"No."

"Constantine—"

"Remember how he stormed into the palace and took you? That was nothing compared to what he's capable of."

"I know, Constantine. But . . . I'm brave."

My entire body stiffened when I heard what she said.

"I'm brave, and I know I could do it."

It meant the world to hear her say that, to hear how much she'd grown since the moment I'd stumbled across her broken pieces. To know that she found herself again after she found me.

But it changed nothing. "I know you are, sweetheart. If I hadn't allowed Darius to outsmart me, we would have had a great life in Rome.

You would have been my empress, and we would have ruled this land. But I'm the one who fucked it all up, and we have to live with those consequences. I'm not going to change my mind . . . and I never want to discuss it again."

A couple days later, our lives began to feel normal again. The episode with Gina was behind us, we didn't speak of President Barsetti's visit, and I started to forget the whole thing. I fell back into my idyllic life in Taormina with my family and my woman. Aurelia continued to work at the restaurant during the day, and I focused on starting our restaurant. I met with the real estate agent to find the right spot. I didn't want to rent from someone else, wanted to own the property so no one could ever take it from me.

I knew I had to confront Isabella at some point, but I waited until my life felt stable before I dealt with that. If I came to her from a place of anger, I was afraid I would rip her into pieces.

I expected the conversation to be brief, so I went to her family-owned gelato shop and let myself into the back. I didn't want to go to her apartment after the workday, because it felt stupid to leave my family and spend that time with my ex.

She was seated at the desk when I walked inside, and she gave a slight flinch when I appeared. "A heads-up would be nice."

"So you can take off and avoid me?" I moved to the other chair by the desk, the same one I'd sat in when I found out her husband had been a cheating asshole.

She finished something on her laptop before she closed it, but she still wouldn't look directly at me.

I knew she was embarrassed—as she should be.

"Look, I'm sorry for my viciousness. No excuse for it, and that's on me. But you also need to make some changes if we're going to coexist in this village."

She sat back in her chair and crossed her arms over her chest.

I waited for an apology, but it didn't seem imminent.

"This is the last olive branch I'm ever going to extend to you, Isabella."

Her eyes finally flicked to mine.

"Then it's no contact, pretend you don't exist, you aren't welcome in my mother's house . . . all that heavy stuff. I don't want that, and I know you don't either. But I can't keep entertaining this circus. I'm going to be a husband and a father, and I can't have this shit show running buck wild anymore." Thank god Aurelia was so understanding about it. Otherwise, this could have destroyed my relationship and chased away the love of my life. "So, can we forgive, forget, and move on?"

She looked away again, her arms noticeably tightening. She took a breath before she looked at me again. "I'm sorry for the way I acted, and I would love to move on. But I can't see us ever being friends. It's hard to imagine a time when I won't love you anymore."

"It'll happen, Isabella. I promise you'll meet someone, and I'll fade so deep into obscurity that you'll forget you ever loved me in the first place." It was the way I felt about Aurelia, my love for her so deep and raw that it was hard to remember a time when I wanted to spend my life with someone else.

"I hope you're right."

I was relieved I'd gotten an apology out of her, because if I hadn't, it would have left a bad taste in my mouth. I needed to know that the woman I once loved wasn't a narcissistic asshole and I was too blind to see it. "I know I am."

Chapter 18

Aurelia

Constantine was himself once again. He always greeted me when I came home from work with a smile, and when he took me to bed, he was all over me, loving me deeply and passionately, just the way he had when we first met. I didn't work on the weekends, so that was the time I lounged around the house with Constantine and Medusa. I would lie on the couch snuggled into a blanket, and Constantine would lift up my shirt to expose my belly that hadn't changed much at all and kiss it everywhere like I was six months along.

He said he'd talked to Isabella and worked things out, but he never gave the specifics and I never asked. His mom would text to check in with me, and she and I started to have our own conversation thread. Instead of feeling like my future mother-in-law, she felt like my own blood.

Constantine took me out to dinner throughout the week, and tonight, we ended up at his favorite spot, Trattoria da Nino. He'd taken me there before, during that first week we met, and he knew everyone on the waitstaff . . . as always.

We had a nice table outside, but it was too dark to see the water now. A summer breeze flowed over us and brushed through my hair like soft fingertips. The dress had been a little tight when I'd put it on, so my body was subtly starting to change. I didn't notice it with the naked eye, but clothes didn't lie.

Constantine merely glanced at the menu before he looked at me again. "What are you thinking, sweetheart?"

"The pappardelle pasta looks good."

When the waiter came over, Constantine ordered wine for himself, the bruschetta to start, and then ordered our entrées. As always, he wanted the fresh catch of the day and requested to clean it himself.

After the wine was poured, he sat with his elbows on the table and stared at me. "Think I found a spot for the restaurant."

"Yeah?"

"It's kinda tucked away off the main street, but I like that."

"The best things in life are always off the beaten path."

"Sometimes," he said as his eyes stayed on me. "Excited for that doctor's appointment next week."

"You're the first man ever to say that," I said with a chuckle.

"It's the start of a new adventure. I'm excited."

"Well, you aren't the one who has to push this adventure out of your vagina."

He gave a quiet chuckle. "That's fair. Wish I could do it for you."

"I wouldn't fight you on that."

He smiled again before he filled his wineglass. "We should take a drive and get some shopping done. There's a lot of stuff we're going to need in a couple months."

"We have like eight months."

"But it'll be here before you know it," he said. "I like to be prepared."

The first man I'd ever met who had his shit together, who wasn't afraid to be proactive about tasks, who was on his game every single day. I loved his boss energy, and I loved his ambition . . . among all the other things I loved about him. "Can't believe this is real."

"Yeah." He looked out to the dark coastline, his eyes warm in their version of a smile. "Pretty great, huh?" He reached for his wineglass and lifted it by the stem. "La dolce vita, right?"

I picked up my water glass and gently tapped it against his. "La dolce vita."

I had that Monday off, so Constantine asked if I wanted to spend the day at the beach.

And there was no way I was going to pass that up. I packed my tiny little bikini that I wouldn't be able to wear in a couple months . . . or maybe ever again. I took my sun hat, my shades, and a cover-up.

Constantine had a driver drop us off at Belmond Villa Sant'Andrea, and we walked down the path and the stairs to the beach club below. It was the same place we'd been to with his friends, and I was excited to go back, especially since it was just the two of us.

He checked us in to a private cabana like last time, but we used the set of loungers closer to the water, right in front of the rock we'd recklessly climbed and jumped off months ago. The waiter came over and brought us drinks, and we lounged in the shade together and watched the boats in the cove.

He was in his black swim trunks, a muscled hunk covered in tattoos, an eleven out of ten. I noticed a few girls looking at him, but I wasn't even mad. Who could blame them, right? He ordered a mortadella and pistachio pizza like the last time we were here, but he was so fit, it didn't look like he'd ever had pizza in his life.

"When your mom showed me your family photos, you didn't look the way you do now."

One arm was propped underneath his neck as he gazed out at the water, a slight smile on his lips. "I left a boy and returned a man."

"What made you make that change?"

"Because no one respects you unless they think you can kill them with your bare hands. When I came home for the first time, my mother nearly didn't recognize me." He released a quiet chuckle. "And then she made all my food portions bigger, like they weren't already big enough."

"Yeah, when I stayed there, she tried to get me to eat about ten thousand calories."

"Yep, that's my ma."

"After I have the baby, you'll have to help me get back into shape."

"I can certainly help you with cardio." This time, he turned to look at me, that big-ass grin on his face.

I rolled my eyes, but it was completely playful.

He patted his thigh, then nodded for me to join him.

"There are people around."

"So?" He snapped his fingers like I was Medusa. "Get your ass over here."

The chairs immediately around us had been vacated, so there wasn't anyone directly next to us. It wasn't private, but it was semiprivate. And anyone who was uncomfortable with it was just jealous they weren't me.

I moved to his lounger and settled between his legs, my back to his chest.

He pulled me against him, his big arms like two safety belts in a car, and he cocooned me between his muscular thighs as the summer breeze moved over our skin. He dipped his head and kissed my shoulder a few times, even though it probably tasted like sunscreen. He flattened his hands over my stomach like he could feel a bulge no one else could see. "I can't wait until you start to show."

I relaxed against his hard chest, feeling him support me from behind while making me feel loved with his big hands and arms. He always smothered me in love that felt so masculine and secure. There were beautiful women everywhere in Taormina, but I never saw his eyes wander once. They were always on me, loving me physically and emotionally with just his stare.

"Turns me the fuck on," he said into my ear.

"Wait until my belly is enormous and I can barely walk."

"Oh, sweetheart." Right on command, his dick hardened and poked into my back. "Don't torture me." He hooked his arms around me again and pressed another kiss to my shoulder as he cradled me to him. He eventually lay back, his chest rising and falling evenly, peacefully.

With a belly full of pizza and mocktails and a beautiful man to hold me like a pillow, I stared at the ocean for a minute or two before my eyes grew tired and I slipped away.

When I woke up, my eyes stayed closed, but I could hear the waves in front of me. They'd increased as the day went on, the tide rising as the afternoon passed. My eyes opened to look at the beautiful sea, and I breathed a quiet sigh, feeling Constantine's slow heartbeat against the back of my shoulder.

I stroked my hand along his arm, feeling all the different muscles underneath his warm flesh. He lifted his hand, then moved for mine, sliding his underneath my palm to cradle it against his chest.

That was when I noticed it.

The enormous diamond ring that he slipped onto my finger while I'd been asleep.

I should have noticed the weight the second he put it on, but I was knocked out cold. Now that I knew it was there, I tilted my hand to look at it better, to see the large princess-cut diamond sitting on a platinum band. It took me a second to react, to understand what was right in front of me.

"If one of my other lovers had told me they were pregnant, I would have been a man and risen to the occasion, but I wouldn't have been happy about the news. But the second I knew we were having a baby, I was the happiest I've ever been. Yes, I'm asking you to marry me because you're pregnant." He tightened his arm around me and pressed a kiss to my shoulder. "But also, because it's shown me how deeply I love you. Because I've never been so excited for anything in my life. Because you're the only person I'd ever want to do this with. Because I look at you like you're already my wife, and I'd give anything to call you that.

So please let me be your husband. Let me love you and support you and protect you for the rest of my life. Please, sweetheart."

I turned in his arms, pivoting my body so our eyes could lock in place.

He automatically slid his hand into my hair and cradled my face as he looked at me, like he hoped and prayed I'd give a different answer than the last time he asked me. His eyes were so assertive and sincere.

If this pregnancy hadn't happened, I didn't know when he would have asked me to be his wife, but I believed that proposal would have come at some point. I believed we would spend the rest of our lives together, regardless of how it came about. It wasn't exactly how I imagined it, but this was the man I loved with all my heart. And I could see he loved me with all of his. "Yes."

His eyes immediately softened when he got the answer he wanted, and his fingers slid farther into my hair as he cupped my face. The most handsome smile he'd ever worn broke out on his face before he pulled me into him and kissed me. Kissed me like there was no one around us except us and the Mediterranean . . . and the large rock we'd jumped off like two teenagers falling in love during a summer fling.

Chapter 19

Constantine

The second we made it home, I had her on the bed in her little bikini and cover-up. I pulled it off so fast that I almost ripped the material. I hooked her bottoms over her ass and yanked on the string around her neck so her perfect tits came free.

I was harder than a teenager who'd just seen his first pair of tits.

I dropped my shorts, then moved over her, my dick anxious to drill into her velvety-soft flesh. My hands tugged on her hips, and I adjusted her underneath me, her head on the pillow, her hands on my forearms, and her eyes on my big dick like she wanted it bad.

Her diamond ring flashed every time she made the slightest movement, a flawless gemstone I couldn't get on the island but had to have shipped from Paris because I wanted her to have the best of the best.

I hooked my arms behind her knees, and I tilted her back as I made my way between her thighs, my dick so excited to be in a place I'd already claimed in my name at least a hundred times. My dick found her entrance, and I sank inside with the least resistance I'd ever felt because she was so fucking wet.

Like that ring turned her the fuck on.

I moaned when I entered her balls-deep, my dick's home for the rest of my life, my oasis between her legs, my heaven on earth. I wanted to take it slow and savor the growing heat, but fuck, I was turned the hell on and unable to control myself.

She didn't seem to want it slow either, her nails scratching into my arms and down my chest, moaning when she felt every inch of me and didn't wince at all as I gave it all to her. Instead of making love, we fucked like we had the night we met, like we just couldn't stop, caught up in the sweat, heat, and desire.

This was how I wanted to fuck my wife the rest of our lives.

Our kid would be asleep down the hallway or at school during the day, oblivious to the two animals they had as parents fucking each other's brains out.

"Con . . ." She couldn't say my full name, not when I made her scream when she came, when I made her nails cut into my skin because she gripped my arms so hard.

"Fuck, sweetheart."

~

My mother was the first person we told. We went to the restaurant together and showed her the ring in the back office. Her scream was so loud it almost shattered the glass in the front window. There were tears when she hugged both of us, and she cupped my cheeks and looked at me like she'd never been prouder of me.

It felt good to bring home someone she loved. If she hadn't liked Aurelia, it wouldn't have changed anything, but it meant the world to me that she did. Meant the world that my mother already loved her like a daughter.

My family had been broken ever since Edric died, and for the first time, it felt healed.

We'd been excited when Beatrice settled down and had her two boys, but after that asshole of a husband abandoned his family, it caused so much duress among the family that a new fracture formed. I pitied my sister, and my mom was a second away from pulling out a gun and hunting down Beatrice's ex. The dust eventually settled, but it wasn't the same.

This felt different.

Medusa was officially out of her cast and running around again. Not with the same speed and strength as before, probably because she was still getting used to having full control of her body again. The leg would probably bother her from time to time for the rest of her life, but at least she had her life back.

Now when we came home, she ran across the house to greet us, to rub her snout in our hands and then follow us to the other side of the house. Aurelia kneeled down to pet her and hug her even though we'd only been out of the house for a few hours, so I excused myself and stepped into the office.

I sat behind the desk and made a call. It rang a couple times before someone answered. "Alberto, the office of the papacy. How can I help you?"

"Hey, Alberto. It's Con. His Holiness around for a chat?"

He covered the phone and seemed to speak with someone in the background before he came back to me. "I'll transfer you. It'll probably be a five-minute hold."

"Yeah, I'm used to it."

He put me on hold, and I had to listen to ridiculous opera music while I waited. I got tired of holding the phone to my ear, so I put it on speaker and set it on the desk as I waited. I stared at the pictures on the wall and regretted the fact that I'd never gotten those explicit photos of Aurelia as a trophy for my walls.

I still wanted them, but with a little one on the way, perhaps that wasn't a good idea anymore.

Pope Zephyrinus spoke over the line. "My son, how are you?"

I took the phone off speaker and put it to my ear. "I'm well. How about you?"

There was a pause, like he didn't know how to answer the question, but after the beat, he found his bearing. "Life is good—and so is God."

"Yeah, ain't that the truth," I said. "I had a favor to ask, Uncle."

"Name it."

"I asked Aurelia to marry me, and I'd love for you to marry us." I hadn't thought about marriage that deeply, but toward the end of my time in Rome, I'd assumed I would get married at Saint Peter's Basilica in a private ceremony with just us and the pope. But now, that dream was beyond my reach because it existed outside my borders.

"Constantine, that's wonderful news. I'm very happy for you."

"And we're also having a baby," I said with a smile, my whole life coming together with a beautiful, big bow.

There was a quiet gasp over the line. "The Lord has truly blessed you, Con."

"Yes, I know he has." All of this could have had a very different outcome, but Aurelia and I were lucky enough to escape to live full and fruitful lives. Was that God's intervention, my intervention, or just plain luck . . . ? Who knew.

"I would be honored to bless your union."

"I knew you would, Uncle. But as you know, I can't come to Rome. I wanted to know if it would be possible for you to come here and marry us. It's a lot to ask, I know it is. But it would mean the world to me to have you marry us—and bless my child."

There was a long stretch of silence as he considered what I'd just asked.

"I understand if it can't be done."

He continued to be quiet, still thinking. "I've committed my life to God, and I work on his schedule, not mine. You know this, Con."

"Yes." I hid my disappointment. "I completely understand, Your Holiness."

"But I will make this exception for you. For everything you've done for the people of Rome—and because your heart is pure. It would be my honor to bind you and the woman you love together in holy matrimony."

I hadn't expected him to agree, and for him to move mountains to accommodate me meant the world. "Thank you so much, Father. I will live by her side for all my days, and my bones will lie beside hers for eternity. I don't need your blessing to know it'll last forever—but it sure would mean a lot."

"Of course, Constantine."

"All right, I'll let you go. I know you're a busy man."

"One moment, Con." His voice sounded distant, like he was dismissing someone from his presence. He came back to the phone. "You should speak with Rocco. I know you two haven't been in touch."

A strange mixture of pain and guilt suddenly gnawed at me, squeezed my windpipe until I couldn't breathe. It was hard to forgive someone if they refused to apologize, and I was too stubborn to let it go on my own.

I didn't want to ask the question. Wanted to double down and let the silence go on until he hung up. But the words came out through tightly pressed lips. "Is he all right?"

"Yes, he's fine," Pope Zephyrinus said quickly. "But I'm not sure how long that will remain the case."

Chapter 20

Aurelia

"Do you think we can pull off a wedding in eight weeks?" I sat across from Constantine at the small table on the outdoor patio of Bam Bar. When he'd picked me up from work, he'd offered to bring me here as an afternoon treat. He always did little things like that to make me happy. I knew he didn't care for sweets, so this was entirely for me.

"Absolutely."

"Really?"

"If you wanted to get married on Saturday, I could pull that off."

"How?" I decided on lemon and orange for my flavors, along with a dollop of cream.

"Because I know everyone, and anyone I don't know, my mother knows. But don't rush it on my account. I want you to have whatever you want. If you want to wait until the baby is born, that's okay too."

I knew he didn't want that, but he was considerate enough to let me have my way.

"No, I want to do it before I get too big. A little bump is fine."

"Any kind of bump is fine," he said with his charismatic grin.

"Trust me, the bigger I get, the less excited you're going to be."

"Trust me, sweetheart. That will *not* be the case." He took a few bites of his granita before he abandoned it, like just a taste was plenty for him. "It's a fetish I didn't know I had. Knowing you're growing my son or daughter . . . it's just unbelievable. Biggest turn-on in the world."

"That's sweet of you to say."

He gave a slight shake of his head. "Not saying it to be sweet. By the way, I found someone to marry us."

"Who?"

"Pope Zephyrinus."

"What?"

He nodded. "He said he'll come down for the ceremony."

"The pope?"

He nodded again. "And my uncle."

"I didn't know the pope left Rome for weddings."

"Not often, but he does."

"That's really nice of him to do that."

"Yeah, it was generous of him. It means a lot to me to have him bless our union and our child. The closest to God we'll ever get, at least on this side of the veil."

"Yeah," I said. "So, is anyone else coming from Rome?"

"Might invite a few friends."

My granita suddenly became less important. I thought of the person who had been painfully absent from our lives. "Is Rocco one of those friends?"

He crossed his arms over his chest, wearing a gray T-shirt with his designer sunglasses on his nose. He didn't seem to be in a bad mood, but he didn't seem enthused by the subject either. "No."

My heart dropped in disappointment. "I thought he would be your best man."

"Antonio is a better fit."

Antonio was family and a great friend, but he wasn't Rocco. "I really think he should be invited."

"Aurelia." He didn't raise his voice, but his tone told me to back off.

"What could he have possibly said or done to make you cut him off like this?"

"Let it go," he said calmly.

"Why won't you tell me?"

He gave a shrug. "Because it doesn't matter."

"I think it does."

He looked down the pathway to the people walking by, ignoring me.

"Then I'll invite him as my guest."

"Go ahead," he said. "Like he would come."

When I'd texted Rocco and told him we were pregnant, he never replied. I hoped that he just hadn't seen it, because the idea that he wouldn't care broke my heart. How could someone Constantine loved like a brother just . . . disappear? How could a friendship that solid just fall apart?

Constantine had a workout session in the morning and the afternoon. His morning seemed to be focused solely on heavy weights, and his afternoon had more cardio and endurance training. I'd see him on the StairMaster or running six miles on the treadmill like it was no big deal.

So while he was occupied with that, I texted Rocco. I know this is a long shot, but could you come to Taormina and talk to Constantine? I don't know what happened between you two, and it's killing me. He won't share anything with me, but I can tell he's hurting. I stared at the phone and waited for his three dots to appear. When I'd reached out to him in the past, he responded with lightning speed, just the way Constantine always did. But now, he was absent, gone like a ghost, gone like he'd never been real.

I continued to stare at the screen and hope for something.

But seconds turned into minutes, and I knew a reply would never come.

Chapter 21

Constantine

I dropped Aurelia off at work and then met up with my mom at the restaurant I intended to buy. There was no one's opinion I valued more than hers in this regard. I walked through the street, then up the stairs to a small grouping of buildings comprising shops, apartments, and restaurants. Mostly where the locals went because it was away from the main road that was always flooded with tourists who didn't know where they were going.

My mom stood there in white jeans and a bright-blue blouse, texting on her phone while she waited for me to show up.

I walked up the last set of steps before I joined her in the quiet courtyard. It was abandoned this early in the morning. "Hey, Ma."

She immediately put her phone away and flashed me a big smile. "Hey, honey."

I gave her a quick kiss on the cheek, and then we walked to the front of the building. The real estate agent was already inside, talking on the phone with another client while he stood in the corner. The place was completely empty because everything had been removed, all the furniture, the ovens and stovetops, paintings that had been on the walls and left shadow marks behind.

Mom moved through the kitchen and examined the space with an expert eye, then walked through the lobby again before she came back to the kitchen once more. "It's a little small, Con."

"It'll be mostly outdoor seating. Was going to build a canopy with flowers and fountains."

"That could work," she said as she looked outside. "There's a lot of space out there. But you're going to have to make it an outdoor-only restaurant because you'll need more room in here to increase the kitchen size if you intend to serve that many people."

"Yeah, you're probably right."

"But I do like it. It's a nice spot. Quiet. Off the main path. What does Aurelia think of it?"

"Haven't shown her yet. I don't think she cares that much about all the details." I knew she wanted to be a part of the business, but she wouldn't have an opinion about the space or the specifics.

"She's going to be your wife, Con. You've got to include her in everything."

I grinned. "All right, Ma."

"Great job on the ring, by the way."

"Thanks. I know a guy in Paris."

She stepped back outside, and the real estate agent continued to talk on the phone. "When's the wedding?"

"She wants to do it in eight weeks."

She nodded like that was easily done. "Let me know who you want me to call. I'm sure we can make anything happen."

"Thanks, Ma."

After I finished up with her and the real estate agent, I headed back home, hit the gym for an hour, and then jumped in the shower to wash off the rivulets of sweat that dripped all over my body whenever I worked out. I set the air to sixty-five degrees and had the fans cranked, but I was still soaked.

When I was done, I put on my sweatpants, made a cup of coffee, and then went outside on the terrace. I sat on one of the couches in the shade of the umbrella, and Medusa hopped up and sat beside me, her chin resting on my thigh while my arm rested over her body.

I was on my phone when Elio's text popped up.

Rocco is at the gate. Shall I let him in?

I read the message three times before I reacted to it, before I felt my heart drop into my stomach with the weight of a brick. When Aurelia and I spoke about the wedding, his name popped up, and I knew his sudden appearance after that couldn't be a coincidence. Aurelia must have said something to him. Must have asked him to come.

I just couldn't believe he'd actually done it.

I sat there for a moment and looked at the sea view before I typed a reply. Yes. Bring him to the terrace.

Of course, sir.

I pocketed my phone, then stood up, forcing Medusa to move aside. I was suddenly warm and needed space, suddenly anxious when I never felt anxious. My heart raced a million miles an hour, and it thumped in my chest like a bass drum. I felt like I was about to face off with Darius . . . not my friend.

Or someone I used to know.

Elio appeared in the glass doorway and opened the door so Rocco knew where to find me. He was in his usual attire, black jeans and a black T-shirt, his dark hair a little longer than it'd been before, the shadow on his jawline darkening into a full beard.

Medusa immediately jumped up when she saw him and ran straight over.

Rocco's serious face softened at the sight of her, and like they were still on good terms, he kneeled down and gave her a rubdown before he patted her on the flank. "Glad you're doing well, Medusa." He rose to his full height again, his expression directly in the sunlight, and he was hard and serious once more. His eyes looked at mine for the first time, and a beat of heavy silence followed.

He crossed the terrace and joined me under the shade of the massive umbrella, his hands sliding into his front pockets.

A silent stare-down ensued.

Medusa joined us, but she picked up on the tension and moved to another couch in the shade, staying out of our way.

The silence continued for a while, like Rocco had made the effort to come all the way here but now didn't have a clue what to say.

To be fair, I didn't know what to say either. I felt a lot of different things at once. I was still mad about the bullshit he'd said to me, but a part of me felt whole in his presence, like the piece of me that had been missing had somehow returned.

"President Barsetti told me he stopped by."

Now I knew the purpose of his visit. "Yeah."

"So you're aware that Rome burns from the flames of our enemies—and you do nothing."

So this was basically round two of our verbal fistfight. "I'm putting my family first—and that's not nothing."

"I thought I was your family."

That stung like a hundred wasps attacking me at once.

"You called me your brother. And yet you abandon me and all your other men while you hide away in your fairy-tale storybook."

"You seriously came all the way here to start shit?"

"I came here to finish it, Constantine. To make sure you're painfully aware of the consequences of your cowardice—"

"You think I won't throw you off this fucking balcony?"

Medusa straightened on the couch and issued a low growl.

I didn't look at her when I addressed her. "Heel, Medusa." I stepped closer to Rocco. "You have no idea how hard it was for me to walk away. The depression that drowned me every fucking day and I couldn't catch a single breath. When you love a woman someday, you will understand. You will watch yourself burn the fucking world with your own goddamn matches. I'm not sorry for turning my back on you or Rome—and I'd fucking do it again."

He watched me with his ice-cold eyes.

"But I wish it hadn't come to this. I wish I hadn't let Darius outsmart me. That regret will haunt me for the rest of my life. I failed everyone I care about, and that will always make me feel like shit. Is that what you want to hear? That I hate myself for letting you and everyone down? That I see the way you look at me right now, and it kills me a little more than it did before. Because yeah, I fucking hate myself."

His eyes shifted back and forth between mine as he listened. "Then come back. Outsmart him. Avenge your brother and save our city. I'm with you in this. I agreed with you from the beginning that Darius needed to be handled, but everyone was too much of a pussy to face him. Let's fucking finish him."

For a brief second, I wanted to do it. Take his offer and return to Rome with guns blazing. Wanted to rip Darius apart with my bare hands for touching my woman and shooting Medusa. Wanted to break open that oil barrel and finally align my brother's headstone with his remains. Finally unleash this rage that had simmered below the surface every fucking day these last seven years.

Rocco's eyes flicked back and forth between mine as if he saw it. "Yes . . . come on."

But then that desire was washed away by reality. "The only reason he let me go was because I gave him my word. And my word only meant something because I always keep it. I can't break it now."

He released a frustrated sigh.

"He said if I ever came back, he wouldn't just kill Aurelia and Medusa, but everyone I've ever known and loved. That means my mom, my sister, my cousins, my aunts and uncles . . . my entire line. I know you think I'm a coward for refusing to return, but I have to protect my own first."

He bowed his head and released another frustrated sigh. He dug his hands deep into his hair and his scalp before he abruptly dropped his arms. Then he looked at me again, his eyes furious. "Con, he can't kill your family if you kill him first. We hit him hard and put his bones in the ground, and everyone wins."

"The second he knows I'm in Rome, he'll make good on his promise."

"Where's the man I knew?" he snapped. "The man who's never even fucking blinked when a gun was pressed to his head."

"The gun isn't pointed at me, Rocco. It's pointed at my wife. At my child. At my mom and my dog. If it were just me, then we both know I wouldn't give a damn. You seriously don't understand that? I thought you liked Aurelia."

"I do like her," he said. "I liked that she accepted you completely and was willing to support you in your reign. That she understood the risks of loving an emperor and chose to stay. I liked that she was fucking brave. But now, she won't let you leave—"

"It's not her." I didn't want to disclose this to him, not when it would just make him hate me more, if that was possible. "She told me she would hide and let me finish this. She's always been supportive of me, even though I know Darius scared her to death. I'm the one who chooses to stay, Rocco."

Disappointment filled his gaze.

"What kind of father would I be if I left?"

"You aren't a father yet—"

"Something else you won't understand until it happens to you, Rocco. My life was forever and irrevocably changed the instant I knew she was pregnant. I'm not a son or a brother or a friend anymore. First and foremost, I'm a father. It's primal and instinctive, and it would go against my very essence to risk the child I haven't even met yet. I can't do it, Rocco."

His arms crossed over his chest, and he bowed his head slightly.

"I don't understand why you need me anyway, Rocco."

He lifted his chin slightly and looked at me again.

"I know you can do this."

He gave a slight shake of his head. "You don't get it, man."

I was too afraid to ask exactly what I didn't get.

"Grow a pair and turn on the fucking news, Con. Maybe then you'll fucking get it." He tapped his fingers against his temple hard enough that I could hear the thud of his fingertips. "Most of our men are either dead or they've fled—or they've joined him. It's me and a few others, with Barsetti's military and police. But it's fucking complicated because Darius has his hands in the Senate now, and he's threatening and bribing everyone left and right. Policies are changing. Did you know he's stripping people of their universal health care? And you want to know why? Because he wants tariffs from the gangs *and* the government. He wants the citizens of his country to pay him to destroy their republic. Tourists have fled, hotels are vacant, motorbikes aren't on the street anymore. Never in my life have I ever described Rome this way—*but it's fucking quiet.*"

It killed me to hear all of that, but I still didn't know what the solution would be. "It sounds like this is bigger than one person, Rocco."

"You don't understand why people left?" he asked incredulously. "It's because they lost all hope when their emperor skipped town. When the person who'd transformed Rome into a goddamn legacy ran off in exile. Not just the men who served the Roman Republic, but the police who felt protected under your regime, the Senate who never had to battle corruption because no one was dumb enough to try. Perhaps you don't fully understand the impact you had on everything and everyone in that city—*but it was fucking massive.* I still believe in the Roman Republic." He patted his palm against his chest. "I still believe in everything we stood and fought for. I will fight for it until it kills me—and in all honesty, it probably will kill me. And that's okay because there are things worth dying for, and this is one of them. So don't be surprised if this is the last time we ever see each other . . . because I know Darius is coming for me, and it's only a matter of time before he finds me."

Chapter 22

Aurelia

When I got home from work, I found Constantine sitting on the terrace with Medusa snuggled into his side. He didn't notice I was home yet, his eyes on the couch across from him, even though no one was there. I wouldn't have stopped to stare at him if I hadn't noticed something was off.

I stared at him for a moment longer, and I could see it in the features of his face. Raw devastation stretched his skin. His eyes were hard and lifeless as they stared at the couch like he was reliving a memory rather than experiencing reality. His skin was gray, like he was sick, and his physicality was different. His shoulders were slouched instead of straight. His spine was slightly bent as if he had no energy to remain rigid. He was hunched and small with empty eyes . . . like he was barely alive.

I stepped onto the terrace, and it wasn't until I was close that he acknowledged my presence with a stare. "Constantine, what's wrong?"

It took him a second to look at me, like he'd been so deep in thought it required time and effort for him to get out of it. "Nothing." He blatantly lied to me and didn't seem to care that he lied, which was completely unlike him. He shifted his body slightly forward, elbows on his knees, falling right back into the hole.

I moved to the couch across from him and stared at him, watched him look at the ground, studied him absentmindedly rub his palms together.

"Constantine . . ."

He inhaled a big, deep breath that made his chest swell like a full balloon. "I didn't realize the time."

"What happened?"

All he did was shake his head.

"Why won't you talk to me? You always talk to me."

He continued to rub his palms together. "Rocco stopped by. Things were said. And I don't want to talk about it."

Surprise flushed through me. My texts went unanswered, but they did have an impact. However, it looked like they didn't have the impact I wanted. "Constantine—"

He lifted his chin and looked at me. "I'm not okay, obviously. And I don't want to pretend I'm okay, but I also don't want to discuss it or dissect it. Nothing noteworthy or new was said. He told me what he thought of my character . . . and left. That's it. That's the whole story. And now, I just want to be alone." He bowed his head again.

He'd never pushed me away like this before. Never completely closed me off. We were so happy before Darius took the palace, and ever since then, our happiness had been waves in the ocean, rising and falling, consistently high and then low.

Now I wished I hadn't texted Rocco. I'd reached out because I wanted them to reconcile—not for him to come out to Taormina and rip Constantine to pieces. This was all my fault. "I'm sorry, Constantine."

"It's fine," he said quietly. "Give me a couple hours, and I'll bounce back . . . like I always do."

I moved to his couch, going to the side Medusa wasn't nestled into. I hooked my arm through his and laid my cheek on his shoulder. My hand rested on his bicep, and I just sat there with him.

He was quiet, staring at the table between the two couches.

"You should know . . . I texted Rocco a couple days ago."

He didn't react overtly, but I could feel his muscles tense under my touch.

"I said I wanted you to reconcile. I didn't expect him to come here and say hurtful things to you. I'm sorry."

He took a deep breath, held it for several long seconds, and then let it out again. To my surprise, he turned to me and pressed a kiss to my head. "It's okay, sweetheart. I know you meant well. It's not your fault you extended an olive branch and he decided to light it on fire."

~

It took a few days for Constantine to bounce back to his old self, but when he did, he had a smile that could be seen a mile away. I loved that despite the fact that he had every reason to be unhappy, he chose to pursue happiness every time. Always rebounded from his funk. Always appreciated what he had instead of dwelling on the past. Never resented me for the circumstances we were in.

On Sunday night, his mother hosted one of her big dinner parties, and when we walked in the door, her home was already crammed with friends, family, and neighbors. The terrace was full of people drinking wine and raiding the ice chests of beers and sodas. Music came from a stereo system, but it was drowned out by the sounds of conversation and laughter.

His mother worked in the kitchen with her sister and her best friend Lucia, Isabella's mother. It seemed like they were on good terms despite all the drama, so that was nice to see. We said hello to them in the kitchen, and all the women came right toward me and touched my stomach like there was anything to touch. I was barely six weeks along and my clothes didn't fit the same, but it wasn't super apparent to the naked eye. But they touched me like I was about to pop.

Beatrice walked into the room with her two sons, and not only did she give me an ice-cold look as she watched my future mother-in-law and her friends shower me with excitement, but she actually rolled her eyes.

"Uncle Con!" One of the boys beelined straight for Constantine, and the younger one followed behind.

"Oh no," he said. "Here come the monkeys . . ."

They climbed him like a tree, and Constantine played along with it, holding out one of his arms so the boy who looked about four years old could climb it like a tree branch and hang down like a monkey in the jungle.

The other looked about two years old, and Constantine grabbed him and threw him over his shoulder, listening to his shrieking laughter. "Anyone got a banana?" Constantine asked. "Because I've got two crazy monkeys on me."

Both boys laughed, clearly thinking their uncle was the coolest guy they'd ever met. They both started to howl like monkeys in the kitchen while everyone tried to finish up the dinner.

"There's gotta be some bananas around here . . ." Constantine walked out holding both boys like they weighed nothing. "Maybe in the bathroom?"

"Ew, not in the bathroom!" one of the boys said as Constantine rounded the corner and headed to the other side of the house.

Beatrice walked forward and poured herself a glass of wine as she leaned against the counter. She looked dead tired behind the eyes and completely mentally checked out. She eventually pushed off the counter with her hips and left the room.

"Need any help?" I asked Sofia.

"No, no, no," she said as she shook her head. "You rest, honey. Go have a seat outside. Dinner will be ready soon."

I made my way down the hallway to see where Constantine had gone. He wasn't in the house, so I headed toward the back terrace, the strings of white lights becoming brighter the closer I came.

Constantine was outside, talking to people while the boys continued to climb all over him like he was a living tree. He didn't seem bothered by it at all, handling two rowdy boys like it was a walk in the park.

I spotted Beatrice drinking her wine by the back door, one arm crossed over her chest, watching Constantine entertain her boys.

I was tired of the animosity between us. This woman would be my sister-in-law in a couple of months, and she felt like a complete stranger to me . . . even an enemy. Constantine told me to ignore her and that he didn't care what her opinion was, but seeing him play with his nephews like he was their father told me he cared a lot more than he let on.

So I walked up to her. "Hey, Beatrice."

She turned to me slightly and acknowledged me with an indifferent stare. "Hey." Then she looked out at the patio again and drank her wine—and waited for me to walk away.

"You know how silly this is, right?"

She turned back to me like she didn't know what I would say next . . . but waited on the edge of her seat.

"To be prejudiced against me because I'm not Isabella. It's not fair for you to hate any woman he brought home just because she's not the woman you wanted him to end up with. It's his life, not yours. You should support your brother and be happy for him. I know if this were reversed and you didn't end up with his best friend, Constantine wouldn't treat your partner like this. He'd take him out for a drink, invite him to hang out with the guys at the beach, completely include him in his life."

She turned back to the door and released a sigh. "It's not because of Isabella."

"Oh . . ." So was it because she really just couldn't stand me? That my presence was that off-putting? "All right, then what did I do that was so egregious, Beatrice? Because I'm generally a lovely person unless someone forces me to be vocal and combative . . . like you have."

"Look." She pivoted her body in my direction, and it was the first time she actually spoke to me like a real person worth eye contact and full attention. "It's not you, okay? You didn't do anything wrong."

"So I did nothing wrong, and I still have to deal with the consequences? Yeah, that sounds fair."

"I don't want to do this here—"

"*Well, we're gonna,*" I snapped. "Because you've had plenty of opportunities every day at work to talk to me and chose not to. Because we've had family dinners, and you've chosen to act like I don't exist. I'm marrying your brother and having his child whether you like it or not, and I know my voice is rising and I'm mad as hell right now, but I would love it if we could find a way to get along. I would love more than that—friendship and sisterhood—but I don't think you'll ever give me that."

This was a version of me she'd never met before, and she was clearly blown away by it. Even had to take a step back. I'd been kind and quiet and nonconfrontational up until this point, but my compassion had officially expired. I didn't understand how his mother could be so warm but his sister ice cold. "I'm tired of watching Constantine be the favorite. I know you're close with my mother and think she's the greatest woman ever, but you don't know her like I do. My whole life, I've watched her favor him. And now that you're pregnant, she acts like she doesn't already have grandchildren. She doesn't spend time with them. When I've asked her to help me with childcare, she tells me they're my responsibility and to figure it out. But I know it's because she resents me for getting divorced. For choosing an asshole she vocally disapproved of. She shuns me and lets me drown just so she can prove her point—*told you so.*"

That was the last thing I expected Beatrice to say, and her words packed a punch.

"You come in here, and she acts like she doesn't already have a daughter. I heard you and Con had a fight, so you stayed here for the night. When my husband left me and I needed her, she told me to learn from my mistakes." Her voice started to rise as it was packed with emotion. "She didn't open her home to me, a home that Constantine bought that I could never afford to give her. It just hurts that she clearly loves you more than me, simply because you're marrying Con . . . than she does her actual daughter. I'm drowning, juggling work and being a single mother, and she never offers to help me, and the only time I get to myself is when my brother lets them climb all over him for twenty minutes so I can have a damn glass of wine." She dropped all of her problems on me in a few breathless sentences, a catharsis she needed for years. "Don't misunderstand me, I love my boys and wouldn't change anything, but I feel like my mother punishes me, when I'm the victim of poor judgment. There's nothing my mother wouldn't do for Con, but there's a very limited number of things she'd do for me."

I remembered when I'd first met Con, he said he was his mother's favorite. Said it in a joking way, but even he recognized it. Now I felt guilty for snapping at Beatrice during the couple of minutes she had to herself. "Beatrice, I'm so sorry."

"It's fine," she said. "You're right, I've been a total cunt to you."

My eyebrows rose at her brutal honesty and emotional intelligence.

"My anger should be reserved for my mother, but the problem is, she doesn't give a shit. When I give her the silent treatment, I never hear from her. When I try to talk to her about it, her eyes fill with so much annoyance like I'm burdening her. There is no solution to this problem. I just have to accept that my mother resents me far more than she loves me."

"Have you talked to Con about this?"

"No."

"Maybe you should."

"It's not his problem."

"I think if he knew this is how you felt, he would make it his problem, Beatrice. You're his sister and he loves you."

She looked out the window to the terrace and took another drink of her wine.

"When the baby comes, I'm going to be home all day. You're more than welcome to drop off the boys a couple days a week. I'm happy to watch them. Constantine will be there too, so it won't just be me."

She slowly turned to look back at me.

"And I'm sure Medusa would love to have someone to play with."

"You don't have to do that, Aurelia."

"I know, but we're family. I'm happy to help you."

She stared at me for a few seconds, her gaze hardening in confusion, then softening when she saw the sincerity on my face.

"I would love to get to know my nephews too. I can tell Constantine thinks the world of them." I glanced out the window. "They're still climbing all over him as we speak."

Beatrice brought her wine closer to her chest, then looked down into the contents.

"We could watch them overnight too, if you want to go on a date . . . and see where that goes." I waggled my eyebrows. "Friends make sure friends get laid."

She burst into a quiet laugh, like she hadn't expected me to say that in a million years. "Yeah, it's been a while."

"Then let's work something out. I know Constantine would be happy to help."

"I don't know. Men aren't usually the ones handling the childcare."

"Well, I know he's different."

"He used to run Rome and hang people from the Pantheon for violating his laws . . . but sure," she said with a chuckle.

"That's not all who he is," I said. "He's very loving and nurturing. You should see the way he cares for Medusa. I have no doubt he'll be a great father, and I have no doubt he'd care for your boys like his own if you needed help."

She turned her attention to Constantine, watching him play with the boys like he was having fun. They'd stopped the monkey game, and now they were playing dinosaurs at the table away from everyone else. He may have seen us talking through the glass and wanted us to have all the time we needed to squash our beef.

"I'm sorry about your mother. She seems so loving and wonderful that I'm sure if she understood her own behavior, she would stop it. She just needs to understand her own disappointment is interfering with her relationship with you."

"I don't think it's that hard to understand. It's been going on for years." She took a drink of her wine. "She doesn't believe in divorce, like most women in Taormina, so she's not only disappointed I chose the wrong man, she's disappointed I divorced that very man."

That didn't sound like the woman I knew at all, but I had to remember that we all had different sides to ourselves. That every person had a distinct and unique relationship with us, so they knew a particular version. "I'm sorry you're in this situation, but I'm really glad we had this talk."

"Yeah, me too." She looked at me again, and this time, her eyes were free of their usual hostility. Now, there was affection in her gaze, a warmth that made me feel like a friend rather than an enemy. "Let's start over." She moved into me and hugged me with one arm.

I hesitated before I reciprocated, not expecting the relationship to accelerate to physical touching so quickly. But I accepted her hug and returned it a millionfold.

~

When we got home later that night, Constantine greeted Medusa with affection, then took her outside to do her business before bed. He used to have staff who took care of Medusa for him most of the time, but he didn't struggle to adapt to the change.

When he came back inside, Medusa headed right for the stairs, like she'd been ready for bed for hours.

Constantine walked up to me, his eyes tired but still so sexy. "Looks like you and Beatrice buried the hatchet."

"Yeah, we did."

"And from what I could discern, it seems you were responsible for that."

"Yeah . . . a little bit."

He smiled at me before he circled his arm around the small of my back and pulled me in for a kiss. "You didn't have to do that, but thank you."

I sank into his touch the way I did when we first met. Turned into a pool of melted chocolate from his warm flames. "She's going to be my sister too. I want things to be good between us."

He kissed me on the forehead and stepped back.

"But she told me Isabella wasn't the issue. It was actually your mother."

"My mother?" he asked, eyebrows rising in surprise.

"Remember when you told me you're the favorite?"

"Yeah."

"Well, you aren't the only one who thinks that."

When the realization hit him, he gave a sad kind of nod. "I see."

I shared everything she'd revealed to me that night. Now I was at a crossroads, loving Sofia for the way she treated me, but also disappointed she could neglect her daughter, who needed her more than ever.

Constantine took a second to absorb all that information. He stepped away and paced the room for a few minutes, arms across his chest, his features hardened in their focus. "I said I was the favorite because of the way she would call and overfeed me and light up every time I entered the room. I didn't realize all of this was happening with Beatrice." He took a seat on the couch. "I wasn't there when that asshole took off. Wasn't there for the divorce. For any of it. So . . . I just missed it all."

"Yeah, I can see that."

"Kinda disappointed in my mother, to be honest."

I moved to the spot beside him. "I was surprised too."

He was quiet for a while as he relaxed on the couch. A moment later, Medusa came back down the stairs, looked at us with that pissed-off stare, and then gave a quiet whine that clearly said *I'm ready for bed*.

Constantine gave a quiet chuckle. "All right, baby girl. We're coming."

Medusa turned and headed back up the stairs.

"Wish kids liked going to bed like that."

He gave a slight smile before he gripped my thigh and gave it a squeeze. "We're going to have a sleepless eighteen years. I'm sure this kid will give me hell as karma, because I was a nightmare for my mother."

"Nothing we can't handle."

He patted my thigh before he got to his feet. "I'll have a conversation with my mother and get this sorted. But for now, let's go to bed."

Chapter 23

Constantine

I texted my mother and told her I was going to swing by. Gave her as little notice as possible. Otherwise, she would bake a lasagna, a full loaf of bread, make a green salad and an entire tray of cannoli, and expect me to eat all of it in a single sitting.

She opened the door for me, greeted me with a warm hug and a kiss, and invited me into her kitchen. "Are you hungry, baby?"

"No, I'm good, Ma." I took a seat at the dining table.

As if she hadn't heard me, she pulled a tray covered in foil from the oven and set it on the counter.

How did she pull that off?

"I had a frozen eggplant parmesan in the freezer." She removed the foil cover and carried the dish to the dining table, placing it on a trivet in the center. Steam wafted from the dish, and it smelled like fresh tomatoes and breadcrumbs.

There was no such thing as not being hungry in this house.

She brought two plates and silverware and set the table. "Wine?"

"Sure." I wasn't going to fight it.

She uncorked a bottle and filled the two glasses before she served me a piece and then herself. "So how are you, baby?"

"Good, good."

"How's Aurelia?"

"The doctor said everything is going smoothly."

"Oh, that's great."

"Hope it stays that way."

"She has nice hips. I think it'll be fine."

She did have nice hips. That was how we got pregnant in the first place.

"Did you show her the restaurant?"

"I did. She's on board, so I made an offer."

"Oh, that's great," she said as she sliced her fork into the tender pieces of eggplant.

I ate half my piece to be polite, knowing I shouldn't eat meals this heavy more than once a week. My dinners were usually simple, just fish and vegetables. "There's actually something I wanted to talk to you about."

"Oh?"

I'd decided to cut Aurelia out of the conversation entirely since this was a family matter. I didn't want my mom getting upset with Aurelia over what Beatrice shared with her. But I didn't lie either. "I get the impression that Beatrice has been having a hard time handling both of the boys on her own lately."

"Being a single mother isn't for the faint of heart," she said before she took another bite. "Your father was around some of the time . . . but mostly none of the time."

The resentment was starting to make a little more sense now. Because my mother had had to do it on her own and run a business, she wasn't particularly empathetic toward someone else in the same position. "Yeah, I remember. I can understand why you wouldn't want that life for your daughter."

"Yes," she said with a sigh. "It's unfortunate that she chose it."

"She didn't choose it, Ma. That spineless prick left. I could have hunted him down and dragged him back here, but I don't think the boys deserve to have a father who doesn't want to be there."

"Well said, Con."

"Aurelia and I are going to start helping her a couple days a week. Just to give her a break."

"Why?" She straightened in the chair. "You have your own on the way, and you're opening a new restaurant. You don't have time for something that's not your responsibility."

"Doesn't matter. She needs help."

"Don't let her guilt you into free childcare—"

"Ma, I love you more than words, but where is this attitude coming from?"

My words knocked her into silence.

"I understand raising two shithead boys and a daughter alone must have been traumatic for you. Had to run a house and run a restaurant, and my father was an asshole. Honestly, I wish he had just left if he didn't want to be there. But don't put that resentment on Beatrice. A parent should always want better for their child, but what I'm hearing is you want the same for her."

She sat back in her chair and crossed her arms over her chest. "Con, where is this coming from?"

I tried to think for a moment, to make sure I handled this delicately. "I think it's too apparent that I'm your favorite, and I think that's affecting Beatrice."

My mother continued to stare at me. Didn't even deny the accusation.

"I know it has nothing to do with how much you love her. You're just disappointed by the choices she made in life and the outcome of those decisions. I know you wanted better for her, but she ended up in the exact same situation as you—and that's a hard pill for you to swallow. I understand all of that, but you need to resolve those issues and let them go because of how it's impacting your relationship with Beatrice."

"Did she say this to you?"

"It hurts her to see how much love you give to Aurelia when she barely gets your attention herself. And to be frank, it hurts me too. Because I'm a grown man who's settled down with my own family, and I don't need that support. But she needs it more than ever. She hasn't been able to get back on her feet because she hasn't had the support even to try."

"How is that my fault—"

"It's not, Ma. But I know if Aurelia woke up one morning and took off, you'd be there every day. You wouldn't want me to hire a nanny because you'd insist my child should be raised by family, not hired help. I know emotions and perspectives and resentments are complicated and layered, and I'm just bringing it to your attention. Because I know how much love is in your heart, and I know how much family means to you . . . and you've just lost your way with Beatrice."

She tightened her arms over her chest, and her eyes flicked away, absorbing everything I said in a long stretch of silence. "The second she brought him home, I told her I didn't like him."

"I know."

"I warned her this would happen."

"I remember," I said simply. "I didn't like him either."

"Told her so many times, and she married him anyway."

I nodded in agreement.

"I'm surprised they lasted as long as they did."

"Beatrice was young when she got married. She probably needed to grow up a little bit before she was mentally prepared for what she was getting into. But I also think she wanted to have a family because of how important family is to all of us. She wanted to settle down. She wanted a traditional life. She just chose the wrong guy, and it's not right to punish her for that, Ma."

She still wouldn't look at me, her eyes directed elsewhere, sitting in the heaviness of the subject.

"She made a mistake—and you made a mistake."

Her eyes flicked back to me.

"It's time to let that go and move on."

"So you think I should talk to Beatrice about all of this?" she asked quietly.

"I think you should talk to her exactly the way you would talk to me. Don't be distant. Don't keep her at arm's length. She's an adult, but she needs her mother right now."

She nodded before she gently rubbed her arm, looking elsewhere for a while as she considered everything I said.

It wasn't a conversation I wanted to have. I didn't want to risk our relationship, but I felt like I had to stick out my neck for my sister. My mother listened to me differently than she did to other people, so I knew I was the one who would make her see what she'd been unaware of. She was a good person and a loving mother—she'd just become blinded by her own trauma.

After a long stretch of silence, she looked at me again. "How have you been?"

I knew she wasn't asking about my general life with Aurelia or the wedding or the pregnancy. She was asking about the event that had brought me back to Taormina in exile. "I have good days . . . and bad days."

She gave a slight nod in understanding.

"A friend of mine came by last week." An old friend—or a former friend—I didn't know anymore. "Said things are bad and I'm a coward for staying here. President Barsetti came by and said the same."

"Things are bad, Con."

My eyes narrowed on her face.

"I watch the news in the morning when I do the books at home." She didn't share what she'd seen, like she didn't want me to know.

I continued to bury my head in the sand, and that did make me feel like a coward. "He told me if I set foot in Rome, he wouldn't just kill Aurelia . . . but my entire family. And trust me when I tell you he'd do it and enjoy every second of it."

She took a slow breath when she realized the extent of his threat.

"If I could take him out before he figures out I'm there, then it's done. But if I fail or he knows I'm coming . . . you're all dead. He outsmarted me once, and that's been traumatic for me. So I'll never be arrogant enough to assume I can outsmart him again. My risk tolerance is different now that I have a woman and a child to think about."

She nodded in understanding. "You said you can't set foot in Rome, but he never said anything about Florence."

I stared at her.

"He wouldn't expect you to go to his original territory. He probably wouldn't see that coming. And I know you're still close to Tommaso and Cosa Nostra. We could always go to Palermo and live under their protection."

The rhythm of my heart changed. Now it pummeled like a speeding racehorse. "What are you saying, Ma?"

She scooted up to the table, her arms moving to the surface as she came closer to me. "I'm saying . . . if you ever changed your mind, I would stand by you. I never really understood what you did in Rome because I wouldn't allow myself to think about it. But now, I see what it's like without you there to protect it . . . and it's falling apart."

Chapter 24

Aurelia

Three months had come and gone. Taormina finally started to grow quiet again as the last tourists returned to their normal lives. The end of summer was here, but the weather was still warm, and there was tons of daylight.

It was obvious Sofia and Beatrice had repaired their broken relationship because I saw them together more often, and in passing, Sofia would say she watched the boys a couple times during the week. At family dinners, they were inseparable.

Sofia and I didn't spend as much time together as before, but that didn't bother me because everything was exactly as it should be. I would be her daughter-in-law, not her daughter, so I was happy to step aside.

But because the relationship between Sofia and Beatrice had improved and grown over the last few weeks, Beatrice was now my best friend. We talked all the time at work, texted after hours, even went out. I couldn't drink and I was obviously pregnant at this point, but that didn't stop us from having a great time.

Constantine was always in a good mood, so he seemed to be happy. Without Rocco or President Barsetti there to remind him of what he'd left behind, he could live in the moment. And he made good on his word, because the bigger my belly got, the more he wanted me.

Sometimes I'd just get up to get a glass of water, and his eyes would pierce me so hard, it was like we met across the bar all over again. His eyes were so intense, they were a little terrifying, and by the time I made it back to the couch, I was thrown onto my back and he was thrusting into me like he was trying to get me pregnant again.

He liked it when I showed my belly around the house, so he preferred if I only wore bras and sweatpants so he could touch and kiss my stomach. I was three months along and definitely showing, but it was still a small bump. But he worshipped me every day as if I would give birth to the next emperor of Rome.

I was at work the next morning, working at the counter, when Beatrice walked inside. "Guess who texted me?"

I looked up from the bowl, my gloved hands covered in food. "No way. He did?"

"Yep." She came around the counter with her phone in hand. "Check this out." She started to read the text out loud. "Sorry, I know it's been a hot minute. But my parents came into town, and then the shop got overrun with work. Free tomorrow night?" She locked the phone and did a little dance.

I was glad she was excited, but I didn't feel the same enthusiasm.

When she realized I wasn't dancing with her, she stopped. "Girl, what's wrong?"

"I don't know if I like what he said."

"What do you mean? His parents were in town."

"Yeah, I get that. But Constantine used to be busy all the time, and I never had to wait for his replies longer than a few seconds. It didn't matter what time of day it was, he always responded to me."

She crossed her arms over her chest as she considered what I said.

"Maybe he's telling the truth and he really was that busy, but you should be with a guy who makes you the priority, no matter what he's doing."

"Sure, but we went out *one* time," she said. "It's early days. Not everyone falls in love during a week spent in Taormina."

"Sure . . . you're right." I used to have such low expectations of men, and then Constantine raised that bar sky high. But he was a one-in-a-million catch. One in a billion, really. "See him again, and see how it goes."

She grabbed her phone again and started to type a message.

Sofia appeared in the alleyway through the floor-to-ceiling glass windows of the restaurant. She approached the door in the corner and stepped inside, her bag over her shoulder. "Stop what you're doing. We're closed for the day."

"What?" Beatrice asked. "Why?"

I started to pull off my dirty gloves, knowing something serious had happened. A family member or friend was in the hospital.

She grabbed the remote for the TV on the wall and turned it on. "Because there's been a terrorist attack in Rome." She flipped the channels until she got to the news station. Two reporters were on the screen, and another window was showing the different clips around Rome. Armed men opened fire in various public places with assault rifles, killing hundreds of people all over the city. It was still an ongoing event, with the police and military attempting to apprehend the assailants. Many more were injured or in critical condition. It was clear it was a coordinated attack by an outside group, but their motivations were unclear. And then to make it worse, the Monumento a Vittorio Emanuele II was on fire. The biggest monument in all of Italy, built to celebrate the unification of Italy in the 1800s, was ablaze. It was a magnificent piece of architecture dedicated to the city and separated from other buildings by the roads, so someone had intentionally set it on fire. "Jesus Christ . . ."

I headed straight home, and when I walked in the door, I ignored Medusa, who came over to greet me. I headed right past her into the living room, but Constantine wasn't there. I looked out the floor-to-ceiling glass windows to the terrace outside.

I saw him standing there at the railing, in just his black sweatpants and nothing else, his hands gripping the iron rail as he looked out at the sea.

All I could see was his back . . . and I knew.

I headed outside and approached him from behind. I knew he could hear me behind him, but he still didn't turn around. He remained slightly bent over the railing as he looked at the view that would have been breathtaking any other day.

I stepped up to his back and pressed my forehead against his shoulder blades before I hugged his waist. I closed my eyes and held on to him for comfort—and to comfort him in return. I was devastated by what had happened, but I was even more devastated by how much this must kill him.

After a couple minutes of silence, he slowly turned around to look at me.

I'd only seen him look like this one other time. When he'd shown up with his crew to rescue me from Pierre and that organization. He'd been maniacal in his anger, ready to burn everyone to ash.

But he'd taken that anger to another level.

His eyes were wet like he'd shed tears, angry ones.

The veins were plump in his forehead in a way I'd never seen before. He had a red tint to his face like he'd gotten sunburned, but it was just the rage making all his tissues inflamed. The cords in his neck popped too, like he'd just gotten done lifting in the gym, but he probably hadn't even had a chance to hit the gym that morning.

I was completely lost for words, having no idea what I could possibly do to make this better.

To make him feel better. To make me feel better . . .

Chapter 25

Constantine

The first person I called was Rocco, but he didn't answer.

I didn't assume the worst. I just figured he hated my guts even more now that Rome was on the brink of ruin and he blamed me for it. I walked back and forth across the terrace as I made more calls. Most of them went unanswered, and others who did pick up said they parted ways with Rocco when I left.

Aurelia sat on one of the couches with Medusa and watched me pace. She didn't try to tell me everything would be all right, soothe my anger with meaningless words, fill the dead air with empty promises.

I finally reached someone who had some answers. "Hey, Roger. I'm trying to track down Rocco. Know how I can get ahold of him?"

The sounds of conversation were all around him, like he was among a large group of people. All the voices sounded male, so he wasn't home with family but still with the crew. The talking died away as he headed elsewhere so we could hear each other. "Rocco got messed up bad. Ambulance took him to the hospital, and I haven't heard anything since."

I came to a halt on the terrace, unable to take in the beautiful sight of the sea in the distance. My heart turned to stone and dropped into the endless pit in my stomach.

"But from what I saw, I doubt he'll make it."

First, there was anger, the kind that made my eyes smart because the rage had no other pathway to escape my body. But the heartbreak came next . . . and then the guilt.

"The Roman Empire has fallen."

I hung up the phone without saying a word and turned to Aurelia.

All it took was one look to get to her feet, to know whatever I had to say was important.

"Rocco's in the hospital. Sounds like he won't make it."

Her hand immediately cupped her mouth, and she gasped. "Oh god . . . no."

"I don't know what happened." The gunmen wouldn't have been able to take him down, so I suspected it had something to do with Darius. Maybe Rocco had taken advantage of the chaos to try to decapitate the king.

Her eyes started to water, and she took a breath before she dropped her hands. "You have to go, Constantine." She looked at me with wet eyes full of sincerity that shone from her soul.

"You know I can't—"

"Save Rocco while you still can," she said through her tears. "He might make it, but he won't last long if Darius comes back to finish the job. Rome can still be saved, but you need to go now in order to save it. The Roman Empire needs its emperor, Constantine."

Her voice was packed with emotion, packed with so much sincerity that I knew she meant every word she said. That she was putting our home and our people before herself.

"Now is the time. He won't see you coming in the chaos."

"If I fail—"

"Then don't." She started to breathe hard, her eyes still glistening. "Kill him, Constantine. Kill him, then come home to us. I know you can do this."

She believed in me without question. Still had faith in me even though I'd let her down before.

She rose on her tiptoes and cupped my cheeks, coming as close to me as her little body would allow. "I know you can."

~

I threw a bag together, but it was mostly filled with guns and ammo. I didn't expect to sleep or eat until one of us was dead, so clothes and toiletries were unnecessary. I tossed everything in the back of the Range Rover parked out front while Aurelia stood there with Medusa, knowing I was about to drive off.

She held herself together, but her eyes betrayed her sadness.

I walked up to her, afraid this wasn't a *see you later* . . . but a real goodbye.

Her eyes watered the longer she stared. Medusa inched closer to her, rubbing her snout against Aurelia's hand and issuing a whine like she knew something bad was about to happen.

I moved into her and cupped her face, looking at the woman who'd stolen my heart across a dimly lit room what felt like an eternity ago. I stroked her cheek with my thumb as I looked at her, and I felt her tremble in my grip as she started to cry. "Sweetheart, our wedding is in two weeks. I promise I'll be there to marry you."

Her hands gripped my wrists, and she nodded as she continued to cry.

"I promise I'll be there in six months when our baby is born."

She nodded again.

"But I have to do this first."

"I know," she said in a whisper.

"Cosa Nostra will protect you until I come back. They'll be here in a few hours."

"Okay."

I pressed a kiss to her forehead and then her lips. "I fucking love you."

"I fucking love you too," she said as she cried harder.

I let her go before I kneeled down to embrace Medusa, my best friend, the only other woman in my heart. I kissed her on the head as I dug my fingers deep into the fur at the back of her neck. "I love you too, baby girl."

She started to pant slightly, like she knew I was about to leave and possibly never come back.

"Take care of them while I'm gone, all right?" I kissed her again. "See you soon."

I turned away from them both and got behind the wheel. I started the engine and drove off without looking at them again. I didn't check the rearview mirror as I pulled out of the gate, knowing if I saw them one more time, I might turn right back around.

~

I sped to Palermo, getting there an hour quicker than I normally would have because I drove like an asshole. I pulled up to Villa de la Sirenuse, knowing Tommaso would be there, that the crew would be lying low in light of the violence infecting Rome like a fucking disease.

I was escorted into his study, and he was already there, talking on the phone to someone, and based on what I heard, they were discussing the events in the capital. He hung up, then turned to me. "Jesus Christ."

I walked right up to him, facing off with him like an adversary rather than an ally. "We need to leave for Rome now."

"We?"

"Yes, fucking *we*. Sicily may be an island, but you're still part of Italy, the Roman Republic—and you should defend it with your life. I'm not going to stand by and watch Darius burn it to the ground. Are you?"

Tommaso took a slight step back, hands sliding into the pockets of his trousers.

"Are you?"

"Constantine—"

"Where is your patriotism? A madman is letting our enemies terrorize our people and set our monuments ablaze and destroy the Eternal City, and you're going to sit on your hands and keep them warm? I'm Emperor Constantine of the Roman Republic, and I order you to bear arms and fight with me."

"Constantine—"

I raised my voice to a new volume, a baritone and an intensity I'd never reached before. *"I'm not asking you."*

Everyone in the room stilled, Tommaso and his two henchmen who guarded him day and night.

I stared Tommaso down, knowing he was capable of more than he showed. He pretended to only care for power and money, but he wouldn't have risked his neck for my brother if he were devoid of empathy. "You think it won't affect you, but I promise his shadow will make its way to Sicily and you'll never see the sun again. Once he realizes exactly how much Cosa Nostra is worth, he'll gut you like a pig. Help me defeat him, and you'll guarantee your perseverance. Either fight with me to protect your own skin or do it because it's the right thing to do—or both."

Tommaso took another step back, looked me over as he remained lost in thought. He rubbed the back of his neck as his eyes dropped before he returned his hand to his pocket. "All right."

I kept my expression stoic, but inside, a burst of relief hit me.

"Because it's the right thing to do."

~

We took the ferry across the channel that connected the southern tip of Italy to Sicily because it was harder to track than a fleet of private planes. It was also a lot easier to transfer everything we needed for the fight to come.

On the way, I made a call to Luca, the First Emperor of the Fifth Republic in France.

It was midnight when I called, so I imagined he was wide awake.

He answered. "Quite the shit show down there. I've been watching the news the way an old lady watches her favorite soap opera. Thought you were dead."

"I'm not."

"Rocco made it sound like you were."

All the resentment I'd felt for Rocco disappeared the moment I knew he might not be alive long enough to see my face again. "Look, you owe me, and I'm calling in that favor."

"I owe you? What the fuck did you just say to me?"

"We don't have time to take a stroll down memory lane."

"I delivered Vladimir on a fucking platter—debt paid."

"One of your men decided to commit his crimes in my territory when he couldn't do it in yours. You fixed your own fucking mess. Your little cult disrespected Pope Zephyrinus and the Vatican and God. That debt has *not* been paid. You owe me."

Luca released an exaggerated sigh into the phone. "What the fuck do you want me to do? I can't come in and put your city back together when I'm not the emperor. That's your job, and I won't do it for you."

"My eyes are on Darius. I need you and your men to come in and control the gangs. They've all gone rogue, and I need them shoved back into their cages. It's a fucking free-for-all, and it's got to stop. Robbery, trafficking, drugs—it's fucking pandemonium. And I need all those assholes who fired on my people dead. The police and military are handling it as best they can, but I'm sure some will fall through the cracks. I can't be everywhere at once, so I need your help restoring order. Do whatever you've got to do to make it happen."

Luca was quiet as he listened to my proposition. He was probably sitting in an armchair, slouched with his elbow propped on the armrest, his closed knuckles against his temple. "Fine. I can get there in twelve hours." He hung up.

Tommaso sat in the back seat with me, against the opposite window. "Bringing in the big guns . . . good."

~

When we made it to Rome, the city was full of sirens. That wasn't unusual on a normal day, but ambulances and police and firefighters were everywhere. The fire from the monument was so bad the entire sky was blacked out by smoke. Destruction from the attack was visible in every direction, lots of roads closed off as the military and police did their jobs.

I was disgusted by it all.

And there was graffiti all over the place . . . not just on the sides of apartment buildings and alleyways, but the Colosseum, the Spanish Steps, everywhere. And strange people crowded all the streets. Not people riding their motorbikes to the grocery store or meeting friends. But drug dealers just waiting for customers to show up on some of the busy street corners. They were visible at every turn—like the entire city was on something. When Rocco had warned me how much the city had changed, I still hadn't expected this.

I was dropped off at the hospital and checked in at the front desk. I feared the receptionist would tell me Rocco was in the morgue in the basement, but she gave me his room number in the ICU.

Thank god.

I took the elevator to the top floor and stopped outside his door. It was a private room and the door was open, so I could see him lying there, wires hooked up all over his body, his face beaten up so badly, he was almost unrecognizable. A doctor seemed to be in the room doing his rounds, so I waited outside until he was finished before I let myself in.

The TV was on in the corner, but it was muted. It showed the news.

Rocco didn't look at me right away, probably because he thought I was another doctor or a nurse who'd come to check on him. His eyes were more interested in the news, but when he noticed I hadn't moved, he turned to look at me.

I watched his reaction to me. Watched his eyes widen at the sight of me like I was the last person in the world he expected to see. It took him a second to process the sight and lower his eyebrows. His expression turned neutral, and he stared at me with his typical poker face.

I approached his bedside and took a seat in the empty chair meant for visitors.

Wordlessly, he stared at me.

I couldn't figure out exactly what Rocco had been through because his injuries were hidden underneath his gown, but if his body looked anything like his face, then he was lucky to be alive. "You all right?"

"I'm supposed to be dead—so, could be worse."

I didn't chuckle, even if it was a joke. Nothing was funny right now. "What happened?"

"Tried to take down Darius. He decided he needed a matching nightstand, so he tried to shove me into one of his oil drums alive. It got rough. Only got away by chance, but not before he messed me up pretty bad."

My eyes moved to the TV because it was easier to look at the news than visualize his tale.

"It's not the first time I've tried to kill him, but he's never alone, so it's hard to manage."

"I'm sorry, man."

"I'll be fine, Constantine."

"No. I'm sorry that you've had to do this alone." I kept my eyes on the TV because it was too hard to look at him. "I'm sorry I turned my back on you . . . our city . . . the Republic."

A long stretch of silence passed, packed with things unsaid.

I didn't expect him to forgive me or even acknowledge what I'd said. But I wanted to say it anyway. Our friendship was probably beyond repair at this point.

"You put your family first—as every man should."

My eyes left the TV to look at him, to verify he'd actually said the words I'd just heard.

"You didn't have another choice. I shouldn't have made you feel like shit about it."

I was stunned into silence, feeling the invisible weight I carried slowly leave my shoulders.

"It's better for you to be there for her than to be in this hospital bed like me."

"You shouldn't be in this hospital bed either."

He looked back at the TV and watched it for a while.

It was tense and awkward, like we didn't know how to talk to each other.

"You came all the way here to see me?" he asked.

"I came all the way here to kill that asshole and protect the Republic."

He looked at me instead of the TV.

I held his gaze. "I've got to kill him, Rocco. I can't let him come for Aurelia and the others."

He stared at me for a while before he gave a nod. "Yeah, I know."

"I know you feel like shit right now and look like shit too—but you've got to get out of this bed and help me."

Rocco signed all the paperwork to indicate he understood he was declining care from the hospital and leaving against their medical advice. He'd just had adnominal surgery due to the lacerations he'd taken from Darius's knife, and he was being held together by long lines of stitches.

He got dressed in front of me, and that's when I saw the extent of the damage. "Damn."

"Asshole got me good," he said. "What's the plan?"

"Tommaso and Cosa Nostra are here to help."

"Good."

"And I cashed in the debt from the Fifth Republic. Luca's probably here or almost here. Told him to handle the gangs."

"You don't think that will piss off Darius?"

"Darius will think twice before starting a war with the Fifth Republic. Right now, I want him to focus on you."

"Me?" he asked before he pulled his shirt over his head. "This fucking rag doll?"

"You think he'll want to finish the job?"

He covered the extent of his injuries beneath his clothes before he started to get his shoes on. "He did say I would make a nice addition to his bedroom set. I've been the one consistently pushing back against him. The last resistance of the Roman Republic. Says I'm a modern-day Marcus Aurelius."

"Quite the compliment."

He released a quiet chuckle. "Pretty sure it wasn't meant to be one."

For a millisecond, I was frozen in time, reunited with the casual banter we'd shared for years. Felt like old times . . . like we weren't in the midst of a war. I blinked, and then it was gone, the present conflict coming back to the forefront. "I don't have much time before he realizes I'm here. I'm not sure if he'll come for me or . . . hit me where it hurts."

"The second one," he said. "So we've got to move quickly."

"You think he's at the palace?" My fucking house.

"I don't know. Our brawl happened outside the Quirinal Palace."

The Quirinal Palace was the private residence of the Italian president. And that meant President Barsetti was either in trouble or he was dead. "What happened?"

"He forced President Barsetti to step down. Darius says there's no such thing as a republic when there's a king. I don't know what happened to Barsetti, because when I got there, I almost died. The military police showed up, and an ambulance took me. Not sure what came after that."

"I haven't seen anything on the news that President Barsetti is dead, so that's a good sign."

“Maybe. Or maybe no one knows he’s dead.”

We walked out of the hospital together, Rocco doing his best to move normally, but his body was unresponsive. I slowed my walk so it was easier for him to keep up with me without overexerting himself.

We stayed in the lobby before we stepped out onto the street. “How do you feel about being bait?”

He winced from one of his cuts before he straightened. “Bait?”

“Sounds like he’s taking the heads of everyone who resists his ascension to the throne. Put yourself out there, he’ll come. I’ll handle the rest. We’ve got to move fast because it won’t take long for him to realize that I’m in the city. Cosa Nostra will be a dead giveaway. You think you can handle that?”

“If he gets his hands on me, you know I’m dead.”

“You know I won’t let that happen.”

He reached for me and clapped me on the shoulder. “I know, man.”

Rocco made some calls and figured out Darius was at the Pantheon—hanging traitors. I called Tommaso, and he picked us up as we headed across the city to the square famous for evening strolls and gatherings. I’d taken Aurelia to dinner there shortly after we’d moved in together.

We stopped a street over and prepared for the shoot-out. I strapped on a vest because I was going to do everything in my power to get back to Aurelia. Do everything I could to live to hold my baby. To be a father to a daughter so badass no man would ever be good enough for her.

“You got this?” I said to Rocco.

He nodded. “You know how he is, likes to play with his food first. He’ll drop his guard, and you’ll have your chance. How are you going to do it?”

“Gonna shoot him in the fucking head.”

“And that’s it?” he asked in surprise. “It’s your chance for vengeance. Your chance to make him suffer.” He didn’t share the rest of his thought, but I knew he was thinking of my brother . . . who’d died a horrible death.

"I've got to think about the living, not the dead. If I see the shot, I'm taking it." I'd brought my scoped rifle and my automatic rifle, a strap over each shoulder, a bandolier of grenades around my hip. "Let's move."

Rocco turned to the few men he had left, and they armed themselves before they headed into the square of the Pantheon.

I took my position at the corner of the building and witnessed the mayhem myself. Hundreds of bodies hung from the top of the Pantheon, all dangling from nooses. The men I'd hanged had been criminals, but when I looked at the people above, men and women, I recognized senators and the mayor . . . and their wives.

Can't wait to kill this son of a bitch.

I watched Darius grab someone by the shoulder and throw him hard across the street in front of the oldest complete monument standing in Rome.

My eyes narrowed when I recognized President Barsetti.

Darius descended upon him. "You're a traitor to your country, denying the king of Italy his rightful place on the throne. Your emperor is gone, your people have turned on you, and you continue to fight me like you have a chance."

President Barsetti said nothing as he looked up at Darius, stone faced.

I turned to Rocco. "Go now before he puts that noose around Barsetti's neck."

"Bend the fucking knee." Darius took a step closer before he looked up at the bodies that hung above. "Or become bird food."

President Barsetti didn't have to resist, because Rocco fired his automatic rifle into the sky as he stepped into the square with his men. He'd limped and grimaced with me in the hospital, but now, he showed no signs of weakness, ready to draw Darius away from his men so I could take the shot. "You're not a king, but a fucking terrorist. A plague on your own country and your own people."

President Barsetti turned to see Rocco, then pulled himself away from Darius, taking the opportunity to get the fuck out of there.

Darius hesitated as he looked at Rocco, his eyes narrowing as he took a moment to understand who was dumb enough to provoke him. The recognition descended on his face, but not an ounce of fear. "Was just about to stop by the hospital and bring you flowers. Glad to see the surgery went well." He seemed to completely have forgotten President Barsetti, who continued to crawl away until he got to his feet. But one of Darius's men stopped him and shoved him back to the ground like the execution would still be taking place.

Darius took several steps into the middle of the square, staring Rocco down like some kind of minor distraction.

I was tucked around the corner of a building, and I lifted the sniper rifle over my shoulder and focused on the lens.

Rocco was flanked by men of Cosa Nostra, but there were only five of them, while Darius had an entire army behind him. He was the king who'd cleared the board, had taken all the pawns, knights, and bishops and kicked off his own queen.

I watched Darius in the scope, but he happened to stop right behind one of our guys. "Come on, move." I kept the gun trained on my target, but I could only get the corner of Darius's shoulder.

Darius trailed his gaze slowly up and down Rocco's body. "Must be on a lot of painkillers."

"Nah, I passed," Rocco said. "Don't want to numb anything—especially the high from killing you."

Darius smirked before he released a laugh. "That's cute. Unless you've got a bomb strapped to your chest and you're about to kamikaze this shit, I don't think that's going to happen. But to be real, I'd respect you for it." The smile remained.

"Jesus Christ, fucking move!" I knew Rocco couldn't keep this up for more than a few minutes before Darius got bored, so I shouldered my gun, ran around the building to the other corner, my heart racing and my lungs aching to get there fast enough. I dropped to my knee and grimaced slightly when the cap hit the concrete. I didn't bother with stealth, so I knew his men had probably noticed me.

I didn't even take a chance to check. I put the gun back on my shoulder, looked through the scope because I couldn't afford to miss even when I was relatively close. This wasn't how I imagined this moment would be. I'd wanted to capture him and torture him until he begged me to end his life. Wanted bloody and violent revenge for my brother . . . but I was prepared to let that go. To live for the future instead of the past. I aimed for his head and squeezed the trigger right when he moved his head, laughing at something Rocco had said or some other thought that had come into his mind.

I didn't see the outcome because gunfire broke out, and I felt a bullet go straight through my arm. "Fuck." I dropped the gun and sprinted away, ducking for cover behind a slab of concrete that comprised the nearby flower box.

I knew they were coming for me, so I ripped off a grenade and pulled out the pin before I tossed it overhead. The second the explosion hit my ears, I ran for it. Sprinted around the building and back to where Cosa Nostra had formed their line of defense. Most of them had moved up to help Rocco when the gunfire started.

I'd just rounded the corner when Rocco ran into me and nearly knocked me to the ground. Blood dripped down his face from a head wound, but he didn't appear to have been shot there.

"You all right—"

"You got him, he's down."

"But is he dead?"

"You hit him in the head. He's gotta be."

I wanted to see his body, to confirm that nightmare truly was gone from this world.

Rocco read the uncertainty in my eyes because he still knew me so well, despite our three-month estrangement. "When the gunfire ceases, we'll burn his body."

I nodded in agreement.

He patted me on the shoulder as the sounds of warfare continued. "Take back the Roman Empire, Constantine."

Both sides were evenly matched, so all the windows of the restaurants and gelato shops were shattered, and glass littered the cobblestone streets. Bullets marked the Pantheon, adding to the graffiti that had already been painted over the Egyptian stone.

Rocco was already gravely injured without the head wound, so he hung back while I moved in with the others, shooting down the Skull Kings and the others dumb enough to fight me.

Luca arrived from the rear with his men, shooting my enemies in the back while they were distracted by me in the front, littering the ground with the traitors who'd chosen a tyrant over an emperor. The second the battle shifted in my favor, so did the surrenders. They dropped their guns and took a knee—and I walked up and shot them each right in the fucking face.

Luca watched me from where he stood, and after he leveled me with a hard stare, he gave me a nod in approval.

I'd never been the merciful type.

Some fled through the streets, and Luca's men chased them down. The men whom I knew were close to Darius were hung from the Pantheon to choke until death, swinging from side to side and bumping into others that had been dead for hours.

There were so many bodies, probably hundreds. Blood filled the cracks between the cobblestones, and the Pantheon witnessed another battle at her steps.

I searched the men for Darius, looking for his black T-shirt and dark hair, turning bodies over when I thought they could be him to get a good look at their faces. But none of them was ever Darius, and I continued my search, kicking every man over to be sure.

"Searching for a loved one?" Luca asked, coming to my side with a cigar hanging out of the corner of his mouth like the shoot-out had been a mere hookup to him.

I looked at the sea of dead men, losing their lives in a battle that never should have been fought in the first place. The Skull King should have been eliminated a long time ago—and I should have been the one to do it. This was all my fault, and not because I'd sacrificed my reign for a woman, but because I didn't kill him sooner. "Darius."

Luca took a drag before he released the smoke in a big cloud. "I'm sure he's around here somewhere."

"Rocco said I shot him in the head, but I need to make sure."

Luca continued to survey the dead like he'd seen it all before. "If he managed to crawl away, he probably bled out in an alleyway somewhere. And if he managed to survive, he's gonna lie low. He's lost his men and is painfully aware of the strength of your allies."

"Fishing for a compliment?"

He took another drag before he dropped the cigar on a dead guy's chest. He raised his boot and smashed it against the body to put out the fire and smear ash into the cotton. "It's good to have friends in high places . . . all I'm saying."

"What you're saying is I owe you."

He gave a shrug.

"Even though you're here because you owe me."

He gave another shrug. "I just gave you back your empire. The debts are not equal in value."

"Instead of owing each other, perhaps we should forge an alliance. It's in our best interest to maintain our respective republics. Not an easy job."

"It's an interesting prospect," he said noncommittally as he looked into the distance.

"I'm sure it'll be even more interesting the next time the Fifth Republic needs assistance."

"We'll require no assistance as long as I'm the First French Emperor. But whoever my successor is . . . they might need a hand." He turned back to me.

"You've just started, and you're already planning to leave?"

He was quiet for a while as he stared at me with a bored look, as if he wasn't sure if he should even bother responding to my question. "I've met someone."

I smirked. "I know how that goes . . ."

"Yeah," he said as he looked off again. "My men have started to round up the gangs. Those who resist will be hand-delivered to you before we depart so you can choose how you want to handle it."

"Thank you," I said. "And even though you're here to pay a debt, the Roman Republic will always come to your aid if you need it." Luca and his men had been critical to this movement, and now that the criminals I policed knew my power reached beyond our borders, there was far less chance there would be another pushback. Even if the Republic was compromised, they would hold their breath and wait. I needed to know that power was in my back pocket, and the best way to do that was to extend an olive branch to Luca—the most powerful ally I could have.

He stared at me for several heartbeats before he barely gave me a nod . . . and walked off.

~

I didn't have time to call Aurelia, but I sent her a text. **I took care of Darius and his men. Rocco and I are fine. Call you when I can.**

Her reply was immediate, like she'd been sitting on the couch with Medusa, the phone gripped in her hand. **Thank god.**

I pocketed my phone and returned to where the cars were parked in the street. The police and the military had arrived, but there was nothing for them to do except help with the bodies.

President Barsetti's suit was covered in dirt and grime, but he looked unharmed otherwise. When he spotted me, he cut short his conversation with one of his military sergeants and hurried over. "You all right?"

I nodded, the wound stitched and wrapped tightly in gauze. It was the same place where I'd been shot for Medusa, and I knew this recovery would be a lot worse since it was the second time. "You?"

"I'm fine," he said like he couldn't care less how he was doing. "You came back."

"Yeah. I did."

He stared at me for a while, as if processing his resentment in order to release it. "Good. Rome needs its emperor."

My decision had been made without needing the time to consider it. It was instinct, something I just knew. "It'll take me some time to get Rome back in order, to put the gangs back on their schedules, and to make sure the Skull Kings are permanently dismantled, but once that's done, I'm done."

Both of his eyebrows rose. "Why?"

Because I'd found my place—finally. It wasn't in the streets of Rome. It wasn't upon an iron throne. It was in Taormina, in the sunshine that reflected off the water, in the small village with everyone I'd known since I was a kid. It was in the glow of my mother's love, in my sister's smile . . . with the woman who would be my wife. "I did what I set out to do—and now it's time to move on."

"You know Rome will collapse again the second you're gone—"

"I know the exact person who should take my place. A far better choice, if you ask me."

I sat with Tommaso on the patio of the restaurant, both of us ordering drinks that we didn't touch. Rocco had checked himself back in to the hospital because he was in no shape to do anything else but recover. I'd been working the whole time, putting the city back in order, removing the graffiti that marked the buildings.

And killing everyone who had become a traitor to their own empire.

"What's next for you, Constantine?" Tommaso suddenly asked.

"Time to settle down in Taormina."

He gave a nod like he'd expected that answer. "You ready for that?"

"Never thought I'd be excited for something so simple." A grin stretched across my face. "But I am. And now that Rome will be in safe hands, I can really enjoy it. Move on and not look back."

He watched the people pass on the sidewalk for a long time. Without looking at me, he said, "And Edric?"

"I haven't gone by the house and grabbed him yet. But I will."

"I can go with you if you'd like." His eyes came back to me. "I dreamed of having you as a son-in-law, but that doesn't mean I don't still care for you like my own."

My eyes dropped at his unexpected affection. "That means a lot to me, Tommaso."

He looked away again.

"And it'd mean a lot if you came with me."

I stopped by the hospital and sat at Rocco's bedside.

He was knocked out, the TV still on in the corner.

I got comfortable in the chair and put my feet up on the edge of his bed as I watched the screen. It was some soap opera where a cougar was having an affair with her stepson, and there was lots of drama and spice . . . pretty entertaining.

Aurelia texted me. I'm sorry to be clingy, but when are you coming home?

I'd been working all week. Collapsing into bed just to sleep for a couple of hours before I was back on the streets again. I hadn't had a chance to call or text much. Be as clingy as you want, sweetheart. You know I'm into it.

God, I miss you.

A warmth like sunshine filled my veins. I loved it when she wanted me. Loved it when she needed me. And I loved that she was so transparent about it. I miss you too. I'll probably head home tomorrow. Just gotta tie up some loose ends.

Okay. Let me know when you leave.

I will.

How's Rocco doing?

He's asleep right now. I'm at his bedside.

Will he be able to leave the hospital soon?

I think so.

The conversation died, so I slid the phone back into my pocket.

A couple minutes later, Rocco blinked a few times as he stared at the TV, the soap opera coming into view. "They haven't gotten caught yet?" he asked in a raspy voice.

"Her husband just found the text messages. Think he's gonna confront her."

"You think he'll blow her head off or just divorce her?"

"I don't think they blow people's heads off in soap operas."

"Well, they should. That'd be great television." He released a heavy sigh as he pushed himself up in bed, then clicked the button to make the top half of the bed lift to support him. "How long have you been here?"

"About an hour."

"You've been watching me sleep for an hour? Fucking creep."

"I was watching the show."

"Right." He turned his head to look at me. "Doctor said I can go home tomorrow. Thank fucking god."

Then the timing was perfect. "Cosa Nostra and I are leaving tomorrow."

"How long will you be gone?"

I stared at him.

He stared back.

It took a couple seconds for it to click, and when it did, his eyes changed. "You aren't coming back . . ."

"No."

He gave another sigh before he lifted himself farther up.

"I thought I would want it, but I don't. I'm a different person now." I wanted to raise my kid in the village, have a quiet life with Aurelia and Medusa, spend time with my mother while she was still around. "Which works out great because I think you'd do a much better job anyway."

He turned his head to me when he heard what I said. He stared, the silence somehow louder than words.

"I abandoned Rome to a psychopathic dictator—but you stayed."

He continued to stare at me.

"I betrayed my country and my people for one person—and you stayed. You continued to fight against Darius and preserve the Roman Republic. Even when you knew it would probably claim your life, you continued to fight back. My reign has ended, and yours has begun."

He continued to hold his silence as he stared at me.

I couldn't figure out how he felt about it, not when his face was as stoic as stone. "Do you accept?"

"You didn't betray your country, Con. A man should always put his family first, and that's exactly what you did. You wouldn't be the right leader for Rome if you'd done otherwise. I think I made you feel bad because . . . I didn't want to do it alone. I blamed you for everything, when it's obvious Darius was always a complicated problem. And what I said about your brother . . . it was fucked up, and I regret saying it.

Would take it back if I could." He looked away when he finished, like he didn't want to see my reaction to the last thing he said.

I'd felt no anger toward him at all, but now, I felt somehow lighter. "You can take it back."

After a hesitation, he turned back to me.

"Because as far as I'm concerned, it never happened. So, do you accept?"

His eyes flicked back and forth between mine, but he let me change the subject and move on from the past. "Yeah."

I smiled. "Good."

"Do I get your place?"

"Fuck off," I said with a laugh.

"Well, what the hell are you going to do with it?"

"Fair point," I said. "I'll make a deal with you. I'll sell it to you—if you let us stay there when we visit."

"Are you gonna visit often?"

"Probably not."

"How much?" he asked.

"More than you can afford. But in a couple months, you should be able to cover it. I'm flexible."

"Sounds like a deal," he said.

"The least I can do for . . . abandoning you."

He looked at the TV again and watched it for a while.

I stayed at his bedside even though I still had a lot of things to do. This story had a happy ending, but I was still bummed I wouldn't see him every day like I used to. He was the closest thing I had to a brother . . . since mine had died.

"Have you gotten Edric yet?" He turned back to me. He pushed the blankets to his waist as if he'd gotten warm in that little bed.

"No. I'll swing by tomorrow."

"Alone?"

"No. Tommaso said he would help me."

"Good," he said. "Do you . . . feel better now?"

I thought about it for a while before I shook my head. "I made my peace with it when Aurelia told me she was pregnant. That made me realize I needed to live in the present and not the past. But it means a lot to me that I can bring him home . . . and lay him to rest. It's closure, the last page in this shitty story."

"It wasn't all shitty," he said. "Pretty fucking epic if you ask me."

I'd met the love of my life, finally put Isabella behind me, and met some of my closest friends on the way. And now, a new stage of my life was about to begin—and I'd never been more excited. "It was, wasn't it?"

The cemetery was located outside of Taormina, a short ten-minute drive. My mom hadn't spoken of Edric in a long time, but I knew she still went there every single morning. That was confirmed when I arrived at his headstone and a fresh bouquet of flowers was there.

He hadn't been gone that long, but time had already made its impact. The stone had lightened from exposure to the sunshine and the salt in the air. Grime had started to build up in the crevices of the engraving.

Tommaso and some of the other guys unloaded the oil drum from the back of the van. They rolled it down a plank of wood to get it to the dirt. They'd drained it in Palermo, and now nothing was inside except for the bones. Even sealed inside the oil drum, his body had still decomposed, and since it'd been over seven years, there wouldn't be much left of him.

I grabbed a shovel and started to dig at my brother's grave site. The others helped me, and an hour later, we reached the coffin that had already deteriorated. It was sealed shut even though there was nothing inside, so I pried it open and popped the lid.

I climbed out of the grave, then moved to the front of the van. I leaned against the grill and stared at the side of Mount Etna, the volcano quiet for the time being. I could hear Tommaso and the guys working, transferring the bones from the oil drum to the coffin before they sealed it shut again.

I didn't have the heart or the stomach to watch. Couldn't see what was left of a man who still felt so real to me.

Tommaso released a quiet whistle to let me know they were finished.

When I walked over, they were shoveling the dirt back onto the grave.

"Thanks, guys." I grabbed a shovel and joined them, putting the dirt back in place and compacting it with the bottom of our shovels, doing our best to make it look like it hadn't been disturbed. But because my mother visited every single morning, she would know something had changed.

Hopefully, she would assume it was just scheduled maintenance. I wouldn't lie to my mother, but this was one secret I would take to the grave. Let her believe her son had been killed by an idiot driver rather than broken into pieces and used as a nightstand.

Now that I was about to be a father, I thought about it differently.

I grieved for my mother in a way I hadn't before.

If that ever happened to me . . . I wouldn't be able to go on.

~

When I pulled into the driveway of my home, I stopped when I got past the gate. I didn't open the garage. Just gripped the wheel and stared at the place that had become home. The place that I had left in search of vengeance, power, and wealth.

I hadn't realized all that was right in front of me the entire time. I just had to get my wife first and bring her here.

I pulled into the garage, then stepped into the house.

Aurelia and Medusa were there waiting for me in the hallway. Aurelia burst into tears at the sight of me and rushed to me to hug me harder than she ever had. Held on to me like she dangled over a cliff with spikes down below. She breathed hard against my chest before she released an unexpected sob.

"Sweetheart." I cupped the back of her head as she cried against me, cried like I'd died instead of lived.

Medusa was right at my feet, looking up at me before she raised a paw and issued a whine.

"In a sec, baby girl," I said quietly, consoling Aurelia first.

She finally pulled away enough to look at me before she reached up and cupped my face. "I'm so glad you're home."

I bent my neck to kiss her, to pull her into me. "And I'm never leaving again."

Her eyes flicked back and forth between mine. "If he's gone, then we can return to Rome—"

"No."

"You can have both, Con."

"I don't want both. This is what I want." I moved my hand to her belly. "Just this." I kneeled down and lifted up her shirt to kiss her stomach. That was when Medusa got impatient, moving her snout under my arm and trying to pull it toward her, demanding attention. She used to be the only woman in my life, but she had two other people to compete with these days.

"Hey, baby girl." I cupped her face with both hands, then ran them back through her fur, making her eyes soften at my touch. Then I kissed the top of her head and gave her body a rubdown, bringing her in for a hug before I let her go. I stood upright and looked at Aurelia again, looked at the eyes that made me soft the moment I saw her. "It's good to be home."

Chapter 26

Aurelia

Constantine didn't say much about what had happened in Rome, but I knew he was in a good place because he had his usual sexual appetite. He relaxed against the headboard with me on top of him, his big hands cupping my pregnant stomach like it turned him on rather than revolted him.

My body changed slowly, but as the changes became more prominent, I became more self-conscious. I was forced to buy new clothes because my hips were wider, my feet were fatter. I gained weight everywhere, even though the only thing that should have gotten bigger was my stomach. My metabolism must have changed because my eating habits weren't any different. My body was just determined to hold on to as much fat as possible, like the baby needed it.

Constantine was rock hard, slabs of muscles separated by indentations of his skin, a god who lived and breathed, but he continued to worship me like I was the hot one in the relationship.

Not even close.

He stared at my stomach as I moved on top of him, felt my belly with worshipful hands, had to edge himself over and over like all he wanted to do was come. He'd never struggled before, but the bigger my stomach got, the worse it became.

As if it really did turn him on like crazy.

My tits got bigger too, and he *definitely* liked that. Groped them all the time the way he used to grope my ass.

When we finished our lovemaking, he spooned me from behind, his hand resting on my stomach. He kissed the back of my shoulder before he buried his face in my hair because he liked the way it smelled.

Then he said the sweetest thing. "I can't wait to marry you, sweetheart."

Just when I couldn't love him more, he made me fall head over heels. The wedding was in a week. It felt a lifetime away but also imminent at the same time. I already had my dress and everything planned because Constantine and Sofia had the connections to make anything happen on such short notice.

I was excited to be his wife, but I was also excited to start this new chapter in life, to finally leave the past behind and turn the page. "Can I ask you something?"

"Anything."

My hand rested over his on my stomach. "Did you get your brother back?"

There was a pause like I'd pressed a button he tried to hide from me. "Yes."

"Good."

He was quiet.

"We should go visit sometime."

"Yeah, we should."

I turned around and faced him, and the second our eyes met, he hiked my leg over his hip to bring us closer together. He looked at me with tired eyes, but eyes that were fulfilled and at peace. "Is this really enough for you?" I whispered. "Us and a restaurant and a dog and two nephews to watch sometimes?"

"When have I ever given you the impression I was unhappy?" His eyes continued to bore into mine with a haze of calm and peace, not exhaustion like he was ready to sleep, just a subtle bit of Zen. "Are you happy?"

"Of course."

"Are you sure?" he asked. "Because maybe once you've had a taste for that life, that's what you really want."

I didn't have to think twice about it. "I never want to feel the way I did a few days ago, when I was terrified you wouldn't come home. I never want to see you with another bullet in your arm. I never want to watch Medusa stare at the door every day, waiting for you to walk through it. Your family feels like my family, and I love our quiet little life here. I just . . . want to make sure it's enough for you. Because I'll go back and do it all if it'll make you happy."

His stare didn't change. He didn't cut me off like he had before when we discussed this. He hung on every word like he wanted to memorize it forever. "There's no doubt in my mind whatsoever that this is what I want. And you know I wouldn't lie to you, sweetheart. I'll sleep just fine knowing Rocco's got it covered."

I could finally relax, be happy without feeling selfish about it. "Okay."

"Rocco asked if he could buy my place in Rome. I said yes, as long as we get to stay there when we're in town. Is that okay?"

"You're going to sell it to him?"

"I can't imagine why we would need it. Unless you have a problem with that."

"It's such a legacy property. Those houses don't come up, like, ever."

His eyes flicked back and forth between mine. "I won't sell it if you don't want me to."

"No, it's your place. You should decide—"

"*Our place.* Come on, you've been my wife since the moment we met. A piece of paper doesn't make that more true. Just true for lawyers."

Sweetest, hottest man alive. "You're right. We probably won't use it. But I guess . . . what if our child ever wants it? What if they want to move to Rome when they become an adult and start a life there?"

He gave a quiet breath like he was in pain. "They aren't even born yet, and I can't stand the thought—especially if it's a girl. I never really understood my mother's perspective about the three of us until I realized

I would be a parent myself. Everything hits different now. She was supportive of me when I decided to move to Palermo, and now I realize how hard that actually was for her. I know she still goes to the cemetery every day to visit my brother, and when I imagine going through something like that myself . . . I can't breathe."

I moved my hand to his arm and squeezed it.

His eyes drifted off somewhere else, his thoughts clouded by his sorrow. "We'll keep it. I'll tell Rocco I'm happy to share it with him. It's such a big place, so someone should live there. And now he needs something of that caliber for protection."

"He gets to live there for free, so that's nice."

"Fuck no, he doesn't," he said with a slight chuckle. "He's gotta cover the utilities and the staff."

"That's fair."

He lay there for a while, the silence trickling by. His eyes stayed on me all the while. "I know we can't go too far for our honeymoon, so I thought we could stay at that hotel where we met."

"Ooh, that's a perfect idea."

"Yeah?" he asked with a smile.

"Room service whenever we want, sex all day, right there at the ocean . . ."

"Good. I like it too."

"What about Medusa? Can she come with us?"

"I'm not taking her on our honeymoon," he said with a chuckle. "She can stay with my mom."

"I'll miss her."

He pulled me a little closer to him, my belly against his rock-hard stomach. "Trust me, you'll be too busy to miss her."

~

The wedding was in just a few days.

Everything had been planned and scheduled. I had my wedding dress in the closet. His mother knew everyone in Taormina, so she had no problem booking everything at the last minute. The ceremony would be at the Duomo di Taormina, the church right in the heart of the village, where Constantine and I met up before he took me on a private tour. He said it was the only request he had because his mother would never forgive him for getting married anywhere else but within the walls of a church.

I didn't care where we got married anyway. As long as Constantine was there, we could get married in a coal mine or a zoo. If it was important to his mother, then she could have whatever she wanted. I was just grateful that she would be my mother too.

The reception would be on an outdoor terrace at one of the hotels, right on the cliff's edge over the sea, an enormous space that could accommodate five hundred guests . . . because that was how many people were coming.

Because, again, they knew literally everyone.

It was my last day at the restaurant. Constantine and I had both decided that we needed to focus on our own restaurant, our honeymoon, and preparing for the baby. I was sad to leave Rosticceria Da Cristina, because it was the place where I became closer to his cousin Antonio and his sister Beatrice. I got to spend time with cousins and family friends. But the bigger I got, the more painful it became to stand all day, and I was grateful that Constantine was able to take care of me so I didn't have to work if I didn't want to.

I finished prepping for the day, so I was supposed to wait tables through the lunch rush. My shirt was a little tight on my stomach and really put my belly on display, so there was no doubt I was pregnant, and everyone congratulated me every day.

Beatrice ripped off her gloves and came to my side. "Can't believe it's your last day. Gonna miss having you around here."

"Me too. I've learned so much and have gotten to know you all so well."

Antonio came from one of the other kitchens. "You can always come back, you know?"

"And if you and Con don't work out for some reason, we'll keep you and drop him," Beatrice said. "He's kind of a prick anyway."

Antonio squeezed his thumb and forefinger together. "A little."

When I'd first come to Taormina, I didn't know where I stood with these people, but now I felt like one of them. "Thank you, guys. It really means the world to me."

"So excited for the wedding," she said. "And honored to be your maid of honor."

"I'm a little irritated that Constantine asked some random guy named Rocco to be his best man, but at least I'm a groomsman," Antonio said.

I smiled. "It was a hard decision, for sure. He loves all you guys."

"Well, try to relax and don't stress," Beatrice said. "Weddings can drive people crazy."

"I'm not stressed," I said. "If the cake doesn't make it or the decorations are wrong or the dress is too tight on my stomach . . . I don't really care. All I care about is Constantine being at the end of the aisle when I get there. And I know he will be."

Chapter 27

Constantine

My mother was blowing up my phone. You can't spend the night together before the wedding, Constantine.

We're already living together and have a baby on the way, Ma.

But it's not tradition.

I'm pretty sure a child out of wedlock isn't traditional either.

Her dots disappeared, but then my screen lit up with my mother's name. "Oh boy . . . code blue."

"What?" Aurelia asked, sitting on the couch beside me with Medusa's chin resting on her thigh.

"Ma's gone nuclear." I answered the call and rose from the couch to step away. I headed out the back door and stepped onto the terrace. "Ma—"

"It's bad luck, Constantine."

"No, it's not."

"It's one night," she said. "You really can't do one night?"

I didn't say what I wanted to say—not to my mother anyway.

"How about you come here and spend the night with me?"

Spend the night with my mother? "Ma, I'm a grown man—"

"Listen to me, Con," she said abruptly, but then there was a long pause afterward. She'd cut me off but had nothing to follow it. "When you were born, my mother told me to cherish this time . . . because I only got to keep you for eighteen years. I know you're a man now, but soon, you'll be married and you'll have your own family, and it'll never be the same. I would love one more night with you, just the two of us."

I felt the breeze move through my hair as my eyes darted down to the floor at my feet, feeling a wave of emotion I didn't expect to hit me so hard. "I have two conditions."

"All right."

"You make dinner."

She didn't say a single word, showed no sign of emotion in her silence, but I knew her eyes were welling with tears.

"And let my friend Rocco join us."

She still said nothing, like she needed a moment to recover from what I'd said. "I would love that."

When I hung up the phone, I returned to the house.

Aurelia was still on the couch. "Everything okay?"

"Yeah." I sat beside her, placing my arm around her shoulders. "She wants me to stay over there the night before the wedding. Says she wants to spend time with me before my entire life becomes about you two, even though it already is."

"Aww, that's sweet."

"So you don't mind?"

"Of course not," she said as she hooked her arm through mine. "I love that idea."

"You'll be okay here on your own?"

"I'm sure Beatrice will sleep over with the boys." She petted Medusa on the head. "And I've got my girl."

"All right. I'll miss you, though."

She smiled as she continued to pet Medusa. "We have the rest of our lives, Constantine. And hopefully eternity too . . ."

~

With my bag over my shoulder, I arrived at my mother's house.

She was over the moon to see me, squeezing me tightly and pinching my cheeks before she kissed me, like I was home for the holidays after being gone for six months.

I put my stuff in the spare bedroom, then joined her in the kitchen. The counters were covered in cutting boards and ingredients, a pot of water already simmering on the stove.

"Handle the tomatoes and the garlic while I take care of the beef," she instructed, like we were at work.

"All right, boss." I washed my hands, grating the garlic and then the lemon zest before I washed and peeled the tomatoes.

She worked on the other vegetables, then put the beef in one of the preheated pans. "Nervous?"

"About?" I asked as I continued to peel the tomatoes in the big bowl.

"Getting married tomorrow."

"Oh." I smirked. "Nope. Not even a little bit."

She worked beside me at the counter, a smile on her face. "She's lovely, Con. I'm glad you found her."

"Yeah, me too."

"Boy or girl, whatever child she gives you will be beautiful."

"I know. Especially if it's a girl."

"What are you hoping for?" she asked.

"Girl—all the way."

"Really?"

"Yeah. The idea of raising a boy doesn't sound appealing to me."

"Why?"

I didn't get into it with her, wanting to keep the conversation light. "Because men ain't shit."

She chuckled quietly. "Ain't that the truth."

"Would love to raise the baddest bitch who's ever lived."

This time, she released a louder laugh. "You and Aurelia can pull it off." She finished chopping her onions and slid them off the plate and into the pan with the beef. Immediately, everything started to sizzle, so she added more olive oil. "How many kids do you want?"

"One, honestly."

"One?" She stopped what she was doing and looked at me like I was crazy. "No such thing as one kid, Constantine."

Every Italian family we knew had at least three kids and a bazillion cousins. "I know, but I like the idea of having one and only. Putting all my love and energy and resources into just them, I don't know. Maybe I'll feel differently as we go through life, but it's hard for me to imagine not falling madly in love with this kid and possibly desiring another."

She turned back to her cooking when that answer was enough to satisfy her.

We continued to cook, and once all the ingredients were ready, we prepped the lasagna together, putting layers of sauce, freshly grated cheese, and noodles over and over before she popped it in the oven.

We sat at the table together and shared a bottle of wine.

"When will your friend be here?"

I grabbed my phone and checked for messages. "Said he just landed. So, probably an hour."

"How do you know him?"

"From work in Rome."

She nodded before she took a drink of her wine. "I'm excited to meet him."

"Yeah, he's cool." He was cool enough that he wouldn't be annoyed by hanging out with my mom tonight instead of going out to a bar or something. "You'll like him."

She swirled her glass, then took another drink, her eyes glazing over like she suddenly went somewhere else. The air around her changed too, suddenly becoming heavy like a storm was moving in over the ocean.

"Ma?"

When she didn't look at me and snap out of whatever funk she was in, I knew she had something to say. "Your brother should be here. He should be your best man . . . sitting right here with us."

My heart dropped straight out of my stomach. I'd finally found my closure, so I felt nothing but joy for my upcoming nuptials. But for her, there would never be closure. She would grieve every single day until God took her soul. "I know."

She continued to swirl her wineglass unnecessarily. "I know I shouldn't make this about me—"

"It's okay, Ma. I know you see his face every time you look at me."

She suddenly sucked in a deep breath as her eyes began to smart. "I loved your father, even if he was a lazy piece of shit, and I was devastated when he passed. But it's nothing like losing a son." She tried to blink the tears away, but her eyelids couldn't move fast enough. "A pain I wouldn't wish on my worst enemy." She took a few breaths before she downed the rest of her wine, the only thing strong enough to pull her back together. Then she grabbed the bottle and refilled the glass once more.

"I've been thinking a lot lately, and ever since I knew I was going to be a father, I feel a lot closer to you."

She turned her head to look at me, her dark eyes tinted with red, the skin underneath puffy even though she hadn't really cried.

"I'm worried about someone who's not even born yet. Worried about how they'll do in school, if they'll be able to make friends easily, if I'll punch a kid if he says anything mean to them, if I'll be able to let them learn to drive, if they should go to college, and if so, where? How I'll react when they bring someone home for the first time, if my heart will break into a million pieces the day they move out. I worry about an entire lifetime every single fucking day. And it makes me realize how much you've put up with from all three of us. That you were a rock star of a mother."

Her eyes started to water again. "Con . . ."

"That I hope I'll be as good as you were."

As if she couldn't take what I said, she looked down into her glass, even though she'd never been shy, never been one to drop eye contact first.

"And . . ." My voice caught before I even said my sentence. "I'm so sorry that you have to carry this pain every single day, and I selfishly pray that I'll never have to know it myself." I hoped I would live a long time, to see as much of my child's life as I could, and then die before them. I loved Aurelia more than words, but the love I already had for this nonexistent person . . . it was just different.

She was quiet for a long time, not responding to what I said, not consoling me or making me feel better like she normally did. Then she said my name, said it in a tone that made my arms break out in bumps. "Con."

I stilled at the table, and somehow, I just *knew* what would follow.

"When I went to visit your brother the other day . . . it looked disturbed."

Fuck. "The caretakers do their maintenance every so often. Perhaps it was that." I'd done my best to level the ground and make it look exactly as it had when I'd first arrived. But she'd been there every single day for the last seven years, so she knew it better than I did.

"No. It wasn't that."

I prayed she wouldn't ask me. But how could she think I had anything to do with that? I was being beyond paranoid but straight-up irrational.

But then she looked at me—dead in the eye.

Fuck.

She looked at my face like she could read it, like there were inked words on my goddamn forehead.

For the love of fucking god, don't ask me.

"Con."

No, no, no. I wore the best poker face I could, but I knew my hand was shit.

"Was it you?" She put me on the spot and asked me, watching my face with eyes that felt like microscopes.

I swallowed, unsure how to respond, knowing she wouldn't have asked me the question if she didn't suspect something deeper. I was a shit liar because it was something I never did, and I definitely couldn't lie to my mother. So the words sat on my tongue but never left my mouth. I held my silence like it was the last defense I had.

She took in a slow breath, her chest rising as her eyes smarted once again. "It wasn't a car accident . . . was it?"

I clenched my eyes closed when I heard her words—my heart shattering into shards like broken glass. I'd tried to protect her all these years, and the moment I put him to rest was the moment the facade was ruined.

She released a quiet yelp as her hand moved over her mouth. And then she cried quietly, cried over her wine with her hand still covering her mouth, the scars ripped wide open and the wounds bleeding fresh.

I sat there and listened to it, listened to my mother cry like she was at his funeral again.

"Edric got mixed up with Darius, the Skull King. Stupid shit happened and . . ." I didn't finish the sentence because it didn't need to be finished. "I became emperor of Rome because it was my life's purpose to get revenge for Edric. But it was complicated, and it never came to pass. Darius outsmarted me, and that was how I lost my position to his regime. He destroyed Rome and the rest of the country, but I killed him."

She continued to keep her hand clamped against her mouth as she processed this, her eyes elsewhere, her cries quiet.

"I shot him in the head, Ma. He's gone."

She was still, her breath still labored. "You got his body back . . . and laid him to rest."

I hadn't wanted her to know she'd visited an empty grave after all these years, but the truth had been unleashed. "Yes."

Now both of her hands cupped her face, and she sobbed. "My boy . . ."

I moved around the table to her side, pulled up a chair and circled my arms around her as I held her close.

She sobbed her heart out. Sobbed as if she'd just gotten the news that he'd been crushed by a semi. Sobbed as if the funeral had just ended but her grief continued.

"I'm so sorry, Ma."

~

I almost told Rocco not to come, but since it was so last-minute, I didn't call it off.

My mom had gone to her room because she wanted to be alone for a while, and I kept the food warm in the oven until Rocco arrived. I greeted him at the door with a smile that I didn't feel in my chest. "Wow, your face looks a lot better. How much makeup are you wearing?"

Rocco grinned at the insult and gave me a hard nudge in the stomach when he welcomed himself inside. "Congratulations, asshole."

I shut the door, and we walked into the kitchen, where the small dining table was.

"Smells good in here," he said as he took a seat and poured himself a glass of wine. "Where's your ma?"

"She'll be out in a bit. Hungry?"

"Why do you think I'm here?"

I chuckled as I pulled out the lasagna and made two plates before I brought it back to the table.

We ate together, not saying much at first, but Rocco seemed to pick up on my mood. Motherfucker knew me so well.

"You doing okay?" he finally asked.

I kept my eyes down on my plate, slicing my fork through the pasta, sauce, and cheese. "I told my mom the truth about Edric."

He stilled when he understood why there were storm clouds in the house. "Why did you decide to tell her that the night before your wedding?"

"I didn't. She noticed that the grave site had been altered, and she kinda put me on the spot. So I think on some level she always knew, you know?" I ate as much as I could with little to no appetite, so I set my fork down.

"So you told her it was Darius?"

I nodded.

"And you told her he's dead?"

"Yeah. At least, I hope he is."

"I checked all the hospitals and called all my contacts. If he's miraculously alive, he's not in the country. And he has no support or reinforcements to retaliate."

"Yeah." I hoped he was dead, among the bodies in front of the Pantheon, taken by the military and burned in the incinerator.

"And I'm sure she appreciates the fact that your brother's remains are now where they belong."

She was too broken to appreciate anything right now. "Thanks for coming."

"Come on. Like I would miss it."

"Well, I've decided not to sell you the house . . . but you're welcome to live there."

"Well, in that case." He started to get up.

I laughed.

And then he laughed before he sat down again. "How's Aurelia?"

"Fucking beautiful. Her pregnant belly . . . the most beautiful thing I've ever seen."

He nodded like he understood, but there was no way he could possibly understand. "Where is she now?"

"Home with Medusa and my sister."

"You think she'll show up tomorrow?"

I smirked and grabbed my fork. "Careful, or I'll stab you with this."

"Come on," he said with a laugh. "She's crazy for you, and you know it."

"Yeah," I said with a grin. "She is, isn't she?"

He rolled his eyes and continued to eat. "So, it's the church first and then the party after?"

"Yeah. And you're my best man, so be there early."

"Whoa, what?" He was about to take another bite of his food, but he put the fork down instead.

"Yeah."

"You're telling me this now?"

"You wanted me to ask over the phone? Through text?" I asked incredulously. "I wanted to ask you in person."

"Well, you didn't ask. You just told me I'm your best man."

"You got a problem with that or something?"

"No—"

"Then we're good, right?"

He leaned back in the chair and stared down at his food for a while before he looked at me. "You're trying to act like this isn't a big deal, but it's a pretty big deal."

I crossed my arms as I stared him down.

"I'm honored, man."

"Yeah?"

"Fuck yeah," he said with a smile. "Didn't bring a suit or anything, though."

"Then what were you going to wear?"

He looked down at himself, in jeans and a black T-shirt. "This?"

I chuckled. "Lucky for you, I've got an extra, and we're about the same size."

Chapter 28

Aurelia

The car pulled up as close as it could to the church, and we walked the rest of the way. I wore flip-flops because I wasn't going to walk down the main path in heels. The cobblestone was cracked in lots of places, and I wouldn't risk breaking my ankle at the eleventh hour . . . or ever.

Sofia held my arm and helped me to the courtyard with the fountain, water spouting from the mouths of horses, right outside the entrance to the church, where Constantine was waiting for me inside, along with hundreds of people.

My friends had made the trip and were my bridesmaids, but I also included some of his cousins, so it was a big bridal party. Constantine had ten guys in his lineup, so I tried to match.

Beatrice pulled out my heels from the bag she carried and got down on her knees to help me get them on.

"Nervous?" Sofia asked as she held me up for balance.

"The only thing I'm nervous about is getting there in one piece."

She smiled. "Like that man would ever let you fall."

"My dress is a little tight . . ." My stomach had gotten a little bigger since my last fitting, or I'd eaten a little too much. Wasn't sure which.

"Good," Sofia said. "You're growing a healthy baby for my son, and that will make him so happy."

The double doors opened, and Rocco stepped out in a black suit and tie, dark hair and dark eyes like Constantine. He came over when he spotted us, and I noticed how silent all the girls fell the second he approached.

"You look beautiful," he said. "Constantine sent me out to check on things. He's impatient, as always."

"I was running a little late," I said. "Had a hard time getting into my dress."

"Definitely won't have a hard time getting it off later," he said.

I shot him a glare, because Constantine's mother was right there.

"Oh, come on," he said with a chuckle. "You're already pregnant. Here, let me help you." He came to me and scooped me up like I weighed nothing, carrying me the rest of the way to the double doors where everyone waited inside.

The girls followed close behind, staring at Rocco as if he'd just stepped out of a magazine.

"I'll tell Con you'll be right in." He put me down, then let himself back inside the sanctuary, making sure the door didn't expose me.

"Okay, I know it's your day and everything," Beatrice said. "But I think I speak on behalf of all of us when we say we want to know *everything* about that man."

I chuckled. "All right, will do."

The girls stepped into the church to take their places, and Sofia stayed outside with me. She fixed my hair and adjusted my dress until I was absolutely perfect. Then she extended her arm to me. "I'm honored to walk you down the aisle, Aurelia."

I was already a ball of excited energy, but she made my heart expand in size. "Thank you for being the best mother-in-law I ever could have asked for."

Her eyes softened. "Seeing my son happy means the world to me. But getting a daughter-in-law whom I truly love is a special gift in itself." She pulled the door handle, both of the ushers propped it open, and we were hit with the organ music.

Once I adjusted to the darkness of the church compared to the bright sunshine outside, I saw all the rows of people standing and staring at me.

And then I saw him.

Standing next to the pope, in his finest suit, he looked at me just the way he did across the bar that night. Rocco was at his side, but Medusa also sat at his feet with a white bow tie around her neck, our rings tucked into a small box in the band.

I stopped as I stared at him, forgetting the room and all the people in it for a second.

Sofia continued to guide me forward, and it was an out-of-body experience, walking to him as his fiancée for the last time. With every step I took, my heart pounded harder, the excitement and desperation growing exponentially. My entire life had led up to this moment, when I would heal from the wounds that had bled me dry for so long.

I finally felt complete, this man loving me in a way no one else ever had, the child we made out of love growing in my belly. The past felt so distant, it was as if it had never happened at all, not when all I could think about was the exciting life that awaited us.

When I was close, he smiled. A full, cheek-to-cheek grin, so sincere and infectious, it nearly brought me to tears.

We came to a stop before him, and I suddenly felt numb and weightless and terrified and at peace . . . all at once.

Constantine kissed his mother on the cheek before he took my hand, guiding me when I'd suddenly lost my direction. He positioned me across from him in front of Pope Zephyrinus, and we stared into each other's eyes while the pope gave a short sermon and blessed our union.

I didn't listen to a word of it, lost in Constantine's dark eyes.

He didn't seem to hear it either, focused on my face with his usual intensity, like he could rip off my dress right then and there . . . or ask me to marry him again.

Pope Zephyrinus turned to Constantine first. "Do you take—"

"Yes, I fucking do."

Quiet laughter filled the church at his enthusiasm.

Then Pope Zephyrinus turned to me, giving a slight chuckle himself. "And do you—"

"Oh yeah."

Everyone in the church chuckled again.

Constantine smiled at me in a way he never had before, like he somehow loved me a little more.

"The rings," Pope Zephyrinus said.

Constantine gave a quiet whistle and turned to Medusa.

She came closer to him and sat at his side.

He reached down and pulled the little box from her bow tie, then pulled out the rings. He took mine first and slipped it onto my ring finger, putting it next to the diamond there. Then he gave me his, which he'd picked out himself, a black band.

I slipped it onto his finger, over his knuckle, and felt an indescribable rush.

I just can't believe this man is actually mine.

And not just today and maybe tomorrow . . . but forever.

The pope stepped back. "I now pronounce you husband—"

Constantine went for it, cupping my face in his hands and kissing me like we were home alone, pulling me into him like I was finally his to take.

My eyes were closed, and I could hear everyone cheering loudly for us, his mother's voice most distinct of all.

Pope Zephyrinus continued with a sigh. "You may kiss the bride."

Constantine dipped me like I weighed nothing and kissed me further, his other hand on my belly. Then he straightened me back up, grabbed my hand in his, and then lifted it to the ceiling, like we'd just won the Olympics or a political campaign.

Everyone cheered so loudly I couldn't have even heard my own voice if I were to say anything. We basked in the glow of everyone's love and excitement, the applause vibrating off the stone walls of the ancient church, people throwing rice into the air, screaming like it was a concert with their favorite artist.

After a solid minute of us standing there together with our hands raised, he dropped my hand and scooped me into his arms before he tossed me up slightly, like a pillow on a bed, and carried me down the aisle, through the crowd of cheering friends and family, on the way to the rest of our lives.

~

Constantine and I had our moment together in front of the fountain as everyone filed out of the church, his arms around me as he held me close, looking at me like I was the single most precious thing in his life.

My sky-high heels were torture on my feet, but they gave me the kind of height that made our eyes somewhat level with each other. I didn't want Constantine to have to bend his neck the entire day.

Everyone continued to stream out of the church and begin their journey to the reception about twenty minutes away. Some people stopped by to congratulate us, but mostly everyone left us alone while the photographers snapped photos of us together.

Pope Zephyrinus approached, flanked on both sides by his personal guards, and everyone scattered like a spooked school of fish. "Congratulations to you both." His hand moved to Constantine's arm, and he gave him a pat. "It was an honor joining you together in your holy union, but I must depart imminently."

I couldn't believe he made the trip in the first place. "Thank you so much, Your Holiness."

He smiled at me and patted me on the arm. "I wish the best for you both."

"Uncle, before you go, it would mean the world to me if you would bless our child," Constantine said.

"Of course, my son." Pope Zephyrinus moved his hand to my stomach, said a prayer, and then gave a short bow. "God is with your child, Constantine. I feel a spirit so distinct within the womb."

Constantine's hand moved to my stomach, and his eyes softened in a way they never had before. Like he would burst into tears at the touch, a sense of joy and pride for someone he didn't know. "Thank you, Your Holiness."

"Congratulations again." He blessed each of us before he walked off, immediately surrounded by his private security like he was the president.

Constantine brought me close and brushed a kiss against my hairline. "Ready to party?"

"Absolutely. Just wish I could drink."

"I'll drink enough for the both of us," he said with a grin. "How about that?"

Chapter 29

Constantine

It was a rowdy party. Everyone was there to eat and drink and have the time of their lives. I sat with Aurelia at the front table with the groomsmen and bridesmaids, the two of us in the center, Medusa at our feet with her own bowl of food and water.

Dinner was served and everyone ate, all five hundred guests, as the sun went down over the edge of the cliff. It was an open bar, so a lot of people enjoyed wine and champagne, while all the guys at the Cosa Nostra table chose stiff drinks. It was a good thing Pope Zephyrinus had left, because this was not his scene at all.

Aurelia laughed with her bridesmaids, and I talked to Rocco and the other guys. I was living on cloud nine, the love of my life and now my wife next to me, a baby whose spirit was so profound the pope could feel it through her flesh.

I was the luckiest man alive.

The conversations died down when my mother stood up and tapped her spoon against her champagne flute. She hit the spoon harder against the glass to get the attention of the people all the way in the back. She wore a sparkling black gown, and I knew she'd chosen the color to honor my brother, who couldn't be there. Her hair was down in thick curls, and she wore more makeup than I'd ever seen her wear—but she looked beautiful. "This is a really special honor for me, because not only am I the mother of the groom, but I already love the bride like my own daughter."

There was a collective "Aww" from the crowd.

"Every mother fears that their daughter-in-law will take their son away, but it's been the opposite with Aurelia. When they came to Taormina, she inserted herself in our lives like she was one of us. Offered to work at the restaurant to spend time with us, even though my son has made sure she never has to work a day in her life if she doesn't want to. Never protested about coming in early or doing the dishes or having the smell of tomatoes in her hair for the rest of the day."

Everyone chuckled, like they knew all too well what that was like, since most of them were in the service industry.

"It became very apparent to me that Aurelia would do anything for my son, and the moment she knew how important family was to him, she did everything to become a part of that world. She's caring, thoughtful, and so kind. I really couldn't ask for anyone better for my son."

My arm moved over the back of Aurelia's chair, and when I glanced at her, I saw the tears in her eyes. I moved my hand to her shoulder over her hair and gave her a gentle squeeze.

"And now . . ." My mother took a deep breath as her eyes started to water. "My son . . ." She stilled as she held the microphone in her hand, trying to keep herself composed for the eyes of so many. "I've watched you grow from a child to a boy, and then a boy to a man. You were a handful and drove me up the wall until I asked God why he'd given me a demon for a son." Everyone laughed, even though she remained deadly serious. "But then you grew into the person you were meant to be. I could describe you with a million words, but the ones that ring the truest are *honest*, *decent*, *kind*, and *protective*. When your father passed, you became the head of the household, took the lead when I couldn't carry on. You helped at the restaurant, respected me always, and told me every day that I was doing a good job when I felt like I wasn't doing enough. Raising you is the hardest thing I've ever done . . . but by far the most rewarding. I couldn't be prouder to call you my son. To see the man before me so strong and true and brave, and I thank God every day that you were given to me. And I thank God that I'm still here, that I get to watch you embark on your own journey into fatherhood. I can already tell how ready you are for it." She gave me a long, hard look, her eyes misty with all the emotions she couldn't fit into a three-minute speech. "I love you so much, baby."

Everyone erupted in applause.

I left my chair and rounded the table to walk to her in the space in front of our table, and I enveloped her in a big hug, holding her close as she squeezed me tight, a foot shorter than me in her heels. "I love you too, Ma." I kissed her forehead.

"You're the best son a mother could have asked for." She pulled away, then cupped my cheek, looking at me like I truly was her whole world.

I knew that look now, because it was the way I looked at Aurelia's stomach. The way I looked anytime I thought of the child I didn't know.

When I felt someone behind me, I realized Aurelia had come over too, and she moved closer to my mother.

I hugged them both before I stepped back, letting them have their moment together. I watched them hold each other before my mother cupped Aurelia's cheeks the way she'd cupped mine and said something quietly to her.

I headed back to the table so they could be together and then sat beside Rocco again.

Rocco immediately turned to me. "How the fuck am I supposed to follow that?"

I shrugged. "Not my problem."

"It's not like I can talk about work."

"True."

"Or how we even know each other."

"Damn, you're right," I said as I clapped his shoulder. "Good luck with that."

The applause had died away a long time ago, and my wife and mother were still talking to each other on the dance floor. *Wife* . . . it had a nice ring to it. Mrs. Constantine Cristina. Then I heard someone clap slowly, so slowly it sounded off-putting, like they were trying to smack their hands together as hard as they possibly could to make the sound pack a punch.

I surveyed the crowd as I looked for the source of the annoyance, realizing it was coming closer. My eyes flicked to the terrace that wasn't under the awning, and then I noticed the men with automatic rifles who seemed to have come from nowhere.

My heart raced, and my eyes flew back to Aurelia first.

And that was when I saw him, moving between two tables, clapping louder and harder and slower, eyes locked on me like I was the target.

I felt Rocco stiffen beside me.

My mother and Aurelia broke apart, and Aurelia's gasp was loud because she recognized him right away.

My mother didn't ask questions, but she instinctively put Aurelia behind her and used her body as a shield.

The room went silent when he stopped clapping. He wore black jeans and boots and a gray T-shirt, and the corner of his head where his temple would be looked odd in appearance, like the side of his head had been shaved off.

Because I'd missed.

He raised his arms wide, then broke into a smile. "Wow, this is one hell of a party. Guess my invitation got lost in the mail."

I shifted my eyes to Tommaso, who was seated with Cosa Nostra, in the hope some of them were armed. But even if they were, their handguns wouldn't be enough against the rifles. Then I turned back to Darius, who had come to a stop feet from the table.

Medusa growled from where she lay at my feet.

"Heel," I ordered, not wanting her to get almost shot again.

Darius glanced down at my German shepherd before he looked at me again. "Your little bitch is still alive."

Medusa growled again.

I slowly rose to my feet and instinctively grabbed my tie and yanked it free.

"Let's take a trip down memory lane, Con." He massaged his knuckles, then his wrists, like he was preparing for a fight as he continued to stare me down. "I let you, your wife—" He looked slightly over his shoulder to where Aurelia stood behind my mother, their backs up against the nearest table covered in a white tablecloth. "Congratulations, by the way." He turned back to me. "And your dog go. And you gave me your word that you would disappear. Or am I misremembering all of that?" He cocked an eyebrow as he leaned in slightly.

I said nothing as I stared him down.

"Man of your word . . . that's what you said to me." He turned to look at my mother. "She said a lot of nice things about you, said you were honest, but you look like a fucking liar to me." He stared at me instead. "And what did I say would happen if you broke your word?"

I continued to stare him down. I didn't have a plan. Didn't know what to do. I could rush him, but his men would probably shoot me. There was likely no way I would get out of this alive, but that was okay if Aurelia did. I spoke low enough for Rocco to hear and no one else. "Save Aurelia."

"Sorry, I didn't hear you." Darius suddenly raised his voice, his temper flaring, and he was louder than the speaker system tied to the microphone my mother had just used. Now his eyes were narrowed and locked on my face with the fires of vengeance. *"What did I say would happen if you broke your word?"*

I'd been happier than I'd ever been just moments ago—and now I breathed my final breaths. I wanted to rip this man apart, muscle from bone, ligaments from joints, but I would probably never get close enough.

"I said I would kill every person you've ever known and loved. Which means . . ." He turned around in a full circle, gesturing to the five hundred guests who had come to my wedding. "All of you are dead. Every single fucking one of you." He made eye contact with me. "Thanks to this pompous fucking asshole who can't shoot a gun straight." He clapped his hands once. "So, how should we start?" Then he took a step toward my mother and Aurelia.

I jumped over the table so fast. Tore off my jacket and cast it aside in a rush. "Darius, I swear to fucking God—"

"Your mother." He pointed at my mother, who continued to guard Aurelia like she was her own daughter. "Or your wife." He grabbed Aurelia by the arm and started to tug her forward, making her stand beside my mother.

"Darius."

The table behind him had a group of men and women, and two of the guys lunged for it, trying to tackle Darius from behind.

Gunfire erupted, and every guest at the table was sprayed with bullets. The room screamed, and everyone ducked under their chairs for cover.

"No one is going anywhere," Darius said calmly. "So, what's it going to be?" He pointed at my mother. "Your mother." Then he pointed at Aurelia. "Or your wife. Who should go first, Constantine?" He turned back to me, arms crossed over his chest. "And yes, I'll stomp on their arms and legs and spine, and we'll all listen to them scream as every single one of their bones snaps in half before I shove them into an oil drum, just like your asshole brother."

My mother couldn't control her pained gasp, learning the truth in the most graphic way possible. She had to grab on to Aurelia's hand for balance, like she might fall over.

There was a malicious glint in his eyes like he was enjoying this, like he'd been plotting this since I'd shot him in the head, like he'd purposely lain low and waited until this moment because it would be far more worthwhile. "And I'll cut out your baby and throw it into the sea—"

"I swear to fucking God—"

"Your wife or your mother. Choose."

My muscles were flexed with rage-soaked blood, and it would take at least twenty bullets to slow me down. I thought I was angry when my brother died, but this was borderline derangement.

My mother and Aurelia shrank back against the table, and Darius and I continued our standoff.

Then Darius moved toward them. "Then it looks like I'll choose for you."

I launched into a sprint, knowing the spray of bullets would kill me, but if I could kill him first, then my mother and Aurelia had a chance to get out of there alive.

A nearby gunman moved in my way, pointing his rifle right into my chest and forcing me back. Then he put the gun to my temple and kicked the backs of my knees until I was forced to the floor, on my knees, the barrel loaded with a magazine pressed right into me.

I felt sweat pour down my face, felt my veins pop until they nearly burst from my flesh. Restrained and helpless, I watched Darius grab my mother by the arm and force her toward the center of the floor.

Medusa continued to growl and then started to bark, mad as hell but still obeying the command I'd issued.

"Darius, name your price. I'll give you whatever you want. Break my spine and make me your new nightstand—"

He continued to grip my mother by the arm, and he sneered at me. "Not enough money in the world, Constantine—"

It happened so fast, I almost missed it.

My mother pulled out a steak knife that she must have grabbed from the table she'd been backed into and stabbed it right into his neck. Stabbed it so deep that the hilt of the knife almost got lost in his flesh. And then she stabbed him again . . . and again.

Darius stumbled for a moment, unable to process the shock of what had happened.

The gunman turned his rifle toward them, but there was no way to shoot my mother without also shooting Darius because they were so tangled together.

And my mom was still going for it, stabbing him over and over. Her eyes were maniacal, and she looked like a bloodthirsty wolf that finally caught its prey in a blizzard and ripped it to shreds. "You touch my son and think you'll get away with it, you son of a bitch!"

Darius finally elbowed her hard in the face, and she hit the floor, the knife still lodged in his neck. He reached for it, and in his insanity, he yanked it out, another squirt of blood spraying like a geyser into the sky. He dropped to one knee, staring at me with a veil across his gaze, like he was already halfway gone.

That was when Rocco and Cosa Nostra leaped into action. Tommaso and the others fired at the gunmen with their handguns, and Rocco picked up a chair and slammed it down hard onto the gunman who had his rifle against me again.

Rocco knocked him out cold before he took the gun and did exactly as I'd asked and shielded Aurelia with his body before he shoved her under the table. Gunfire erupted throughout the terrace, and people ran for their lives. Cosa Nostra tried to tackle Darius's men even though they were outnumbered.

I wasn't taking any chances this time, so I ran to Darius to finish the job.

But right when I got there, Medusa jumped on him—and literally ripped out his throat.

He barely screamed before his windpipe was gone, and he was done. When she pulled away, her white teeth were covered in blood, her fur soaked in it. Even the bow tie that had been white was now bloodred. She growled at his body as if what she'd done wasn't quite enough.

I went to my mother, who hadn't moved since she'd hit the floor. "Ma." Her eyes were closed when I found her, and I gathered her in my arms and sat her up against me.

The movement made her stir, and she sucked in a deep breath and released a gasp.

I felt the back of her head, and my hand came away with blood on it.

She let me support her as she stared at Darius before her, a massacred corpse now.

"Ma, are you okay?"

"Yeah . . . yeah . . . I'm fine." She suddenly left my arms, crawled across the floor, picked up the knife Darius had yanked out, and started stabbing him in the chest with it—over and over—a mother unleashing a catharsis of grief.

I let her be. She deserved to do whatever the fuck she wanted to his body after what he'd done to Edric.

The gunfire receded, and it seemed as if Rocco and Cosa Nostra had either taken them all out or run them off.

I moved to the table where Rocco had shoved Aurelia and lifted the tablecloth to find her, clearly in shock, judging by how snow white her face was. She trembled from head to toe, and when her eyes found mine, she immediately started to sob.

"Sweetheart, it's okay." I pulled her into my arms under the table and clutched her tight. "He's dead. Everything is okay . . . it's okay."

Her hand moved to her stomach like she needed to make sure our baby was all right, that a stray bullet or a knife hadn't come close.

I felt her hyperventilating against me, afraid not for me or for herself, but for the person we both already loved with our full hearts.

"Everything is okay," I repeated. "Everything is okay."

"Your mom?" she asked through her tears.

"She's fine." I could hear her continue to stab Darius through the tablecloth.

Then Medusa ducked her snout underneath the white material and lifted it as she came to us, blood all over her face from getting her revenge against Darius for breaking her leg . . . and to protect my mother.

Aurelia didn't care about the blood at all and brought her into her arms like Medusa was our child, a seventy-pound baby covered in fur. She got blood all over her dress as she snuggled Medusa, sobbing into her fur because she was relieved she was okay.

I'd fucked up again. I'd never gotten the irrefutable evidence that Darius was actually dead, and it had nearly cost me my entire family. "I'm so sorry." Tears sprang to my eyes when I mourned what I'd almost lost. "I'm so fucking sorry."

Chapter 30

Constantine

There were no further casualties other than the family seated together at that table. It was the Renaldo family, who operated one of the souvenir shops in town. My mother had gone to school with the father, so he was an old family friend.

They were brave for trying to help, but I wished they hadn't.

When Tommaso and the other guys moved Darius's body, my mother was still stabbing it, creating a huge pool of blood underneath her that soaked her dress and got into her hair . . . everywhere. She was literally soaked in blood, sweat, and tears.

The brightest day of my life turned into one of mourning.

When they took Darius away, my mother started to scream because apparently she wasn't quite done massacring his remains.

I kneeled down next to her and grabbed her by the shoulders as she tried to yank Darius by the arm to continue her carving. "Ma." I pulled her into me. "Ma, it's done." I took the bloody knife out of her hand and handed it to Tommaso, who set it on one of the tables.

She still looked pissed off as fuck, glaring at the body like it was still Darius, living and breathing, and she wished vengeance upon him like the head of the mob.

"Ma." I tried to bring her back to me, tried to help her process the rage that couldn't be satiated. "Ma . . ." I rubbed her shoulder and then her back.

She finally calmed herself and looked at me, blood splattered all over her beautiful face.

"He's dead. It's done."

She shook her head slightly. "It'll never be done for me, Constantine." Then her eyes started to water as the grief replaced the rage. "I don't care what Edric did, if he deserved it or not, it'll never be done for me."

I continued to rub her back. "You aren't alone, because it'll never be done for me either."

Her eyes watered so much that tears dripped down her cheeks. She closed them before she nodded.

"But you gave that asshole what he deserved and saved everyone here, Ma."

"I wasn't trying to save everyone," she said quietly. "I just . . . I heard what he said . . . and I fucking lost it." Tears continued to stream down her cheeks. "Like I'd ever let him walk free after what he did to my boy. I'd do it again . . . and fucking again."

"I know," I said gently.

She breathed and sniffed, her eyes on the tile, and it was only then that she looked at herself and realized she was soaked in another man's blood. "How's Aurelia?"

"Shaken up but okay. She'll be all right."

"The baby?"

"I felt them kick a couple minutes ago."

"Good."

"I'm sorry about all this. I thought I'd killed him, but clearly, I hadn't."

She watched me, eyes still watery.

"Lost some good friends today because of my stupidity—"

"And you've served this country and protected our people for a long time, Constantine. I'm sorry that it ended this way—but at least it ended." Now her hand moved to my arm to console me. "I know you've hunted this man for a long time for what he did to your brother, and I want to apologize for taking a life that you should have taken—but I can't."

"You deserve it more than anyone, Ma," I said. "And truth be told, if you hadn't, I'm not sure if any of us would be here right now. Because you're a fucking badass. I know exactly where I get it from."

Her eyes softened in their wetness, and she looked at the floor. "The love of your child will make you the most powerful person in the room. You'll see, Constantine. You'll see . . ."

I found Aurelia sitting on a bench in the courtyard at the clock tower. She must have slipped off on her own to get some space. She was still in her bloody wedding dress, Medusa sitting on one side of her, while Rocco sat on the other, his arm wrapped around her shoulders like he was consoling her in my absence.

When I approached, Rocco shared a look with me, then a nod, to let me know she was doing okay. He wordlessly left the seat, patted me on the arm, and then walked off.

I took the spot next to her, wrapped my arm around her shoulders, and pressed my palm to her belly like my hand was bulletproof.

"How's your mom?" she asked.

"She's okay. The adrenaline and rage are fading, and reality is creeping in."

"I'm glad she killed him. She earned that."

"Yeah."

I rubbed her arm as I held her close, the night cool as the ocean breeze blew over the cliffs and into our hair. "I'm sorry about all of this. I should have done more. I should have known . . ."

"Con, it's okay. It's over now."

"But friends as good as family are dead . . . and our wedding day is ruined."

She stared toward the ocean, the lights from the mainland distantly visible on a clear night like this. "Our wedding was in that church in the eyes of our friends and family and God. It was beautiful and special, and I'll never forget it. That was our wedding, and nothing could ever tarnish it. I'm just grateful that the outcome of this night wasn't worse. A lot more people could have died, and at least now he's really gone. Our country can start to heal from the wounds he inflicted. The Republic is secure under a new emperor. And you and I can raise our baby in this beautiful village without having to look over our shoulders. I know it hurts right now . . . everything hurts . . . but it'll be okay."

The heaviness continued through the week, through the joint funerals, and it was only then that people started to move on from what had happened. Taormina was a quiet and safe place where nothing violent or dangerous ever happened, so I knew the village would be forever scarred by what had taken place.

I carried that guilt with me every single day, but I knew I needed to move on.

My mother asked me to visit Edric with her, so Aurelia and I went along. It was Aurelia's first time visiting the grave, and we all stood together in silence as we looked at the lettering on the headstone.

Now that I knew his remains were there, I felt closer to him than I had in a long time. I felt like his spirit could truly be free, knowing what was left of him had been honored. He wouldn't want us to be sad over his death. Would much rather we move on . . . especially my mother.

She stared at the headstone in silence, the flowers cradled in the crook of her arm, not a hint of a tear on her face. Then she stepped forward and placed the flowers on his grave before she kissed her palm and placed it on the top of his headstone. "I hope you can find peace now, baby." She held her hand there for a long time before she stood upright and moved back. "Every day I've visited him, I've cried myself dry. The wound has always felt so raw, years and years afterward. A part of me wonders if I always knew he wasn't here, that I couldn't rest or truly grieve until he was exactly where he belonged. Because the moment I came here and felt the disturbance in the ground, it felt different. Felt like someone else was here with me. And now . . ." She took a breath, the breeze moving through her hair. "I feel like I can finally find peace."

I sat on the couch on the patio with Medusa beside me, staring out at the sea in the distance, the wedding band on my left hand where I would keep it forever, night and day, in the gym and at work. And even though I was happy, I wasn't quite healed from what had happened. It might take longer than a week . . . or a couple weeks.

Medusa turned when the back door opened, and she immediately leaped down to greet the person.

I knew it wasn't Aurelia because Medusa wouldn't jump off the couch if it were, not when she'd just seen her in the house a couple minutes ago. I turned to get a look at the person and saw it was Rocco. "What are you doing here?"

"Decided to drop by and catch up." He gave Medusa a quick rubdown before he sat down on the couch across from me.

"Just decided to drop by?" I asked suspiciously.

"It's only an hour flight. As convenient as it gets."

"You gotta get there two hours early, and then it's an hour drive here—"

"Not when you fly private."

"But still," I said. "It's not *that* convenient. So why are you really here?"

He sat forward slightly, rubbing his hands together, and then gave a slight smirk. "Your wife texted me."

I gave a slow nod in understanding.

"She said you've been down lately."

"Hard to bounce back, I guess."

He stared at his hands as he continued to rub his palms together. "It sucks it happened, but what are you going to do? Feel guilty forever? There's not a single person in your life who wants you to feel that way, Con."

"A lot of bad shit happened under my watch."

"And you think bad shit won't happen under mine?" he asked. "I absolutely guarantee you it will. It's a tough job, Con. You're running all the criminal enterprises of the country yourself. You police the guys the police can't even police. And Darius was a well-connected, rich, corrupt motherfucker. Look, I thought he was dead too. Everyone thought he was. And even if he wasn't, no one thought he'd pull that trick out of his hat."

"Rocco, I appreciate you trying to make me feel better—"

"It's all done now, Con." He cut me off with his tone. "You can keep living in the past, but where's that going to get you? You've got a beautiful wife who wants to fuck your brains out, and you're sitting here staring off into space. You've got a baby on the way—"

"Whoa, what did you just say?"

He shut his mouth and stared at his hands again.

"She told you about that?" We hadn't actually consummated our marriage yet. After everything that had happened, I just wasn't in the mood, and when she'd tried to get something going a couple days ago, I told her I wasn't ready.

"She may have mentioned it."

I shook my head as I chuckled. "Wow, woman's got it bad, huh?"

"She said she just got hit with a new batch of hormones, and she's . . . a bit frisky."

"She told *you* this?"

"Yes."

"You?"

"We talk," he said with a shrug. "And friends always help friends get laid."

I chuckled again, unable to picture my wife texting my best friend, saying how much she missed riding my dick.

"So, give your wife that D, all right?"

I'd been miserable a few moments ago, but now the grin on my face felt permanent. "I'm glad you guys are close. That makes me happy."

"I'm glad it makes you happy and not want to punch me in the throat."

"Pigs would fly before either of you betrayed me." I trusted both of them implicitly. My wife was a good woman with eyes only for me, and Rocco was like a brother to me. He'd rather take a bullet in the arm than lie to me.

"I'm gonna check in to my hotel. Let's meet at Daiquiri in a couple hours."

"Why don't we just go now?" I asked.

He glanced behind me at the glass wall of the house. "Because your wife is giving me the death stare, so she's not gonna let you leave the house until you service her." He winked before he stood up. "Hit me up."

~

When I returned to the house, Aurelia wasn't on the couch where I'd last seen her. The TV was off, the kitchen was quiet, and Medusa jumped on the couch and curled up like she expected me to sit next to her.

"Sweetheart?" I called through the house.

"Upstairs," she called down.

She was usually on the main floor during the day, only going upstairs to shower or sleep or use the gym. I made my way up the stairs and reached the next landing before I headed down the hallway to our bedroom that had a set of double doors.

They were wide open, so I walked on the hardwood floor into the room, then stopped when I saw her propped up in bed.

Wearing a two-piece white lingerie set and white sheer stockings up her legs, she had her four-month pregnant belly on display because she knew it did some serious shit to me. She had darkened her makeup and thickened her lashes, and her hair was fluffed up like she'd done something to make it enormous.

My breath stopped the instant I saw her, a fucking wet dream just waiting for me. Rocco must have texted her when he left and given her some indication that he'd gotten through to me.

I looked her over, pitching a tent in my sweats, hard as ever.

Fuck, can't believe this is my wife.

She continued to stare me down, confident and mysterious, her hand moving over her belly.

My shirt was already off, so I dropped my bottoms in one swoop, my dick at full salute for the queen in my bed.

Her eyes lowered to look at me, and the arousal and excitement and joy in her eyes were too potent to hide. She even bit her bottom lip absentmindedly, her enthusiasm raw and pure. "Get over here."

I crawled up the bed then grabbed her by the ankles and gently tugged her down so her head moved to the pillow. She looked so damn fine that I didn't want to take any of it off, but now that this door had been opened, I wanted to sprint through it.

I moved down and kissed her belly, the belly that was small compared to what it would become in a few more months, but it felt like the sun to me. The center of my universe, the soul to my body. I kissed her belly before I rested my forehead against it, feeling the life we'd made together out of the love we shared.

Biggest turn-on of my life.

I slipped off her little white thong and left the stockings in place before I scooped my arms around her thighs as I moved my mouth to her entrance, which was perfectly shaved like she'd hoped today would be the day.

"No."

I moved up again, never having heard that word from her in my life.

"I want you." She started to pull on me, too anxious for foreplay, wanting the deed to be signed and delivered.

I did as she asked and moved up her body, bending her into place, her pregnant belly between us. My head dipped, and I kissed her, kissed in a way I hadn't in the last two weeks, her breath growing rapid as our tongues occasionally met in a seductive swipe.

She didn't let me guide myself inside her. She grabbed my length and put me in place, like she meant business.

I couldn't help it. I smiled against her mouth before I pressed inside, recognizing the pool of slickness that had been filling for a while. This was the horniest she'd ever been, for sure. I didn't have to push through her tightness like I normally did. I was immediately drenched in her desire so I could sink effortlessly.

She gasped against me like this was our first time rather than our first time as husband and wife.

I was immediately engulfed in her flames, brought into the fiery heat that had been burning beneath the surface. I felt myself set ablaze as I rocked into her, my core just inches away from her distended stomach, watching her take my dick for barely a minute before she came all over me, like she hadn't touched herself while I'd refused her advances.

She'd waited for me.

I felt her come around me and watched the pleasure and relief enter her gaze like she'd been waiting day and night for this. Like an addict who'd finally gotten that first hit after being clean for far too long.

Her eyes came back to me, glistening in satisfaction, but still heated like that wasn't even close to being enough.

I kissed her again, my mouth dancing with hers in a slow embrace, my arms still pinned behind her knees to keep her in place. Then I started to move again, feeling her fingers slide into my hair and then down my arms.

"I love you," she said into my mouth during our embrace, a whisper just for me to hear.

I kissed her again before I pulled away to look into her eyes, seeing my whole world in a single person. The person I'd spotted through a window one sunny afternoon in Taormina . . . and just knew. Knew she was my person, my future wife, the woman who would give me a child and somehow make me ready to be a father when I didn't even know if I wanted to be one. She brought me back to who I was, who I'd always been, back to where I belonged . . . with her, in this special place. "I love you too."

Epilogue

Constantine

I stood in the kitchen, gripped the handle of the pot, and gave it a hard shake, mixing the pasta noodles with the tomatoes, basil, onion, and garlic. "All right, Julia. Hit me."

Julia carried the bowl of freshly grated buffalo mozzarella and stepped up onto the wooden step I'd made for her since she was only five years old and could barely reach the counter. She kept the bowl steady as she stepped up and placed it on the counter.

I very rarely helped her with things, wanting her to think for herself from a young age. She could make as many mistakes as she wanted—the more, the better—because she learned from all of them. And learned she didn't need anyone. "All right. Add the cheese."

She reached her hand inside.

"Gloves, remember?"

"Oh yeah. Sorry, Daddy."

"It's okay, baby girl." God, I loved when she called me that. One day, she would just call me Dad—and I dreaded that moment. When she wasn't a kid anymore but a teenager or an adult or a middle-aged woman . . . and we would never have this again.

She took her time getting the gloves on, because, again, I didn't help her. Then she reached into the bowl, grabbed a handful, and tossed it into the pot, where it immediately melted on the hot food.

"Perfect." I turned off the burner and set the pan on the counter to cool for a minute.

"All right, let's do it." I stepped away from the counter, and she hopped off the step stool.

I wrapped the pot handle with the cloth slipcover, then handed it to her. "You got it?"

"Yeah, I got it."

Aurelia walked toward us from the main dining area in her black T-shirt with the restaurant name on the front, Osteria di Cristina, her hair in a high ponytail that showed off her elegant neck. "Constantine, are you sure she should be handling that?"

"She's got it."

"She could get burned—"

"She's got it. Show your mother, baby girl."

"I got it, Ma." She carried the hot pan to the right table, using both of her little hands, and put it on the colorful trivet bearing our restaurant logo in front of the correct person who'd ordered it. "Here you go," she said sweetly.

The couple sitting there clearly thought she was the cutest thing ever. "Thank you so much," the woman said.

"You're welcome," Julia said in the same sweet voice. Then she walked back to us, her dark hair in the same high ponytail as her mother's. "See? I did it."

Aurelia's eyes squinted with affection, and she gave Julia a pat on the shoulder. "Good job, honey."

Julia hopped onto the step stool, then reached for the basket of bread that had just been prepped by one of the other cooks. She carried that over to the couple's table too, except they hadn't ordered it and it should have gone to someone else, but that was just fine. Looked like they got some free bread.

"I admit she's a natural," Aurelia said.

"It's in her blood."

"She's also got the blood of emperors too."

I grinned. "And if she wants to do that someday, she'll be ready for it."

"God, let's not even joke about that."

"Con."

I looked into the dining room and saw none other than Rocco entering the restaurant, a tall behemoth in the little place, his eyes lit up in joyous affection at the sight of me. "You didn't tell me you were coming into town."

He came to me with arms wide, and we embraced outside the kitchen. We exchanged hugs and pats on the back before we broke apart. "Rome's been quiet, so I thought I'd take a little holiday."

"And you had to pick Taormina, of all places?" I teased.

He shrugged. "Just looking for a free meal, I guess."

I chuckled. "I've got you covered, brother."

Julia came over after she delivered the bread. "Uncle Rocco!"

"There's my little princess." He scooped her up with a single arm, then hoisted her over his shoulder like a sack of potatoes.

She laughed as she was held upside down, kicking her legs toward the ceiling.

"Wow, you've gotten heavy." Rocco returned her to the floor. "I can barely lift you anymore."

"Well, I'm *five* now," she said with a bit of sass. "And you didn't get me a present."

"Julia," I said with a tone, telling her she was being rude without actually saying it.

"Actually . . ." Rocco pulled a small box from his pocket and popped it open for her. Inside was a little golden bracelet with a maroon pendant.

Her eyes lit up at the sight of it. "Whoa."

"Only for a princess." He smiled before he got it out and clasped it around her wrist.

"Wow, Daddy, look!" She showed it to me and then her mother.

"Beautiful," I said before I gave Rocco a pat on the shoulder, appreciating how good he was to my little girl.

"Why don't you two have lunch, and Julia and I will handle the kitchen," Aurelia said.

"Works for me," I said. "I'm starving."

"The only reason I'm here is to eat, so sounds good," Rocco said with a smile.

We headed outside to one of the quiet tables under the awning, and my little girl immediately brought us a basket of fresh bread like the good little waitress she was. I gave her a gentle tickle, and she giggled before she headed back inside.

"Jesus Christ," Rocco said. "She's so damn cute."

"I know . . . it kills me."

"Why?"

"Because it won't always be this way," I said sadly. "I hate being this happy sometimes."

He watched me for a while before he crossed his arms over his chest. "You could have another one."

I shook my head. "I really love it being the three of us. Well, four, if I'm including Medusa."

"And you better include her. Otherwise, she'll rip out your throat."

I chuckled. "Yeah." She was starting to slow down because she was ten now, but still as feisty as ever. "I love Julia so damn much, I just can't picture loving another kid. I like that she's my one and only. I'm sure a parent loves their kids all the same, but you only have so much time in life, and I don't want to share that time with anyone else but her."

"I think if it actually happened, it would be okay, Constantine."

"Maybe," I said with a shrug. "But I wanted a girl so bad, and I got her. So . . . I don't need anything else." Most people wanted boys and were disappointed when a girl came along, but I couldn't have felt more differently about that. "I always wanted to be a girl dad. And I live in a house with three of them."

"Sounds rough, honestly."

"Nah, I fucking love it." Julia came out again with a bottle of red wine and set it on the table. But it was still sealed, and there was no corkscrew, so we couldn't even drink it. Then she brought two glasses and left.

Thankfully, Aurelia came out and opened it for us. "You know what you guys want?"

"Whatever Con is having," Rocco said.

"We'll share the rolled swordfish," I said. "And then the seafood pasta."

"Are we on a date?" Rocco teased.

Aurelia walked off.

"Does that pasta come with octopus?"

"No. We don't have it on our menu."

He nodded. "That's right. You don't eat that."

I never asked Aurelia to change her diet to accommodate me, but I'd noticed ever since I'd told her I respected the octopus, she didn't eat it either. And when we designed our menu together, we had a silent agreement not to feature the item, even though it was a popular dish in Taormina, a village that was proud of its seafood. "So, how's Rome?"

"No complaints. Been pretty quiet."

"Rome is never quiet."

"It is under my watch," he said with a smirk. "Guess I'm better at the job than you ever were."

"I won't argue against that," I conceded with a shrug.

"Come on, you know I'm just being a dick."

"Doesn't mean you're wrong." I opened the bottle and filled our glasses. "And I don't mean that disparagingly. Seeing anyone?"

He shook his head. "Nah."

"Do you ever see anyone?"

He shook his head again. "Not my cup of tea."

"It'll be your tea once you find the right woman."

He gave a quiet chuckle. "Just because you fell in love and popped out a kid doesn't mean I will. Or will ever *want* to."

"True," I said. "But if you meet *that* woman, doesn't matter what you want. You're fucked. The second I met Aurelia, I was *so* fucked. Fucked in every way imaginable. But a good fucked, you know. And you're great with Julia. You'd be a stand-up dad."

He chuckled quietly. "Hanging out with a kid for a couple hours is not the same thing as being a full-time dad."

"Yeah, it's better."

He grinned. "Well, I'm glad you're happy, Constantine. You're a good guy."

"Thanks, man," I said. "You think you can hold down the job for another twenty years until Julia is old enough?"

His eyebrows furrowed at the question as he studied me. "I can't tell if that's a joke or not."

"Does it sound like a joke?"

He studied me again, his eyes flicking back and forth. "I thought that would be the last thing you wanted for her."

I shrugged. "I mean, if she wants it, she wants it. Unless you have a kid or someone better suited to the position."

"Look, I don't mean to sound like a sexist prick, but I'm not sure a woman is the right person for the role."

"You do sound like a sexist prick," I said. "And if she wants it, I'm sure she can handle it. I'm raising her to be a tough chick. A bad bitch, some might say," I said with a grin.

"Then how about we cross that bridge when we come to it, all right?"

At that moment, Julia came out and put the swordfish rolls on the table between us. "Here you go."

"Thanks, baby girl." I gave her a little smack on the butt, and she ran off again. "Besides, if someone ever gives her trouble, she's got a scary-as-fuck dad to call and a psycho uncle to clean up her messes."

"You know we'd be fifty-nine in this scenario."

"So? I'm sure I'll still be able to lift a tree by then. You're gonna let yourself go? Eat a pint of gelato in front of the TV every night?"

He smirked. "I do like gelato."

"Augustus denied his daughter Julia the throne and handed it over to his fucking nephews. I wouldn't repeat the same bullshit. If she wants power and wealth and to be the baddest bitch in Rome, it's hers. I'm not gonna tell her there's something she can't do, because she sure as hell can do whatever she wants."

He grabbed his wine, took a drink, and then held it up toward me. "I'll drink to that."

I gently clinked my glass against his. "To Julia, the First Empress of Rome, the baddest bitch who's ever ruled."

He chuckled and took a drink. "To Julia."

OTHER WORKS BY PENELOPE SKY

Golden Retriever in Another Republic

Fifth Republic Series

The Butcher

The Carver

The Saint

Golden Retriever in a Mafia Romance

The Betrayal Series

It Kills Me

It Breaks Me

It Ruins Me

It Hurts Me

It Pains Me

It Destroys Me

Morally Gray Hero in Organized Crime

The Buttons Series

Buttons and Lace

Buttons and Hate

Buttons and Pain

Buttons and Shame

Buttons and Blame

Buttons and Grace

Morally Gray Hero That Doesn't Care About Boundaries

Skull Series

The Skull King

The Skull Crusher

The Skull Ruler

Arranged Marriage with Alpha Protector

The Wolf Series

The Wolf and the Sheep

The Wolf and His Wife

The Lone Wolf

Alphahole That Falls First

Banker Series

The Banker

The Dictator

The Tyrant

Alpha Male That Wants Revenge Through Arranged Marriage

Betrothed Series

Wife

Husband

Lover

Committed

First

Second

Forever

Lie

Secret

Truth

Morally Gray Alphahole

Lesser Evil Series

Lesser Evil

Better Man

Harder Betrayal

Golden Retriever Mafia Romance

Empire Series

Bartholomew

Barbarian

Morally Gray Antihero in a Romantic Thriller

Chateau Series

The Chateau

The Camp

The Boss

The Palace

Alpha Male Protector in Romantic Thriller

Cult Series

The Cult

The Catacombs

Alphahole Captor Falls First

Queen Series

Protect Your Queen

Love Your Queen

Worship Your Queen

The Barsetti Clan from the Buttons Series Continues

Beyond Buttons Series

Buttons and Revenge

Buttons and Betrayal

Buttons and Devotion

Buttons and Power

Buttons and Despise

Buttons and Beauty

Buttons and Loyalty

Buttons and Blood

Buttons and Death

Buttons and Lies

Buttons and Deceit

Buttons and Hope

Buttons and Belief

Buttons and Desire

Buttons and Shadows

PENELOPE SKY WRITING AS PENELOPE BARSETTI

Morally Gray Alphahole Necromancer

Death Series

The Death King

Blood of Dragons

The Dragon King

The Dragon Queen

Princess of Death

Empire of Death

Alphahole Hell-Bent on Revenge

Forsaken Series

The Forsaken King

The Broken Queen

The Three Kings

Obsessed Golden Retriever Vampire

Dirty Blood Series

Bite The Woman That Feeds

Bite The Terror That Feeds

Bite The Power That Feeds

The Forsaken Vampire

The Broken Prince

Clash of Kingdoms

About the Author

Penelope Sky is an international phenomenon and multiple Amazon Charts, *New York Times*, *Wall Street Journal*, and *USA Today* bestselling author. She's best known for her dark romance, mafia romance, and romantic thrillers, and with books translated into dozens of languages around the world, she's sold more than five million copies worldwide. Sky also writes fantasy romance under the pen name Penelope Barsetti. Follow and connect with the author on Instagram or TikTok at @penelopeskyauthor.